Mr. Rosette

Anthony D. Phillips

DREAMERPUBLISHING®

Cleveland, Ohio

Library of Congress Cataloging-In-Publication Data is on file at the Library of Congress, Washington, DC.

Printed in the United States of America

Copyright © 2012 (Revised 2013) by Anthony D. Phillips

October 2013

Published by

DREAMERPUBLISHING®

ISBN: 0991058208

ISBN-13: 978-0991058204

Visit us at www.adpbooks.com

Dedicated to my future, with love

ACKNOWLEDGEMENTS

Thanks to God, mom, dad, Tonia, Javon, Alicia, Anthony, Aaliyah, Alexandria, Reggie, Sierra, and Miles.

God – created me in his image and gave me the gifts needed to succeed as an author

Mom – always believed in me, even when I didn't and helped me get closer to my dream

Dad – gave me the inspiration to seek something better than working a sucky job

Tonia – tolerated my addiction to success and helped me get on the right track

Javon – gave me the insight and radio promotion, my brother from another since day one.

Alicia – for believing in your big brother

Anthony, Aaliyah, and Alexandria – gave me the need to get to a higher level.

Reggie, sierra, and miles – accepted me into the fold.

PROLOGUE

"Go away!" I scream at the top of my lungs, all the while hoping that Heaven, Hell, and everything in between will hear. I know what these things in my house want. They want me! It's not all in my head. It can't be all in my head, they're here right now. My dreams are coming true, unfortunately not in a pleasant way. I can see my breath in front of me as it escapes my warm ninety-eight degree body. I feel the sting of the cold numbing air. The temperature in the room has dropped significantly. Death or something like it is present. Max stands near me paralyzed with alertness; his fur is standing on end, his growl guttural. I feel an icky crawling sensation invade the surface of my skin as goose bumps form on it. I'm flooded with intense fear as I stare deep into something that is there but not there. A shadowy semitransparent creature with red piercing eyes stands in front of me. Its eyes are like small intense fires burning their way into my core. I feel helpless and alone. I know that there is no way to escape; this is it. I wish Aiden were here. I wish I had his protective courage to rescue me in my darkest hour.

"It is your time, you must transcend. You must become what we need you to be. Spill the blood of the unworthy one and fulfill the divination. He is near. Sacrifice him to your cause." The menacing figure says in unison with the others surrounding me. Who or what they are referring to is unclear. I feel their strong cold hands grab my wrists. I attempt to break free, but my efforts are futile. The more I struggle, the stronger they become.

"No, get off of me!" I yell while struggling for freedom. Suddenly, the creature that I'm directly facing removes its hood and reveals its identity. It is… me! We appear to be the same person, which is utterly impossible. *"How can there be two?"* I ponder as my heartbeat intensifies. My other self, has a sinister look of glee. It is as if she is feeding off my fear.

I never really did take much stock in ghosts, demons, angels, or the paranormal world at large. I figured that only people craving attention or afflicted with mental illness believed in those types of things. Now I don't know what to believe. I really thought that ghost-hunting shows were just a bunch of Hollywood hyped entertainment. Orbs, EVPs, doors opening, mysterious footsteps, haunting reoccurring dreams; these things didn't happen to someone like me, Talia Rhodes. I was the type of person that stuck strictly to facts. If I couldn't see, taste, smell, or touch it, it didn't exist. Now I'm trying hard to cling to my belief system. *"What's really waiting for us on the other side? Where do we go when our time is up? What happens when the clock stops ticking, when we leave this world? When bills become irrelevant and saving for the future ends."* All of these thoughts are rumbling around in my head as I stare face to face with a woman that is not supposed to be there. She reeks of brimstone. Her eyes are filled with an all-consuming malevolence. She extends her hand towards my head. As she extends it, her form begins to change. I jerk back, a futile effort to prevent her from touching me. I watch in horror as she turns into a grotesque oddity, the likes of which I have never seen. The sheer horror of her appearance is indescribable! She turns into an exact personification of evil. I fight and frantically move my head. I mustn't let her touch me. She looks as if she is enjoying every moment of it. The shadow creatures grab my head and hold it still as my dead ringer's hand gets closer and closer. I feel an intense burning sensation as her fingertips touch the skin on my forehead. Her fingers begin to merge into my flesh, which is something I know there is no known explanation for; the laws of science are being broken as I cry and wince from the intensifying pain forming in my head. My head starts to throb and a loud ringing sound begins to bounce around in my ears. The pain is so intense. It's like having an earache to the tenth power combined with cramps. I feel myself getting weak. My legs are getting heavy. The muscles in my abdomen tighten and throb as well. My posture begins to slump. The pain is unbearable. She merges further and further into me. A dizzying sensation sweeps over me as everything begins to fade.

The sound of birds chirping and rays of sun sneaking in through the slats of the window blinds work collaboratively to awaken me. I try desperately to rustle out of my semi-comatose state. I'm in my living room sprawled out over my couch in a weird unnatural manner. I notice dark red spots smeared in its fabric, as well as on my hands, arms, and torso.

At first, it doesn't really hit me. However, as I continue looking myself over, I begin feeling uneasy. My feet have caked on dirt and remnants of dead leaves stuck to them. "What the…" I sit up. My body feels rigid and my head is throbbing uncontrollably. I manage to stand sloppily to my feet. I look around the room and begin to assess the situation. The room is in complete disarray. The coffee table is broken and lying scattered in pieces across the once pristine carpet and someone or something has made a huge hole in the chocolate colored accent wall. Something definitely isn't right. I try to remember the night before but most of it seems like a dream. It's all pretty much a blur. I can't distinguish the difference between reality and fiction.

Panic begins to set in and my body starts to tremble involuntarily. *"Keep it together."* I think while on the verge of hyperventilating. I tightly wrap my arms around myself as I try to calm down. I desperately want to close my eyes and not accept what I am seeing but a weird compulsion forces me to do exactly the opposite. I continue glossing over the room. My eyes stop at a trail of bloody footsteps leading into the dining room. I lift up one of my feet and check the bottom of it. It's covered in dried dirt and blood. The footsteps appear to be my own. I lower my foot and continue my trek. While walking through the dining room, I look over myself again; this time checking for any cuts or other fresh wounds. I don't find a single scratch. "What have I done?" I mumble as I reluctantly follow the mysterious trail out of the room.

I step into the kitchen, and immediately notice a shovel with pieces of fresh dirt caked on it. I can tell that it's fresh because it still has a clumpy, moist appearance. *"Did I kill someone? And how did I dig through the cold hard pre-winter soil?"* I question mentally as I try to CSI the facts. I walk through the kitchen and head out the back door. I examine the backyard for any freshly dug or covered holes. I'm glad that my backyard has a tall wooden fence that encloses it. The last thing I need is a neighbor to see me covered in blood looking like a deranged killer. I see a small hole near a tree. I proceed over to have a look in it. It's empty. Now I'm confused. *"What did I remove from the hole?"* I rack my brain trying desperately to retrieve any memories of what transpired the night before.

I try to recall the last person with whom I came in contact. *"Kenna,"* quickly illuminates in my mind. In a panicked haste, I run back into the house and scramble around for my phone. I begin removing every couch cushion and metaphorically leaving no stone unturned. I find it of all places, in my back pocket. I swiftly swipe in the pass code and scroll through the recent call list. I tap on the last call log with Kenna's number. Her contact info pops on the screen, accompanied by the sound of ringing. The phone picks up.

"Hello," interrupts the silence.

"Kenna," I respond feeling partially relieved to hear her voice.

"Hey Talia what's up?" She says, while obviously in the middle of something, I can tell by the amount of noise in the background on her end. "So did you have a good night?" She inquires.

"Uh yeah sure," I blurt out, not really giving my full attention to the question.

"You know I miss you," she says warmly.

"Hey let me call you right back okay?" Like a flash of

lightening, another person pops in my head, *"Aiden,"* I quickly hang up and scroll until I locate his number. I click on it and it begins to dial. I say hello as soon as the rings stop.

"Hey, I was waiting on you to call me," Aiden says in longing sincere, somewhat angry manner.

"Hi honey," I reply.

"Why didn't you tell about everything that's been going on?"

"I see somebody is happy to hear my voice," I respond sarcastically.

"You don't have to be a smart ass! All I'm saying is that you could've filled me in, I'm sick of finding out things after the fact! Kenna told me everything. I called you like I don't know how many times and it kept going to voicemail!"

"I'm sorry," I reply, which is a rather weak response given the circumstances but I can't think of anything to else to say. Most of my attention is preoccupied with the mystery from the night before. "Hey honey..." I pause, midsentence. In the midst of panic, I clearly forgot to check for one thing, *"Where is Max?"* is the latest addition to the mystery. "Hey Aiden baby, let me call you right back okay?"

"Okay," he responds angrily before abruptly hanging up.

"Max," I yell as I search throughout the house. I check the rest of the rooms on the first floor, no Max. I check the upstairs rooms, still no Max. I make my way to the basement… surprise, no Max. The sound of scratching stops me dead in my tracks. I follow the sound; it leads me to the front door. I open the door and see Max!

CHAPTER 1

The room is dark. It would be pitch black if not for the moon light faintly shining through the slits of the partially closed window blind. The sparsely furnished living room reflects that of a lone occupant. I lay frozen on my sofa, paralyzed by some unknown force. The room is ice cold. I am a prisoner in my own home. My eyes are the only things I can move. I focus my vision. I can't believe what I'm seeing in front of me. Three tall hooded menacing figures are standing over me. A forth is kneeled down directly in front of me. The darkness helps to conceal all of their features, all except one, their piercing intense red eyes. The kneeling figure begins to make an unrecognizable otherworldly sound. The sound is a deep growl, unlike anything I have ever heard. After growling, it begins to speak. "You will know!"

"Talia... Talia, wake up! You're going to be late!" I jump up, drenched in sweat. "I'm up!" I blurt out in a sleep drunken state. I sit on the edge of the bed for a few moments to get my head together and shake off the remnants of the horrific nightmare. Once I'm fully awake, I rush to get my things together and head off to the bathroom.

After a quick shower, I get dressed and start brushing my teeth. While brushing my teeth, I find myself doing an involuntary habit that I'm sure most people do when in the same situation. My eyes become glued to the mirror, noticing something that definitely needs to be addressed—my hair, I am irritated by the wild dark curly flowing mess on my head. *"I really need to do something with my hair!"* The thought completely captures my attention as I run my fingers through my untamed locks. Other than my desperate need of a salon, I am what most would consider an attractive female. I am twenty-four with hazel eyes, golden skin, a slender frame, a slightly toned physique, and exotic features. My physical appearance, made me quite popular in high school and college, which wasn't always a good thing, especially when your friend's boyfriend develops a crush on you. It has happened more times than I care to remember, and why is it that the friend gets mad at you? I mean, shouldn't they get mad at the boyfriend? The average person doesn't understand how much of a curse beauty actually is. I mean sure it can help get you further in life but it can also be a dangerous asset. Other than the aforementioned scenario occurring a few times, my college life was a great experience. I enjoyed it much more than high school, the parties, the freedom, my sorority… I'm reminiscing like it was twenty years ago, when it's really only been close to four. Seeing as how I'm somewhat pressed for time, I decide to do the go to thing that most women having a bad hair day do, I comb it through, and bunch it all into a ponytail.

With my hair temporarily taken care of, I head back to the room to finish getting ready. I make sure that I grab all of the necessary items and put them into my brown leather coach bag. It was a gift from Aiden, my high school sweetheart. He gave it to me our senior year as an anniversary present. After I have everything that I need, I put on one of my favorite jackets. Despite showing signs of wear, it's still in somewhat fair condition and the brown color matches the coach bag perfectly. My mom doesn't understand why I've held on to such a relic for so long. Like the bag, it was gift from Aiden. He gave it to me as a Christmas gift our first year together. The sentimental value alone is the reason why I'll probably keep it until all that remains is a shredded, worn ghost of a jacket. I stumble and barely catch myself before making my way down the stairs and into the front room.

"Make sure you have everything you need for your appointment." My mom says in a manner that is not quite irritating but borderline redundant, while giving me that doting motherly look.

"I know mom, I know," I murmur before planting a kiss on her cheek as she puts her suit coat on. People tell me I favor her a lot. Her light golden brown skin, soft facial features, and deep green eyes make her a stunning sight at forty-five. I completely understand my father's pain. As a child, I hated going places with her. For some reason, she would always attract hard up losers with cheesy lines and no respect. Even when she would flash her wedding band and politely decline their advances, most would still attempt to steal the fire. When I say steal the fire, I mean try to possess something that they know can never rightfully be theirs. Over the years, my experience with men has been somewhat similar, which is probably why I'm currently single. I guess the curse runs in the family. Beauty is quite the overrated trait. According to my mom, my father has gotten into quite a few fistfights over her.

"I'm probably going to be in meetings all day and your father should be in this evening. Try to be back. He really wants to see you." She announces while grabbing a bottle of her favorite juice from out of the refrigerator.

"Aye, aye captain," I say jokingly as I walk out of the front door. "Love you, see you later."

I make my way outside. The cold air brushes over my face. The smells of early fall bring back fond memories of the forthcoming season. Helping Grandma Mariana bake delicious homemade pies and going on hunting trips with Grandpa John. Oh and going through old photo albums with the both of them while

14

Grandma Mariana told the stories associated with each photo. Periodically Grandpa John would interject with what he felt were the correct details. Oftentimes, it would lead to a cute little spat between them that always ended in grandpa being wrong and everyone laughing about it after the fact. The stories Grandma Mariana told, really gave me a better understanding of her homeland and the things that she kept close to heart. It was through her that I learned that my mom's side of the family is from Brazil and Seattle.

Grandma Mariana was from Brazil and Grandpa John was from Seattle. According to Grandma Mariana, they first met when Grandpa John came to her country while on vacation. She was a waitress at a local bar and grill that received a great deal of business from tourists. One day while she was working, she said the weirdest guy came in with a look in his eyes that was much different from anyone else she had ever encountered. He told her that he and a couple of his friends were on a two-week vacation. His friends ended up finding the company of lady friends. He didn't want to be the fifth wheel so that's how he ended up alone at the bar where she worked. He purposely spent the night ordering drinks from her just to stay in her company. By the end of the night, he was so drunk that he could barely stand, let alone make it back to his hotel. My grandma knew that some of the locals would take advantage of him in his drunken state, so she ended up taking him back to her place to look after him until the next day.

When he woke up, he told her "I must be in heaven because the most beautiful angel is standing over me." After that day, the two of them were inseparable. As his two-week vacation was nearing its end, he pleaded with her to come back to Seattle with him. He said he felt complete for the first time in his life and that he could provide her with a better life if she were to do so. After some intense pondering, she agreed on three conditions. First he had to make sure that she was able to visit home at least twice a year, second she made him promise to never get drunk like how he had gotten the day they met, and last, to always make her feel special like how he had done up to that point. I guess love doesn't have a time limit or stringent rules because she left with him and they lived happily ever after. He lived up to all the promises. Actually, he did even better. Once his business really got off the ground, he made sure she got to visit home three to four times a year, he quit drinking other than on special occasions, and he kept finding ways to make her feel special. One of the ways he made her feel special was that he would prepare her favorite breakfast every Friday morning. The breakfast consisted of a scrumptious selection of bacon, ham, provolone and smoked cheddar cheeses, and whole grain wheat bread with some type of fruit that he would sculpt into the shape of a flower. Since I was their only granddaughter, they let me enjoy the delightful meal on a few occasions. I absolutely fell in love with it.

They stayed together for forty-three years until Grandpa John passed away. Grandma Mariana knew something was wrong that particular Friday morning because she didn't smell the familiar smell of her favorite breakfast being prepared. It turns out that he died while on his way back from the grocery store. He had forgotten a key ingredient and rushed out to get it before she awoke. Less than ten minutes from home, Grandpa John had a heart attack and his car ended up going head on with an eighteen-wheeler.

After his death, Grandma Mariana was never the same. She

was completely heartbroken. It seemed as if she had died when he died and was just waiting for her body to catch up. Visiting their once happy home post Grandpa John's death was like visiting some sort of memorial. Pictures and memorabilia of Grandpa John were present in every room of the house. Grandma Mariana became reclusive. She entertained her family less and less with each year that passed. Thankfully, for her sake she died a few years afterward. My eyes always get watery when I think about them. They really meant a lot to me.

My dad is from Cleveland. I have never met his father. I'm not sure what their relationship was like because he's never talked much about him. One day I tried to get information out of him about his father and he completely shut down. He wouldn't talk to me for the rest of the day. I also know very little about his mom. I remember visiting her a few times as a child. She was a small black woman with deep hazel eyes. She was nice, but weird. According to my mom, she was originally from somewhere in Haiti and relocated to Louisiana before settling in Ohio shortly before my father was born. I think her weirdness came from the fact that she was into black magic or voodoo. The last time we visited her, she and my dad got into a real bad argument. I was too young at the time to understand the cause of it. It got so bad that he threatened to never let her see me again. She left town shortly after. To this day, I don't know what happened to her. I don't even know if she's still alive. All I know is that she was very weird. More than likely, she probably went back to Haiti or her second home, Louisiana.

Cleveland is an okay place. I work there now at "Central Insurance". The only major gripe I have is that sometimes, the commute to work can be nerve-racking! Driving from North Olmsted to downtown Cleveland is an adventure in itself. I shouldn't really complain, considering the fact that getting to work and school in California was ten times worse! My car is a modest late model Toyota corolla that I affectionately refer to as "Lindy". She isn't the most attractive car in the world but she's lasted me throughout my college days and up to the present. I got her as a high school graduation present. She's dependable and inexpensive to repair. I love her.

I start Lindy up. One of my favorite songs by "Maroon 5"

greets my ears. I sing along with Adam Levine while waiting for her to heat up. After lindy warms up, I head off to start my day. I still can't quite seem to get the nightmare out of my head. Just thinking about those creatures, sends chills up my spine. "You will know... what the hell does that mean?" I say aloud while stopping at a light. My attention shifts as I notice someone in the distance. Someone very familiar, I notice... him. He still looks the way I remember. His thick black wavy hair complements his handsome chiseled face, his strong blue eyes sparkling in the sunlight. His tight long sleeve shirt looks as if it's painted on his buff muscular physic. His slightly loose boot cut dark blues match his rugged dark brown leather footwear. He is still as amazing as I remember. I feel a little tingle just looking at him. His face glows radiantly in the sunlight. Yep, he is still a sight to behold; so ruggedly handsome and sexy. The moments we spent together replay in my mind like highlights from a TV show, as I watch him casually stroll down the sidewalk. *"What went wrong with us?"* I wonder as I contemplate stopping to say hi. I have a few minutes to spare so I figure I might as well take advantage of it. I park Lindy and approach him.

"Aiden," I call out to him. He smiles when he recognizes me.

"Talia, I was just thinking about you."

"So I see you're back in town," I say while trying not to get too excited or lost in his gorgeous smile.

"Yeah, I'm back permanently." He responds, as his ocean blue eyes captivate me. "I just got a place over near Lakewood."

"Oh okay, great. How was New York?"

"Hectic, non-stop, you know typical city that never sleeps,"

"Okay. So how are your mom and Ashley? I heard about your father and you know…"

"They're okay. My mom is holding up well considering…" he looks away briefly, I feel like kicking myself.

"I'm sorry—"

"It's alright; it's a part of life."

"How are you taking it? I mean, are you sure you're okay?"

"Yeah, I'm okay. I'm just taking it one day at a time."

"Your dad was pretty cool."

"Thanks. He always thought you were going to end up being his daughter-in-law."

"He and I both, you know—" before I can finish my sentence,

Aiden's lips connect with mine.

"I missed you Talia." He says in a low breathy masculine tone. I'm shocked. I don't really know what to say or how to react. My heart still longs for him but I'm still not sure why we ended. The flame of love that I have for him is still burning strong in spite of all of the dating that I've done afterwards. Even when I went away to school in California, my heart stayed with Aiden. He is the one guy that I couldn't replace.

"I missed you too. I missed us." I say before kissing him back. His lips are warm and exceptionally soft. His taste is intoxicating.

"What are you doing later? Maybe we can catch up a little bit more over dinner." He slyly slips out the invite while flashing a charming smile.

"That sounds great. I just have to take care of a few things. I should be free after six."

"Okay well I have to stop by my mom's house and help rearrange some stuff so you can meet me over there if you'd like. I'm sure her and Ashley would love to see you, unless you want me to pick you up?"

"Well I'm kind of staying with my parents until I get my

house so meeting you at your mom's will be perfect."

"Alright well I guess I will see you later." He says in a warm extra friendly manner. I give him a hug and a kiss on the cheek before walking off. I sense his lusting gaze on me while I lightly switch back to Lindy. I make sure to walk at a slow enough speed to keep his attention. Once I reach Lindy, I look back to see if I still have is focus. His eyes are still fixated, which is the desired effect I was hoping for; I flash him a quick smile before opening my door. I feel the effects of nostalgia as I get back inside.

"Wow he is just as I remember." I think to myself while turning the key in the ignition. I feel a big smile form on my face. Lindy revs back up and I continue on my way to handle my affairs of the day.

The drive is smooth as "Heart" blares through the car speakers. I love their old classic rock sound. I'm too young to remember when they were out, but I'm still a fan never the less. I wish I were around during that era. A lot of the musical acts nowadays don't compare to their predecessors. For some odd reason or another, I've always favored listening to older music over the new stuff. I remember when I used to go hunting with Grandpa John and he would play a lot of classic rock and funk. I think that's where my love for old music stems from, from good Ol' Papa John. Even though I was a girl, he never treated me differently. He showed me the same hunting techniques that he showed my male cousins Jacob and Caleb. He always said, "When it comes to survival, gender doesn't matter, some of the greatest killers are ladies." I can still picture his trademark half-cocked smile and the seriousness in his eyes that would often accompany the statement.

I arrive at my first destination right on schedule. I pull into the driveway of my soon to be home. I step out and Mr. Hal Reynolds, a real estate agent greets me. Mr. Reynolds is an older guy with salt and pepper colored hair. He's a little on the obese side. He looks kind of like Reed Richards, you know "Mr. Fantastic" from the "Fantastic Four" movies. Well, more like a bloated non-super version. The fact that he's noticeably overweight makes his choice of vehicle comical. I mean picture a three hundred something pound guy in a two-seater sports car.

"Hello Talia, it's good to see you."

"Hello Mr. Reynolds I'm all set to go." I'm eager to get things finalized. Today is the first day that I will be handling things by myself. My dad insisted on coming along but I fought tooth and nail with him to get my way. I need to show him that I'm capable of handling my own affairs like the adult that I am.

"Okay, go on ahead inside. I have to grab a few things out of my car and then we can get down to business."

The house is a cozy white colonial with dark burgundy trim and awnings. I enter the house followed by Mr. Reynolds. We step into the vestibule. I notice the hardwood floor has indications of recent work. I also notice it is extremely cold. I shrug it off, attributing it to the change in season and the heat not being on.

"Okay Talia if you will follow me into the dining room, we can get this process underway." We walk through the living room. It is a nice inviting room with a decorative fireplace and built-in bookshelves. A lone picture hangs up on one of the walls. The picture is strange. In fact, it's downright creepy. The carpet is cream and the walls are off-white with one of them painted chocolate brown as an accent. When I first saw this room, it instantly made me think of the furniture that I wanted to get that would match it perfectly. We make our way to the dining room. It has hardwood floors similar to the vestibule. The only furnishing in the room is a slightly worn dining room table and a floor lamp in the corner.

"So before I sign these papers, is there anything you have to tell me about the house? Any deaths or gruesome murders I need to know about?" I say with a wily grin.

"No Talia, nothing like that has ever happened here. Trust me your father and I already had a long talk about it. You're quite lucky to have him as a father."

"I know. He definitely wants the best for me." I respond with a smile. "If not for him having to work, he would've probably insisted on coming today."

"I know the feeling. I'm the same way with my daughter but anyway, the previous owner was a real quiet guy. He kept to himself. Other than that, the house was a family owned house passed down two generations. The original owner was a guy by the name of Jerry Graftmore. He came here as an immigrant and built the place from scratch. When he got married, he moved in the Mrs. and the rest is history. To my knowledge, there haven't been any deaths, murders, or anything of that nature. A lot of love and care was put into this property. The last owner had some major renovations done to it before putting it up on the market."

"Well you know I had to ask. I regularly watch some of those ghost shows. Not that I believe in them but why chance it."

"I got you trust me. This one lady I grew up with her and her husband bought a place and there were all kinds of weird things going on there, lights turning on and off, footsteps, weird noises at night, the whole shebang. The lady almost lost it completely!"

I continue talking to Mr. Reynolds and going over the paperwork. Once we're finished, I take a second look around the house.

"It's a pretty big space for just me maybe I should get a cat, a dog, or a roommate? Who knows, maybe if things go great, Aiden will end up moving in." I think to myself while giving the place a once more look over. I still feel a distinct chill. It seems as if it is following me from room to room. *"Whoa Talia, relax it's just a little draft, perfectly normal for the season."* I try to reassure myself. I go back into the living room for one last look. The creepy picture, steals my attention again. I can't explain it, but there is

something about it. It's creepy, but not in the conventional manner. Even though it's only like my third time in this house, I feel like I've been here a thousand times before. I can't figure out why it looks so familiar, especially this living room.

"Wow this is weird, déjà vu." I say in a low voice. I just can't seem to shake the feeling but I won't let it overshadow my joyous moment. As of today, I am officially on my way to becoming a homeowner. Remembering the rest of my schedule, I leave the house and get back on the road to my next destination, work.

CHAPTER 2

The drive into work seems a bit more pleasant. A sense of accomplishment overwhelms me. Within thirty minutes, I arrive in downtown Cleveland. My favorite parking spot is open, the sun is starting to shine, and I have a date with the love of my life, everything feels right. Oh how I've missed him. I take the stairs that lead into the main lobby. I reach the lobby, and see Hank, the older heavyset security guard doing his usual afternoon patrol.

"Hey beautiful what's going on," Hank asks in his normal flirty manner as we greet one another.

"Nothing but the usual handsome," I respond playfully as my eyes inadvertently shift to look in the direction of the little coffee shop located a few feet away. I see my ex-friend, Kenna. We work for the same company but in different departments. I really want to avoid her.

"Alright Hank I gotta run so I'll talk to you later okay?" I murmur as a way to cut the conversation short. We say our goodbyes and I quickly make my way to the elevators. Since it's around noon, I assume that she's just grabbing a few things to snack on as opposed to going out for lunch. I notice the items as she places them on the counter a cup of yogurt, an apple, and a bottle of flavored water. She is rather intimidating, with looks and sex appeal that in my opinion slightly exceed my own. She's a fiery red head with ambition to match. She has nice legs, a slim waist, and bright green eyes to die for, I still remember how close we once were, until the one night that changed everything. She really was a great friend but… it's not like that now. Things were going great between us at one point but after that unfortunate night, the friendship came to a screeching halt. In spite of feeling awkward in her presence, I secretly hold out hope that we can salvage our once blossoming friendship. I wait anxiously as the elevators take their sweet time reaching my floor. Kenna notices me and starts heading in my direction.

"Hey Talia," she says as she waves.

"Dammit," I mumble under my breath as I force a fake smile.

"How are you doing today?" She says with her eyes cooing, I catch on to her flirting but I choose to play it cool.

"I'm good and you?" I say smoothly without showing the slightest hint of interest.

"Here going through the motions, I thought you were on vacation?" Her lips release her words gracefully.

"Oh, I am. I just stopped in to deliver some paperwork that Mr. Beck has been hounding me about; I'm gone for three days and the whole place is falling apart!" I joke as a means of being friendly.

"Gotcha," she retorts. Kenna is definitely a good person, well other than that one flaw that ruined everything. After waiting for what seems like an eternity, one of the elevators finally reaches our floor. I contemplate letting her take it and waiting on the next one. She gives me a weird remorseful look that instantly appeals to my softer side. Before I can step on, a weird man walks off. He is abnormally pale with short-cropped black hair. He reeks of strong unpleasant cologne. He stares me down as he walks past. Then he turns and flashes a quick smile at Kenna. "Fuckin' creep," I mumble to myself as I watch him walk away. We both get on the elevator simultaneously as if we have some unspoken agreement. Once inside, we go to opposite ends of the elevator. I go right into the corner closest to the buttons and the door, and she goes to the back and practically hugs up against the wall. While riding in the elevator, my mind starts to drift. It never really occurred to me why thirteen is such an unlucky number. I work on the thirteenth floor. I had my first kiss when I was thirteen; I won a raffle with the number thirteen. It's been nothing but lucky for me. I guess waiting in silence makes one reflect on such things. It helps little to keep my mind off what's bothering me. I feel Kenna's eyes staring at me. It's so weird. I try to ignore it but it's uncomfortable not knowing what she is thinking. Based on that night, I'm thinking the worse. I hope it's not what I think it is. The elevator reaches the floor and I quickly exit, not looking back.

"See you later Tally," I hear Kenna blurt. I ignore her and keep walking.

I step into my office and see all the usual suspects. Jessica, my partner in crime, is a chubby fast-talking busy body with a severe addiction to reality shows. She knows everything that there is to know about them. From "Dancing with the Stars" to "Bad Girls Club", if the show is reality based, she's seen it. Personally, I think that she has way, too much time on her hands. When it comes to talking, she definitely has the gift of gab. When I first met her, I told her she should be in sales instead of general office work. Ironically, it turns out her dad was a car salesman for years and her mother was and still is a "Mary Kay" sales rep. It's safe to assume that they contributed to her chatty ways. I guess she found a perfect match in her husband, seeing as how they've been together for almost seven years. That's a lifetime by today's standards!

"Hey Talia, see you can't stay away huh?"

"Yeah, right Jessica. I just love work," I respond sarcastically. I have to get these papers to Mr. Beck. Besides, I'll be back tomorrow anyway so it's no big deal."

"Oh okay, well I have to tell you about the "Bad Girls Club" reunion! O-M-G, they were going at it for real!"

"That sounds really interesting but I'm really in a rush so how about you tell me all about it tomorrow okay?" I respond hoping that my lack of interest isn't too apparent.

"Yeah alright," she says with a look of disappointment. I keep walking and run into Kathy the receptionist. Kathy doesn't really strike me as the clerical type. She's a blond with most of her ambition and focus outside of work. She has had a few small breaks in her pursuit of fame and fortune, mainly public access appearances and radio commercials. She really aspires to be a pet whisperer/reality star. She claims to understand exactly what her cat named Tuna wants simply by watching the way her ears move. She also thinks that her looks and talent will make her a mega superstar. She is super quirky.

"Hey Talia how are you?" She asks in a friendly manner.

"I'm good. I just stopped in to drop these papers off to the boss. Is he in?" I respond as I adjust the coach bag's shoulder strap.

"Yes he is,"

"Okay thanks. Oh by the way, how is Tuna doing?"

"She's okay, you know typical tuna,"

"That's good to hear." I respond before making my way into Mr. Beck's office.

Mr. Beck is so anal-retentive. He overly worries about everything! He gets anxious or distressed over minuscule problems and he hates change or anything that deviates from the normal flow of things. However, for some strange reason we seem to get along. As usual, his office is meticulously organized. Everything is in an exact spot or location, even his pencil and pen holders. I remember this one time, a guy came in for an interview and moved something on his desk, needless to say, he didn't get the job.

"Hello Talia, have a seat." He says as he makes a gesture towards the seat in front of his desk. "Do you have what I need?" He questions as his eyes shoot towards the brown coach bag hanging from my shoulder.

"Of course sir, have I ever let you down?" is my response as I unzip the bag and retrieve the paperwork. I make sure to put the papers in his hand. I don't want to risk accidently shifting anything on his desk. He looks them over and places them down on his desk.

"Thank you for bringing them in for me Talia. How is everything going with the new house?"

"Great actually, we finalized it today."

"Okay good. Congratulations."

"Thanks Mr. Beck, I will see you tomorrow." I humbly reply as I get up to leave.

"Wait Talia before you go…"

"Yes?" I respond and shift my attention back towards him.

"There is another reason why I wanted you to stop in. I've been thinking. Since victor's promotion to another department, we have been in dire need of a new Office Manager. Now at first, I was considering absorbing the duties of the position among several other positions. However, after careful consideration I've decided that a new Office Manager would be a better solution. Do you remember the company expansion that I mentioned last month?

"Yes, I recall you mentioning it in the last meeting."

"Well now because of the expansion, I'm going to be overseeing three different departments; which means that I really need the right person to keep this office running smoothly. I need a good capable individual to take Victor's place, be my right hand, my go to person. I've been noticing your business ethic and the quality of work that you have been producing and well… I would like to offer you the position." The offer surprises me. I was not expecting it at all. I take a few seconds before responding.

"Oh wow sir I am honored, um… I will gladly accept your offer." I respond as I try to contain my excitement.

"Great," Mr. Beck says as he extends his hand. We shake, and I get up to leave his office. "Enjoy the rest of your day."

"I will sir."

After leaving Mr. Beck's office, I see Jeff. Jeff is just your average Joe. He does the minimum to get by, anything extra, don't expect to get it from him.

"Hey Jeff,"

"Hello Talia, what brings you up here?"

"Mr. Beck,"

"I knew there was something going on between you two… that's probably why you never gave me a chance."

"UH… no, and you already know why we never got to that level."

"No I don't actually, enlighten me."

"You know you're like a weird slacker brother to me and besides you have a thing for Kathy."

"Okay fair enough, well everyone from the office is planning on hitting up the "Dirty Rascal" Friday. You know, shoot some pool, throw back a few Buds… see how far I can get with Kathy…" Jeff has the hugest crush on Kathy. He's been trying to get things going with her for the longest. He's gotten close a few times but something always happens to prevent it. "Oh and Jessica is probably going to bring her husband too." He says as a means of further enticement. I've been wondering what Jessica's husband is actually like. Jessica always talks about him, well when she's not talking about TV shows. She does impressions of him in a hysterically, low pitched voice. I want to see how close the caricature is to the real thing.

"Alright well maybe I will go too. I'll let you know Friday." I respond, as I seriously give the invitation consideration.

I run into a few other people around the office before leaving. I see Brad. He handles all of the finances for our department. He's cool but doesn't talk much. He's the quiet, skinny, brainy, analytical type. He looks sort of like Napoleon Dynamite. I also see Tasha. Tasha is a cute woman with a warm personality. She reminds me of the actress Meagan Good. Tasha was one of the first people that I befriended when I started working for central a couple of years ago. She has a good heart; I just wish she had good judgment to go along with it. She seems to be a magnet for losers and douche bags. She always has a new story to tell me about some jerk doing her wrong. She's like a slightly older sister to me. I think the feeling is mutual. Sometimes when we hang out outside of work, she tells people that we're sisters. I have a lot of love for her. I sincerely hope she finds someone to treat her right.

"Hey Tash," I acknowledge her with a warm smile, a quick hug, and a friendly kiss on the cheek.

"Hey Talia, how is your vacation?" She asks after equally reciprocating my greeting.

"It's going good. I just stopped in to give some paperwork to Mr. Beck." I respond as my mind thinks about the things that I have to do before my date tonight. "Are you going to the "Dirty Rascal" Friday? Jeff told me that the usual suspects him included, will be there."

"No unfortunately, I've got a lot of school work to catch up on. I really don't care much for school but since the company is reimbursing me for it, I'm going to do the best I can."

"I understand completely. I might not make it either. Well

anyway, I gotta run but I'll be back to work tomorrow."

"Alright, well it's good to see you sis." She says while placing her hand on my shoulder.

"It's good to see you too sis." I give her another hug before continuing to make my way out of the office.

I'm almost out of my department when Shane calls after me. I really want to ignore him and keep walking but that probably wouldn't be the best thing to do, considering that we work in such close proximity. We really don't see eye to eye. He is very cocky with asshole tendencies. He's your typical meathead. He looks like the ex-jock type. Every time I see him, my high school stalker/ex-boyfriend Blake comes to mind. He and I have bumped heads on more than one occasion. Whenever everyone from the office hangs out, we never socialize. I think it has a lot to do with the fact that I rejected all of his advances while he and Kenna were fooling around, or maybe it's because she told him about the night. If looks could kill, I would've been dead after he found out about it. It played a major part in the unraveling of their relationship. For some reason, he couldn't seem to let it go. Shane gives me the usual look of disdain covered up in a smile. The phony son of a bitch can't wait to see me leave.

"Hey Talia, I see you're working towards that "Employee of the Quarter" award." He says in a condescending tone. I'm really close to hating him.

"No actually Mr. Beck entrusted me with the task of finalizing some time sensitive paperwork. He didn't want to jeopardize it by assigning it to an employee that lacks the proficiency to complete it." I respond in a manner that is not so subtlety directed at him.

"Oh okay." He says before walking away. He probably has to think about it before he really gets it. He's such a fucking brick head.

I finally leave the office and make my way back home. I think of all types of things to kill the monotony of the drive. Sometimes driving to the same destinations can get a little old. I think about the stuff I want to buy to go in the new house, I think about the new promotion, about Aiden, and for some strange reason, Kenna comes to mind as well. I recollect how good it felt to see her earlier and how we obviously still have some type of bond. An image of us together with Aiden pops into my head. I briefly entertain what it would be like to spend the night with the both of them. Having them at the same time would perhaps be the best of both worlds. "Geez, Talia you really need to get laid!" I mumble, not paying any attention to what's playing on the radio. It's been like a month and a half since the night with Kenna. I'm surprised that it hasn't crossed my mind sooner. I guess I've just been too busy with work and the new house to think about it, or maybe it's because I was somewhat traumatized by the whole ordeal. Some people may chalk it up to being experimental, which is exactly what I hope it was, but deep down I have a nagging dose of doubt. I really need to do something about it.

At this point, my mental black book is blank. I can't really think of anybody that's available or that I would even want to bother giving the time of day to, or maybe it's because subconsciously I'm hoping my reconnection with Aiden will turn into something. I must admit he really is the greatest lover I have ever had. I definitely wouldn't mind spending some more time in is big strong arms. Thanks to having sex on the brain, my desperate need for the salon almost slipped my mind. I haven't been there in a few weeks. I decide to give my hairdresser a call. I dial the number and turn on my Bluetooth headset. *"Maybe I should wear that new outfit I've been dying to wear?"* I think as the phone rings. Last year, I bought the cutest dark red skirt outfit. After bringing it home, I tried it on again with a new pair of boots and then put it away in my closet. I haven't taken it out since. My dad calls me a hoarder. He says that I have more material things than I know what to do with. Personally, I think it's because he's a man and men in general tend not to understand how or why women do the things that we do. I like to have options and when it comes to clothing, shoes, and accessories, I like keep an abundance of them.

"World famous hair studio, Tanya speaking,"

"Hey Tanya, please tell me you have an opening today it's an emergency!" I blurt out while slowing down at a red light.

"Whoa slow down Hun, where's the fire? Who am I speaking with?" She responds.

"It's Talia,"

"Oh hey Talia, I might be able to squeeze you in within the next hour. Let me guess, you have a hot date tonight."

"That would be correct," I respond in a giddy tone.

"I see said the brown cow. Okay well head up here and I'll be sure to take care of you."

"Okay, thanks a million sweetie."

"No problem."

I step inside the salon, the same one I've been going to for years. I see Mrs. Graves the owner talking to Mrs. Randal one of the shop's regulars. I try not to overhear their conversation. More than likely, they're talking about the latest gossip as usual. Shania, another one of the shops regulars is there as well. She's the type that's always bragging about something. If she's not bragging about her rich husband, she's bragging about her jewelry, their cars, his business, or the latest gift he bought her. She is a major attention whore. I guess she needs it to feel some type of validation in her otherwise shallow life.

"Talia, how are you darling?" She asks as I walk closer to her. She gives me a superficial hug and fake kisses on each of my cheeks. The smell of her perfume chokes me; it's so strong that it smells as if she took a swim in it. Her pricey outfit and gaudy jewelry makes it obvious that she is dressed to impress. She reminds me of one of those rich house wives made famous by reality TV. I know she doesn't really care about what's going on in my life, she's just happy to have someone else to brag to, I fake my politeness as usual.

"Oh I'm good, how—" I stop myself in mid-sentence. I dare not ask her how she is doing. All that will do is open up the Pandora box of bragging. I pretend to have an incoming call on my cell phone. "Excuse me for a second I really have to take this." I say as I pretend to press the button on my Bluetooth. My award winning acting skills work like a charm, mission accomplished thirty minute bragging conversation averted. I see Tanya and head towards her. She's a cool lady that always looks like she's ahead of the latest trends as opposed to following them. She appears to be in the middle of doing another customer's hair.

"Hey Tanya," I give her a quick wave and smile.

"Hey honey, have a seat and I'll be right with you. As soon as I get done with her, you're up next." She responds.

"Okay thanks," I walk over, take a seat, and search through a pile of magazines on the table next to me. I see a few issues of "In Style", a few of "Cosmopolitan", and a couple issues of "US Weekly". I'm a sucker for celebrity gossip, beauty, sex tips, and fashion, so the choice is obvious. I start flipping through the magazine and notice an article about perfect pickup lines. I read them and find out that I have heard a few of them. One in specific I remember hearing last week. A gas station attendant used it on me. I chuckle as I reflect back on the incident. I make a mental note of the rest of them before continuing my journey through the mag.

"Talia you're up." Tanya says as she collects payment for her services and begins getting the seat ready for me. Once she gets all set up, I put the issue of "Cosmopolitan" down and take my seat in the salon chair.

"How do you want it?" She asks as she preps me for the treatment.

"I need it straightened out a little and I guess add some highlights to it oh and take care of the split ends."

"You really don't like curls do you?" She asks while taking out a mild relaxer.

"I think my natural curls make me look too young and naïve. I just reconnected with my old high school sweet heart so I want to have the look of an older, more sophisticated woman. I think it

46

would be sexier."

"I gotcha, so you must have high hopes for the two of you hitting it off again huh?"

"Yes and no, I don't know. It's just that… when I saw him to today, all of those old feelings came rushing back, plus he surprised me with a passionate kiss on the lips."

"Oh wow, you might have a hot night tonight." She responds with a devilish grin. "Don't worry; I'm going to give you a hairstyle that he won't be able to resist."

Tanya straightens out my mess of curls, adds subtle highlights, and takes care of my split ends in less than two hours. When she's done she hands me a mirror, takes the cover from around me, sprays my hair, and then I'm good to go.

"How much do I owe you?" I ask as I pull my wallet out of my coach bag.

"Eighty-seven," she responds. I pull out a one hundred dollar bill.

"Keep the change. I appreciate you taking care of me in such short notice."

"No problem, anytime. Now go and get than man wrapped around your finger girl."

"Okay," I reply, as I get ready to leave.

CHAPTER 3

I pull up to the house of Aiden's parents. It still looks the same. Even with a few minor alterations. The one difference that really catches my eye is the updated color of the trim and awnings. I park Lindy and go up to the front door. Before I get a chance to ring the doorbell Ashley, Aiden's sister opens the door. *"Wow Ashley has really grown up."* I think while trying not to stare too hard at her because let's face it, that would be weird. She has really turned into a knock out. I pick up a familiar vibe from her almost instantly. There is something different about her that I can't seem to figure out.

"Hi Talia," she says to me in a sweet soft voice. I swear she's a dead ringer for a young Megan Fox. Her bright blue captivating eyes, her full pouty lips, her long dark hair, she is definitely a dead ringer for her.

"Hey Ashley," I respond. She gives me a warm hug and welcomes me in. I walk into their front room and make myself comfortable. Their front room was always a warm inviting room. Now it seems different. The warmth that I felt on previous visits is definitely missing. For some strange reason I feel cold like how I felt earlier in the new house. Aiden's mom walks into the room.

"Hi Talia, how have you been?" She says before giving me a big hug.

"I've been okay Mrs. Daniels. How have you been?"

"I've been better, it's just so difficult… you know… I still feel like he's here with me."

"I understand. My grandmother went through the same thing. Mr. Daniels was a good man."

"So where are you two kids headed?"

"Our favorite place Mrs. Daniels, "Tasty Bones" ", then we will probably head to slams. You know just to catch up."

"Aiden will be up in a few, I needed help with his father's things. Brian always wanted you to stick around."

"I know. Me too," we continue talking for a few minutes before Aiden makes his way up from the basement and into the front room. He looks so amazing. He has on a black sweater and a handsome pair of slacks. His hair is cut low on the sides. A strong smell of one of my favorite scents "Engage for Men", hangs in the air. It's an intoxicating scent. Engage is the type of fragrance that never gets old. His deep blue eyes are like melting ice kisses. I still feel a chill around me but the energy in the room forces it to take a back seat. We make our exit and the cold evening air greets us. The evening sky looks quiet and foreboding. I can hear the wind blowing through the dying leaves.

"Would you like to leave your car here, at your place, or at my apartment?" He asks as he walks me to Lindy. The choice that I make will indirectly decide how it ends. A quick thought of sex pops into my head and helps me make the decision.

"Um, I'll follow you to your place." I respond as I try to contain my excitement. Aiden opens my door and helps me in before going to his car. Before starting the car, I look back at the house. A shadowy figure in one of the upstairs windows catches my attention. Thinking my mind is playing tricks on me, I forcefully blink my eyes. I look at the window again. The figure is gone.

Within twenty minutes, we arrive at Aiden's apartment complex. From the outside, it seems decent enough. I park my car. Aiden gets out of his car and opens his passenger side door. He was always such a gentleman. I see that he hasn't changed.

Driving through our hometown brings back many memories for the both of us. We begin reminiscing on our high school days. I recall the first time we met. It was a few days before he joined cheerleading squad. We both laugh at how ridiculous he looked in a male cheerleader outfit. He confesses that he joined the squad to get girls, which makes sense considering that he only lasted half of a season. He puts on the charm by adding that after he got me, he no longer had a reason to be on the squad. He joined the soccer team the following year. I love soccer. It's a great sport. He was good at it too. If it weren't for his career ending knee injury, he would've definitely gotten a full ride scholarship. Every now and then, he says he pops in the old highlight tapes for nostalgia.

After a brief moment of silence, Aiden goes into one of the most memorable parts of cheerleading practice, toss extensions. The first time he hoisted me into the air, I had to use every fiber of my being to keep from shaking due to nervousness. I knew he really didn't know what he was doing. We laugh a little about before he brings up our first kiss, or rather how he stole his first kiss from me. It was bold I must admit, it was a game changing move, one that could've got him pulverized by my then boyfriend Blake who was the captain of the football team. It's apparent now but at the time, it puzzled me as to why I didn't spill the beans to Blake. He already had it out for Aiden because he was on the cheerleading squad. According to Blake, real men play sports while girls and sissies cheerlead. The kiss changed things for the better. I broke up with Blake shortly thereafter.

As we get on the freeway, a strange song comes on the satellite radio station. It's strange because I've heard it before but I can't recall where. The rest of the ride is smooth. We arrive at "Tasty Bones". I can smell the food as soon as Aiden steps out of the car. My stomach lets out a small growl in anticipation of the meal. As Aiden walks over to open the passenger side door, the song starts to play in my head. *"She said, she said I'm watching you/she said she said I got my eye on you."* I have no idea why or how the song is stuck in my memory. I don't even know who made it.

I'm giddy with delight as we walk into the restaurant. As seniors in high school, we practically lived in the place. Almost every Friday, you'd be sure to find us at "Tasty Bones" stuffing our faces. My mouth waters at the thought of tasting those sweet succulent ribs. Peggy, the woman at the greeter podium remembers us. She is a sweet lady. Actually, she is the aunt of one of my high school friends.

"Hey, I haven't seen you folks in ages." She says while grabbing two menus from behind the podium.

"Hello Mrs. Thornton." I respond, followed by Aiden's response.

"You guys look like you want a booth am I right?" She asks as walks from behind her station.

"Yes, we would. By the way, how is Shelly?" I ask. Her niece Shelly was one of my closest friends. We lost contact a short time after I went to college.

"You don't have to be so formal, just call me Judith. Oh and Shelly has done quite well for herself. She's married and has a two year old with another one due by next spring."

"Wow really?" The news is shocking considering the fact that Shelly never wanted kids. Back in high school, she seemed to have her whole life planned out they weren't included.

"Yup, she's officially in the motherhood club." Judith says. "Follow me." She instructs as she turns and begins to walking toward the dining area. She shows us to a small booth nestled in the corner with a view of the bar and the entrance to the kitchen. "Your server Tina will be with you shortly. Oh and I'll tell Shelly that you asked about her." She says before heading back to her post by the door. Hearing that Shelly is married with kids makes me feel old. As thoughts of days gone by cycle through my head, I glance over at the bar. There are several TVs stationed around it displaying various sporting events. The barmaid a young girl with purple highlights is preparing a drink and holding conversation with a man in all black sitting on the opposite side of the bar. I take a closer look at the man and almost do a double take. He looks like the same creep that stared me down before I got on the elevator at work. Aiden has just started a conversation with me but I'm so distracted that I don't hear a single word he is saying. My eyes connect with the stranger and an uneasy feeling comes over me. Something isn't right about him.

"Talia," Aiden finally manages to get my attention.

"Huh?" I respond.

"Is everything okay?" He asks with a concerned look on his face.

"Yes everything is fine. I'm just day dreaming about ribs." I respond while managing a quick smile and giggle. I look back at the bar and the man is gone! Tina comes to the table and takes our order. Aiden orders his usual, a full slab of ribs with a side order of fries and a draft beer. I order a half a slab with broccoli, fries, and a glass of pink lemonade.

During the meal, thoughts about the ominous mystery man occupy my mind. A curiosity as to his identity is beginning to develop. *"Was our two encounters merely a coincidence? Does he know me? Why did I feel so uneasy in his presence?"* Are some of the unanswered questions lingering in my mind?

"Is everything alright? You seem to be bothered by something." Aiden says while wiping barbeque sauce off his hands.

"Yeah, I was just thinking about Shelly being married and having kids." I murmur before taking a sip of my pink lemonade.

"Makes you feel old huh?"

"Yeah I guess. I'm just now getting my first house and she's married with kids." I state before taking another sip.

"Things have changed a lot." Aiden says before taking a hefty swig of his beer.

"Well luckily for us, some things haven't." I utter as I flash a smile. "I really missed you."

"I missed you too." He replies. We finish our meals and head out to our next destination.

After a thirty-minute plus drive east, we arrive at slams. The parking lot is semi packed. "Slams", is a cool place. It has a special made volleyball area (sand included), where in the warmer months, customers can play. A few people are hanging out around it. Most of them have lit cigarettes in hand. I'm glad that there's a ban on indoor smoking. I used to hate going to house parties and sorority socials. The smoke would be so thick that it felt like I was walking through a burning building! I know the comparison is a bit much but cigarette smoke clogs me up and makes my clothes smell awful. When we get out of Aiden's car, I feel a few drops of rain.

"Let's hurry up and get inside." Aiden says as he grabs my hand.

Once inside, the bar and grill atmosphere is just what I expect it to be. Some random current top forty hit is blaring through the sound system. A few people are dancing to it on the medium sized dance floor. The barmaid is dressed for success. She has on a tight fitting shirt and I assume a push up bra as well, considering the full appearance of her cleavage. Her noticeable rack is sure to help with the tips. I sneak a quick glance at Aiden to see if her appearance has caught his attention. He appears to be looking in a different direction, completely oblivious to her. Aiden was never the disrespectful type, so that's one thing I never had to worry about with him. Besides, even if he did sneak a quick peak, I couldn't really be mad. To be honest, I can't imagine what man wouldn't want to steal a quick glance.

"What would you like to drink?" Aiden asks as we go towards the bar.

"Well I'm not really big on drinking. Just get me a sex on the beach." I respond in a flirty tone. We reach the bar and the barmaid's attention focuses right on me. She is clearly attracted to Aiden. I myself have done the same thing when I was in the presence of an irresistibly handsome man. I found myself staring at his wife the entire time.

"Hey guys what can I get ya'?" The barmaid asks as she acknowledges our presence. She looks at Aiden for a split second and then focuses back on me.

"A sex on the beach and a "Red Bull" and vodka," he says as he pulls out his wallet and draws her attention back onto himself. It appears that he still is not really paying attention to her hotness, which is crazy because she is stunningly attractive.

"Okay," the barmaid says before she begins making our drinks.

"So do you wanna shoot a quick game of pool?" Aiden asks as he does a quick scan for an available pool table.

"Sure," I respond with a forced smile. I hate playing pool. I swear that he purposely lets me win. When I first started playing him in his basement, Aiden used to whip the pants off me literally, we used to play for sexual favors, where the winner took all, or rather received all from the loser. I guess he realized that doing so discouraged me from playing. After a while, he wised up and started letting me win a few games to keep me playing and to keep himself getting regular after school action. We were quite the devilish pair. Some of my questionable teenage activities really make me dread the day that I have kids.

"That'll be ten-fifty." The barmaid says as she brings us our drinks. Aiden pays her fifteen and tells her to keep the change.

We make our way to the pool tables. We play a few games, most of which he ends up winning and then I convince him to go out on the dance floor with me. A few songs in, we order a couple more drinks. We quickly down them and head back to dance around some more. Three drinks in, I feel myself becoming uninhibited. Once I consume my fourth of the night, I start having this undeniable urge to grind my body against his. I begin to weave my web of seduction with sultry moves as we continue to dance. I press myself lustfully against him. I feel the heat of his body and smell the scent of his masculinity as we melt on the floor. He places his hands on my waist and asserts his dominant position. Our show of eroticism motivates others. The medium sized dance floor fills with ambitious bodies. We begin to melt in the crowd of enthused beings. As Aiden maintains his grip on my waist, I start to feel that special tingle indicating the awakening of my sweet spot. I turn to face him and we engage in a passionate kiss. Our tongues caress one another while our lips stay locked in a forbidden dance. We are oblivious to everyone around us. The explosive kiss further intensifies the tingle. I'm ready to go and I can tell that Aiden is ready too. When the song ends, we waste no time leaving. We reach the car, and Aiden urgently unlocks it. Once inside, he starts the ignition, docks his iPod, and puts on some slow music. Within minutes, we are on the freeway headed back west.

"So are you excited about your new house?" Aiden asks while keeping his focus on the road.

"Yeah for the most part I am but I know that having one is a huge responsibility. I just hope I don't over think or over do things. I've got a lot on my mind." I respond.

"Well maybe this will help get your mind off of everything." He says before extending his arm and placing his hand on my thigh. He begins rubbing it and gently moves it up my skirt. I'm glad that I finally decided to wear it. I want to resist, I want to state that it's too soon, but I have been denied the touch of a slow strong hand for far too long. I gladly accept his advances. Blood quickly rushes to the appropriate spot. I feel his fingers shift over my panties and make their presence known. They slowly but firmly massage me. The sensual touching intensifies the tingling sensation. The caressing motion instantly brings back memories. I'm deeply engaged in a fantasy when the flash of a dark evil face interrupts. Except for its glowing red eyes and maniacal smile, the dark face is featureless. It causes me to flinch involuntarily. Aiden reacts by temporarily losing control of the car. It swerves slightly and forces him to slow down and shift to the farthest right lane.

"Is everything okay?" He asks with a troubled look on his face.

"Oh yeah I'm good baby. It's been a while since I've been touched like that." I reply while trying to hide my nervous fright. I put a smooth tone in my voice and a slight, relaxed giggle. The confirmation of its effectiveness is evident when Aiden begins smiling and resumes. We finally reach his apartment complex and I'm ready to explode. I have weeks of pent up frustration just waiting to be released. He smoothly pulls into the parking lot and glides into a parking space with one hand on the wheel and the other on me. He is such a pro.

"Are you sure about this?" He asks before turning off the engine.

"Uh huh," is the only response that I can muster. My lust is boiling over. His masculinity is overwhelmingly difficult to resist.

"Okay," he exits the vehicle and opens my door before I have time to regain my composure.

"Wow he wants it as bad as me." I think as I slowly step out of the car. I am definitely feeling the effects of the stimulation.

"I'm right on the first floor." He says as he clicks his car alarm.

After getting inside his apartment, we instantly get hot and heavy. Clothing comes off, lips kiss, and tongues connect in a sensuous display of young burning passion. Aiden lays me on his bed and thoroughly begins placing kisses on me with his warm soft lips. I release low moans of pleasure. Then without warning, I feel a warm wet sensation on my secret garden. I grab at Aiden's dark locks as he gives me a rightfully deserved, long overdue tongue-lashing.

I feel my drive rising. I shift from grabbing his hair to gripping the sheet beneath me while his tongue maintains its steady sensuous pace. It dances effortlessly on my sensitive region like a graceful ballerina giving the performance of their life. I lose track of time as Aiden continues placing deep kisses down low. It's getting insanely good. I arch my back and tighten my grip and then, Aiden abruptly stops.

"Ugh, keep going!" I utter while looking down disappointedly at a gorgeous pair of baby blues accompanied by a devilish smile moving closer towards me.

"Get ready baby," he instructs before his love invades my raging waters. His movements are intense and rhythmic. He navigates his way through my choppy waves like a veteran sea captain. I cling to the skin on his back with my freshly polished red nails. I moan uncontrollably as Aiden grinds steadily inside of me.

I feel myself nearing an explosive long overdue climax. *"Whoa"* I think as I regain my sensibilities. It's too soon. I'm not ready to give up the ghost so easily.

"Aiden stop," I expel in a low breathy tone.

"Huh," he utters, completely thrown off by my command. "Is everything alright?" He questions as a look of concern forms on his face. The moon light beaming through the window illuminates his glistening ripped form.

"Everything is perfect but..." I pause and regain my composure.

"But what," he is undoubtedly perplexed.

"It's time for me to take over, on your back now!" I command. In one slow steady motion, I magically manage to get on top while keeping Aiden inside.

"Wow." is all that he can manage to discharge from his lips.

"You ain't seen nothing yet, hold on tight," I utter before grabbing his hands and guiding them onto my soft curvy backside. He grips two handfuls as I ride the waves of euphoria. We dance the dance of lust, both working towards the sweet eruption of climax. His manly moans fuel my lustful ambition. My grinding intensifies and my lower muscles tighten around him. I am on the verge of exploding. My leg movements become tense and precise. Then, I hit the jackpot. I dig my nails into Aiden's chest as my orgasmic bomb detonates within. Shakes and shivers travel like express trains from the top half of my body to the bottom half. My nails break his flesh as I involuntarily claw for dear life. Seconds later, Aiden follows suit and joins me on the cloud of satisfaction. His face shrinks up as he releases a low manly groan. I dismount and roll over to rest beside him.

"That was amazing baby." He whispers in a breathy sexually charged voice followed by a short masculine laugh.

"Much more than amazing," I add. My senses are numb and my body is limp. All I want to do is curl up like a cat and go to sleep. I'm on the verge of passing out when Aiden gets up and sneaks off to the bathroom. Minutes later, I hear the sound of running water. I'm almost asleep when he returns. He quietly slips back into bed, snuggles up next to me, and wraps himself around me. His presence helps me drift right off to sleep.

CHAPTER 4

The room is dark. The only visible light is the soft glow from the moon. I lay frozen on my sofa, paralyzed by some unknown force. The room is ice cold. This time I know where I am. I am in my new house. My eyes are the only parts of my body that I can manage to move. I can't believe what I'm seeing in front of me. Just as before, three tall menacing hooded figures are standing over me with a forth figure kneeled down directly in front of me. The moonlight shining through them lets me know that they are semitransparent. The shadow men have a holographic appearance not at all solid like a typical living being. In addition to the shadow men, I notice what appears to be a normal human being behind them with a solemn expression on his face. I'm still afraid but now

I feel a sense of curiosity rising from within. I look deeply into the hot red eyes of the creature closest to me. I see an intense indescribable energy. The eyes are brighter than hot coals. Just as before, the figure begins to make the same unearthly sound although this time I listen to it more attentively. It sounds like some type of strange foreign language. After it stops speaking in what I assume is its native tongue, it begins to speak in English. "You will know."

The buzzing of my alarm causes me to stir. My eyes open to reveal Aiden still asleep beside me. Covered in sweat, I can feel my heart pounding like it's about to burst through my chest. I'm glad it was only a dream but it's odd how I have had almost the same dream twice. Who was the man in the background? Why did he look familiar? Why wasn't he like the rest of the figures? I guess I will try to figure it all out later. Right now, I have to get ready for work.

I get up and start going through the motions. It's time to get back to the daily grind. I have a slight hangover but a night like last night was absolutely worth it. Aiden looks so peaceful asleep it's a shame I have to wake him.

"Wake up sexy," I whisper in his ear while my hand gently rubs his chiseled chest. He starts to rouse then looks over and smiles at me.

"Good morning, so what's on your agenda today?" Aiden ekes out between stretches.

"Not too much, just work." I murmur as my fingertips glide along his smooth firm skin.

"Well I was thinking, how about we play hooky so we can spend more time getting reacquainted?" He utters as he adjusts himself into a sitting position. His offer is too irresistible to refuse but that wouldn't be wise considering I'm coming back from mini vacation.

"I would love nothing more than to spend the day wrapped up with you but I'm up for a promotion and my boss Mr. Beck is counting on me." I respond. What happened last night was somewhat unexpected but completely enjoyable. I know I'm going to need a strong cup of Joe to stay alert at the office and a couple of aspirin to knock out the slight headache but as I said before, it was worth it. The things we do for love and/or lust.

"I understand." He responds before rising off the bed. "Give me a few minutes to throw on something and I'll see you out." He adds.

Once Aiden is dressed, we walk out of his apartment hand in hand. The semi cold air dancing on my exposed skin does little to dampen the moment. I'm still on cloud nine from last night. Aiden gave me exactly what I needed. His energy feels as good as ever and is precisely what I've been missing. We reach Lindy and share a brief PDA moment before I get inside. I start up Lindy and watch as Aiden walks back to the apartment. As Lindy warms up, my thoughts shift to the big move. With only two more weeks left to go, I'm excited and anticipating the change. I entertain how I will decorate each room. The color schemes, the furniture, the accessories.

I arrive home and waste no time getting myself together. I'm glad my parents have already left for the day because having them ask me a million questions about last night, would only put a damper on the magic that was made. *Who were you with? Why did you stay out so long? Remember what happened to you about a year ago."* are some of the things that I will definitely hear upon their return home. I might be spared if I inform them that I spent the night with Aiden. They've always loved him. Heck, if they had it their way Aiden and I would have said our nuptials years ago.

Once I have myself all together, I leave a note for my parents letting them know that I am alive and not a sex slave in someone's basement, before heading back out. I start my trip to work. The drive to work is hectic as usual. People act like driving is so difficult. I'm shocked that they even have their licenses! I manage to avoid three possible accidents before finally making it to work. I park Lindy in my favorite spot and hastily speed walk to escape the chilly morning air. Once inside, I make a beeline to the coffee shop before heading up to my department.

When I step off the elevator, the great time that I had with Aiden is the center of attention in my psyche. Wow, I forgot how great it was being with him. I'm not just talking about the sex, it's the whole vibe I get when we're around each other; he has to be the one.

"Hey Talia," my thoughts are interrupted by Kenna's unmistakably alluring voice. I turn around and take notice of her. She looks like a goddess in business attire. She is every bit of seduction. If I had to make a list of other women whose looks I admire, she would definitely be on it. Her eyes are like sirens singing a seductive song. Her smile is like a glimpse into heaven. Her body is a deal closer.

"Good morning Kenna." I respond while trying to avoid checking her out. My feelings are mixed. I'm on the fence as to whether I have a genuine attraction to her. I try to flee and keep my jumbled mush of thoughts at bay but she is persistent to make me suffer them a little longer.

"Wait!" She says, while desperately trying to keep my attention. "I…" she stops and thinks before finishing her thought. "I really miss hanging out together Talia. Why haven't you been calling me?"

"Hmm Kenna I don't know you tell me. Is it because we don't really have much in common or is it because you took advantage of me?" I say in a cross manner.

"Hold on, so you're blaming it all on me?" Kenna asks in disbelief. "As I recall, you weren't complaining about it until after the fact." She retorts. Her response makes me pause and think. Based on the way the conversation is going, I decide to try a different approach.

"Look Kenna I'm not blaming you for everything. It's just— I don't know what to make of it." Kenna grabs my hand and stairs into my eyes. It feels weird but I can't seem to muster the spirit to fight it.

"Talia , I know how it may have left you feeling unsure and I know our friendship sort of got derailed by that incident but we all make mistakes so please accept my apology."

"Kenna I really wish I could but that's not my thing. You and I have different definitions of friendship. I don't think it will work and besides, I've kind of started seeing someone. I mean well not officially… but the situation between us," I do a quick gesture at the both of us, "would only complicate things."

"Perhaps you have a point. I understand and respect what you're doing right now. Just keep in mind how I feel about you. I want to renew our friendship and if it means playing according to your rules then I'm fine with that. So can we still be friends and will you accept my apology?"

"Um..." I take a moment to think. I quickly assess the pros and cons before giving her my decision. "Yeah sure, as long as the friendship stays within certain borders and you know what they are. Are you going back up?"

"No I have to step out and run an errand for my boss. Maybe I'll see you later." We smile and give each other a friendly hug before going our separate ways. There is still a definite something between us. I feel partially relieved to have her back in my circle.

The elevator reaches my floor and I get off. I enter my department and see Kathy sitting at the front desk doing her usual.

"Hey Talia congratulations," Kathy says as I step into my department.

"Thanks." I respond with a smile.

"Mr. Beck needs to have a word with you right away."

"Okay." I wonder what he has to discuss with me. Maybe he has a few more details or things to tell me about the position. I run into several pit stops as I head to Mr. Beck's office. First, I chat with Jessica. As usual, she talks about a lot of reality TV stuff that's like a foreign language to me. I try to keep up as best I can but I don't really watch reality shows. I'm more into scripted television. I may watch a few casually but that's as far as it goes. I cut the conversation short because I really want to see what Mr. Beck has in store for me. I see Jeff doing his usual. Trying to look busy while somehow managing to get work done and avoid the chopping block. He's somewhat cute in a slacker surfer dude type of way. Brad is quiet as always analyzing expenses and crunching numbers, you know typical financial accounting, and Tasha… well, something is pleasantly different about her. She has a smile on her face from ear to ear.

"Hey Tasha, what's with the smile?" I inquire assuming good news will follow.

"Well, I think I've found the one. I think I've found my Mr. Right!" She expounds as she tries hard to contain her giddiness.

"I'm glad to hear that sis. So, how long have you and Mr. Right been seeing each other?" I ask.

"A little bit over a month."

"Okay, so how did you guys meet?"

"Um well it's a funny story actually, remember that asshole Grayson?"

"Yeah the jerk that stood you up?"

"Right, well the same night that Grayson stood me up is when I met him. After waiting for over an hour, I finally decided to leave the restaurant where we agreed to meet. As soon as I walked towards the door, it started to rain. Seeing as how I had just got my hair done earlier that day, I waited until it let up. Once the rain stopped, I made my way out of the restaurant. As soon as I begin walking to my car, this asshole drives too close to the curb and splashes a puddle of muddy water all over me! I was furious. First, Grayson stood me up, and then I got drenched. I wasted no time firing off a barrage of expletives. While I'm busy yelling obscenities at the air like a raving lunatic, I fail to notice that the car has stopped and the driver has gotten out. The next thing I hear is "Excuse me, are you okay?" in one of the sexiest voices that I have ever heard. I stop mid rant and the sight of a tall dark Modelesque stranger rewards me. My anger starts to subside as I take in his breath taking looks."

"Mmm hmm I see, tall, dark, and handsome huh?"

"Exactly, just the way I like 'em!"

"So what did he do?" I ask as I study Tasha's movements. I notice how animated she is as she talks about her new beau.

"He began apologizing profusely. He explained that he was distraught after leaving his girlfriend's place and failed to pay attention to the puddle."

"So he already had someone?"

"No, well at the time he did but…well see it's a pretty fucked up story. He stopped by her place to surprise her with an early anniversary gift but he was the one that got the surprise. He walked in on her giving some other guy a blowjob!"

"Oh shit!"

Exactly, so that's why he was speeding and not paying attention. Oh and guess what the gift was?"

"Um I don't know what was it?"

"The gift was a new dress, which actually went perfect with my shoes and purse. He was so sorry for ruining mine that he offered it to me as a peace offering of sorts I guess. At first, I was apprehensive about taking it, so I rejected his initial offer. After a brief debate, I reluctantly accepted it. He parked his car, wrapped his coat around me, and escorted me back into the restaurant. I went to change in the ladies' room and when I came out, he was still there so I asked him if he wanted to talk about what happened. Even though I was feeling like crap, something told me that he was feeling far worse. We stayed to talk and ended up having a late dinner."

"Wow."

"I know right! After dinner, we went out dancing and left all of the emotional baggage on the dance floor. We danced until the place closed and have been hanging tight ever since."

"Awww, that sounds like something out of a movie."

"Yeah it does, which is exactly why I'm keeping my fingers cross until we get to the happy ending."

"Which is?"

"Marriage maybe,"

"Okay so have you had a test drive yet? I know it's a pretty private question to ask but it would be a letdown if Mr. Wonderful wasn't wonderful in the sack." I can be brutally honest at times, but I think it's one of my best qualities.

"Well… yes and that's another reason why he's so wonderful.

The things that man does with his hands, tongue, and…" Tasha pauses and begins to blush, "let's just put it this way, he's a triple threat!" She expounds.

"I see, well if he meets all of your needs, it should definitely work. You just have to believe. I'm happy for you and I would really like to meet him. Maybe we can do a double date or something. I have to see Mr. Beck so I'll catch up with you later okay?"

"Okay well just let me know when Talia."

"Alright Tash,"

I resume my journey to Mr. Beck's office. Of all the days that I try to avoid Shane, I run right into him.

"Hey Tally. How is it going?" He asks as he smiles wryly at me.

"Everything is fine Shane." I murmur in a fake polite tone. "I don't mean to be rude but Mr. Beck wants to have a word with me." I blurt out before quickly walking away. His less than favorable vibe always gets to me. Thank God, Mr. Beck never put us on a project together. His whole demeanor is so snaky. I don't know… maybe I feel too strongly about it or maybe he really is that way. It's hard to tell. I'm glad that I didn't have to have a conversation with the loser. He always finds some way to bring up Kenna, insinuate that Mr. Beck and I have something going on, or spew some other nonsense that's borderline sexual harassment. My recent advancement to Office Manager is really going to send him off the deep end. I find it weird that Shane is so focused on what I have going on in my life. If not for him being so pressed over Kenna, or making slight passes at me, I would swear he was a closeted homosexual and jealous of the fact that I'm a woman.

I finally make my way to Mr. Beck's office. His office is neat and organized as usual.

"Hello sir, you wanted see me?"

"Yes I did. We are going to have a department meeting today and I will be announcing your new position."

"Great."

"Hold for just a second," Mr. Beck says before picking up his phone. "Hey Kathy, I need you to please get everyone together for an impromptu meeting—conference room A—thanks." Mr. Beck hangs up the phone.

"Okay Talia, now the reason I called you in here is that, as the new Office Manager I'm going to really need you to get on a couple of people's cases. Their work has been drastically insufficient. The first person is Shane. A smile begins to form on my face as soon as his lips release the name. "I have him working on a special project so I really need you to stay on him. I've had to clean up quite a few of his mistakes and frankly; I'm reaching my limit. He's two seconds away from the unemployment line!"

"I understand sir."

"The second person's case that I need you to get on is Jeff. He thinks that I haven't noticed him slacking off. He's been doing it for a while and as a company moving forward, we don't need the dead weight. I need you to have a serious talk with him. Tell him to shape up or collect his things and have a nice life."

"Yes Mr. Beck." is the only response that I can muster up. I could care less about getting rid of Shane but Jeff is different. Truth be told I know Jeff is a bullshitter but he's a good guy and I've grown quite fond of him. On the other hand, business is business and it should never be personal.

"Alright Talia we're going to have a meeting to go over all of the changes, including your promotion. So be ready in like fifteen to twenty minutes. Oh and by the way, I forgot to tell you about your new office."

"I get my own office?"

"Of course, you're getting victor's old office."

"You mean the one with the great view of the city?"

"That would be the one,"

"Thank you sir,"

"No. Thank you Talia."

I leave Mr. Beck's office and rush to clean out my cubicle. Thank God, no more sharing office space. Jessica sees me cleaning out my cubicle and her nosy ways get the best of her.

"Is everything okay Tally?" She inquires as she rolls in her office chair over to my work area. I decide to play a trick on her.

"Yeah everything is just great." I verbalize in a sarcastic manner as I continue the task of clearing out my former claustrophobic workspace.

"You're still employed here right?" She utters desperately trying to dig up information. The concerned look on her face lets me know that it's time to lay the gag on hard.

"Nope, it was nice working with you." I respond as I put on my most disappointing facial expression.

"Are you serious?"

"If I wasn't would I be boxing up all of my stuff?" I lay on the deceit flawlessly.

"Damn, what happened?" She asks with concern heavily evident in her tone. I really have her going. The look on her face is priceless. I gather the rest of my things before responding.

"I don't feel like talking about it. I'm sure it will get out. Word travels fast around here." My response stuns her. I gather up the last of my things and walk away in a hasty manner to keep from laughing my head off. I can't believe she fell for it.

Once I get to my new office, I close the door, put down my things, and laugh so hard that my eyes start to water. After a few moments of semi hysterical laughter, I hear a knock on the door.

"Yes," I croak out as the laughter partially chokes my response. The door opens and Kathy pokes her head in.

"Hey Talia, it's almost time for the meeting." Kathy says as she mutes her headset.

"Okay I will be right there." I respond before pulling myself together and leaving the room.

I walk into conference room A. Everyone has arrived except for Mr. Beck and Kathy. I take a seat close to the door. Kathy rushes in with handouts in hand, Mr. Beck trails in behind her. Kathy starts passing out the handouts, while Mr. Beck prepares his things. After all of the handouts are dispersed Mr. Beck gets right down to business.

"Good afternoon everyone, I called this meeting to go over some changes that have taken place and a few others that will be implemented in the near future. Now in case any of you haven't heard, we have expanded our operations into three new markets. After the recent promotion and relocation of Victor, our former Office Manager, we were considering absorbing his former position among several other positions but we have chosen to fill it instead. So with no further ado I would like to introduce your new Office Manager, Ms. Talia Rhodes!" The announcement catches everyone off guard. I glance over the entire room. Everyone except Shane has cheerful well-wishing expressions on their faces. Shane has a weird forced expression. I can see right through his fake halfhearted attempt at a smile. The announcement will only give him more of a reason to hate and annoy me.

"You really got me good," Jessica whispers as she nudges me. I flash a quick "I gotcha look" at her before standing to my feet and acknowledging the announcement.

After the meeting, as I'm being showered with congratulatory words, handshakes, and hugs, I notice Shane trail Mr. Beck out of the room. I politely make my way through the crowd of the well-wishers and follow. I reach the hallway and see Shane walking at a hurried pace to keep up with Mr. Beck, who obviously doesn't care to hear what he has to say. Even though I'm at a distance, his mannerisms clearly show that he's not too pleased with the announcement. I want to catch up and butt in but I decide not to y about it, I have more pressing matters to tend to like fixing up my new office, which by the way is almost twice the size of Shane's. Size does matter.

As I make my way to my new office, my mind shifts gears to Kenna and our weird relationship. I miss hanging out with her, at least that's what I believe the longing feeling I'm experiencing is. She has left an undeniable impression on me. Perhaps it's something more, something that I'm afraid to fully acknowledge. I step inside of the office and quietly close the door behind myself. With the door closed, I immediately set to work. My thoughts bounce back and forth between Aiden and Kenna. While in the midst of thinking, something unexpected happens. A voice appears from out of nowhere.

"I'm here," it says in a whispery tone, startling me in the process and halting my train of thought.

"Huh?" I murmur as I quickly turn around only to see nothing. I'm completely alone. *"Where did that voice come from?"* I wonder as I attempt to come up will a logical explanation. I feel a distinct coldness as well. My eyes search around the room nervously. I walk to the door, open it, and peek out into the hall. Both directions are clear and the only sounds I detect appear to be coming from another office a few doors down. Tasha is discussing something in Spanish with another female on speakerphone. The voice that I heard was in English and clearly that of a male. "Wow you're letting your work get to you old girl." I utter as I duck back in and close the door. Not coming up with a clear explanation, I dismiss the incident and resume the task of organizing.

Within the next hour, I manage to organize the bulk of my things as well as figure out a way to approach Jeff and Shane and the order in which to do it. With most of the work completed, I decide to put the remaining portion on hold and address them. I figure that I will go to Jeff first given the good nature of our relationship. I put everything down and head out of the office and straight to Jeff. When I arrive, I catch Jeff doing his usual. I take a deep breath and push my personal feelings aside.

"Hey Jeff, got a minute?" I ask in a calm neutral tone.

"Uh yeah sure Tally,"

"Okay great, well look I'm going to get straight to the point, you really need to get your act together. Mr. Beck isn't too pleased with your performance. I'm telling you this as your friend. Now as your new supervisor, I'm telling you that you are in the hot seat and you need to improve ASAP, because you're running out of grace."

"Um okay, well thanks for letting me know, I will definitely get my shit, I mean stuff together Talia. I promise you I will beautiful."

"I'm serious."

"Okay I gotcha."

"Alright good, because if you don't, well I don't even want to think about it; just handle it. Oh and another thing,"

"Yes,"

"You're going to have to stop with the flirting and comments, is that understood?" I say in a firm authoritative manner.

"Yes ma'am, as clear as a window." He responds with a goofy expression on his face.

"Jeff!" I give him a serious no nonsense look. He straightens his demeanor and responds.

"I gotcha, sorry about that,"

"Apology accepted." I utter before leaving his cubicle. *"Okay one down and one to go, now for the hard part, Shane."* I think as I head towards his office. I contemplate finishing my office as a way to buy myself more time before the confrontation. The guy already dislikes me and after the announcement, he probably hates me! I rejected his advances, I get the promotion that he obviously wanted, I'm almost a decade younger, and to add further insult to injury, I'm a woman! That fact alone probably burns his pickle. He seems like a chauvinist. Some of the comments I've overheard him say to others in the office firmly makes me believe so.

I slowly precede to Shane's small, "not nearly as cool as mine" office. As I reach the doorway of his office. I can see him through one of the glass side panels. He is sitting slumped in his chair with his head cradled in his hands. I lightly knock on the door. "Come in," he yells as the knock rouses him out of his slumped state. I take a deep breath and get my confidence in order before entering. Under normal circumstances, I would definitely try to avoid going into his office. Since I started working for Central, I have only had to visit it a handful of times.

I slowly step in and cautiously close the door. Shane doesn't look too pleased to see me. Oh and besides Shane there's another reason why I loathe visiting his office. As a browns fan, the décor is aesthetically displeasing. The office like a make shift Pittsburgh Steelers shrine. The black and yellow color motif runs rampant throughout it. Bobble heads and other fan boy memorabilia clutter the tops of files cabinets and shelves meant for books. Framed posters and jerseys cover the walls like a collage of pigskin devotion. The sight of it makes me want to regurgitate.

"Can I help you?" He asks in a less than friendly, closer to "why the hell are you in my office?" tone. I waste no time getting straight to the point.

"I'm here to check on the special project that Mr. Beck assigned to you."

"It's getting done." He responds coarsely.

"Well I'm just making sure because he needs it completed by the end of the week so—" he cuts me off before I can finish.

"I told you, it's getting done."

"I'm just making sure."

"Okie Dokie boss," he says sarcastically, mocking my authority.

"Yeah okay, well just make sure it is." I respond before abruptly leaving the room. I don't even wait to hear his response. On the way back to my office, I feel a slight headache coming on.

Other than the nagging headache, the rest of my workday goes smooth. I actually manage to complete my office and get ahead in my work. At the end of the day, I say bye to all of my coworkers and head out of the office. On my way to the elevator, I bump into

Kenna.

"Hey Kenna see you're done for the day too huh?" I ask. For some reason, can't help but notice how appealing her features are.

"Yes indeed, I can't wait to go home and unwind with a nice hot bubble bath and a glass or two of chardonnay." She says as she searches through her purse. I have to stop myself from holding the mental image of her in a bubble bath for too long.

"What's the hell is wrong with me?" I wonder. "Just got promoted today," I gush out proudly, quickly changing the subject.

"Oh wow really?" She says while still fumbling in her purse. She finally finds what she is looking for. "What is your new position?" She asks as she draws her hand from out of her purse with keys in tow.

"I'm the new Office Manager for my department."

"That's great!" She exclaims in a bubbly manner."

"Okay well I don't want to keep you too long. I hope you enjoy the bubble bath and I will see you tomorrow." I say as I begin to walk away. Kenna stops me mid stride with a hug.

"What—" I respond, completely thrown for a loop by the unexpected embrace.

"It's just a hug relax," Kenna says before I can finish my sentence.

"I know I just wasn't expecting it." I respond as I gaze into her warm green eyes. She knows what she does to me. She knows how strong our chemistry is.

"See you later Tally." She says before walking away. As I watch her walk away, an overwhelming pain shoots through my brain. The pain is so intense that it brings me to my knees. I cradle my head in my hands. A loud ringing sound invades my ears and the sharp pain turns into an intense throbbing. I hear voices around me chattering with concern. Due to incessant throbbing and ringing, it's hard to make out what they are saying. I feel someone place a hand on my shoulder. The voice accompanying it is barely audible over the ringing in my head. I look up and see Kenna standing over me. I feel lightheaded and dizzy. Everything goes black.

CHAPTER 5

I regain consciousness and find myself in a strange bed, a hospital bed. The stark sterile room that houses the bed gives off a sense of seriousness unlike any other environment. When you wake up and happen to find yourself in one of them, you know that things have definitely taken a turn for the worse. The hospital bed that I'm resting on is cold and impersonal. I take into mental inventory an IV and other random cords running from my body. I look to my right and see Kenna sitting next to me. Her face shows signs of crying. I look to my left and see my parents and Aiden. Aiden and my mom look like they have been crying too. The dry tearstain telltale trails on their faces are confirmation.

"How are you feeling?" My mom asks as she caresses my

forehead.

"I'm okay I guess. I'm just a little groggy." I respond as I try to crack a smile.

"Your coworker Kenna called 911 and stayed by your side the entire time." My mom says.

"So much for going home and relaxing," I joke as I turn towards Kenna.

"Yeah, I had to give the bubble bath and chardonnay a rain check." She responds with a slight giggle and smile. I turn towards Aiden. Judging by the look on his face, he doesn't know what to make of the joke.

"Hey Tal, I'm going to go have a talk with the nurse and try to track down the doctor. Come with me honey." My father says before grabbing my mother's hand and leaving the room.

"Thank you Kenna for helping her." Aiden says in a sincere manner. "I wish I could've been there." He adds.

"It's okay I understand. It's like that when you really care for someone." The way Kenna is looking at Aiden is strange. I can't tell whether she's admiring his physical appearance or if she's sizing him up.

"Well I think Aiden's got it from here so you can go home to your bubble bath and chardonnay." I say in a weak somewhat humorous voice. It feels weird having the both of them in the room. I think that my history with Kenna has something to do with it.

"Are you sure?" Kenna asks.

"Yeah, I'll be fine. Go home and relax." I reply as I place my hand on hers. The way she looks at me is comparable to a lover not wanting to leave their companion. It's a little unsettling.

"Alright well keep me posted okay?" She says before giving me a hug. "Aiden it was nice meeting you." She says as she extends her hand towards him.

"Likewise," Aiden responds as they shake hands. Kenna leaves the room.

"Nice coworker," Aiden says.

"Yeah she's cool." I respond with my eyes fixed on the doorway.

"How long have you guys known each other?" He asks as the door closes.

"I've known her for about six months." I respond.

"So what happened, I mean how do you pass out?" Aiden asks as he grips my hand.

"I don't know. I was getting ready to leave and then it just… happened."

"So there weren't any symptoms prior to it."

"Well earlier, I came down with a slight headache but I'm not sure if that had anything to do with it."

"I see. Well, hopefully it's nothing serious."

"I don't know Aiden but I'm scared. Please hold me." Aiden draws in close and wraps his muscular upper body around me. He feels warm and comforting in contrast to the stark cold bed. Tears begin to fall from my eyes as I hold on to the love of my life. I feel the wetness penetrating the fabric of his shirt. His manly scent is soothing. My parents return and Aiden releases me from his arms.

"Hey Tal, I talked to the nurse and the doctor. They think that an MRI and a CAT scan should be performed to make sure that there aren't any signs of infraction, tumors, cancer, calcifications, hemorrhaging, or bone trauma." My father says with a concerned expression on his face. My mother's eyes are watery.

"Mom I'm going to be okay," I say as an attempt to comfort

her. "It's not like I've been having a series of episodes, it's just one isolated incident."

"Are you sure Tal?" My dad says as he rubs my mother's shoulders.

"Yes dad I'm sure." I answer.

"The doctor says they're going to keep you overnight to monitor you and run a few tests. I have some PTO so I can stay if need be and—"

"Dad I'll be okay, really." I state firmly. The last thing I need is for them to be worried any more than they already are.

"Okay well I have a lot of work to finish so I will be back in the morning to check up on you before I go to work. Your mother and I will have our phones on us at all times so if anything goes wrong, you or Aiden need to definitely give us a call okay?"

"Yes dad." I utter.

"Yes Mr. Rhodes" Aiden responds. My mother and father walk over to me and smother me with affection.

"I can stay here Tally." My mom offers. Having her stay would do more harm than good. I know my mother. If she stays, she'll spend the whole time crying and bugging the hell out of me.

"Mom I think you should go home and get some rest. I will be okay, I promise." I force a smile on my face.

"Okay Talia but I will be back to check on you." My mom responds as she wipes her eyes and hesitantly grabs her coat. She gives me a kiss on the forehead before reluctantly making her way out of the room. Having Aiden next to me gives me comfort but for some strange reason I can't stop thinking about Kenna. I try blocking her out of my mind as I look into Aiden's warm loving eyes but it's no use. It's as if she's placed a spell over me. My brain feels drained. Too many things are going on. I just need some rest. I don't want to think about anything.

"I'm going to try to get some rest Aiden. I'm so groggy and drained. You're welcome to stay if you want." I say as he resumes holding me.

"Okay well I just want to stay a little while longer, I mean at least until you fall asleep." He responds while tightening his grip around me. "I'm sorry for ever leaving you Talia. I never want to be away from you again!" He states with sincerity. I look into his eyes before placing a warm passionate kiss on his sweet soft lips.

The next day of testing is far from fun. The barrage of tests that they perform on me, make me feel like a human lab rat. MRI, CAT scan, bone density test, blood work and like a few other tests. I feel far worse afterwards. It's a good thing I have excellent medical coverage or I would be running up a hefty tab! I start to feel grogginess set in after all of the testing is completed. So much so, that my mind begins to play tricks on me. As I lay in bed recuperating on verge of drifting off to sleep, a cold chill invades the room and something in the hallway catches my eye. A thin slow moving man, which at first, I assume is just one of the medical staff going about their normal affairs. That changes seconds later, when the same person walks past again headed in the same direction! This time, he appears to be moving slower than the last.

"Wow I'm tripping," I state as I shake my head in disbelief. At first, I attribute it to the stress of the whole ordeal, a hallucinatory side effect from the meds. I am on the verge of writing it off when the stranger appears in my doorway a third time. Panic sweeps over me. Something definitely isn't right. Although I didn't get a complete view of the person's face, I'm quite sure that it is the same man. How the bed is positioned and the fact that the door is partially ajar makes it hard to get a definite clear view but I'm quite sure it was the same person. "What the fuck…" I mumble as I sit up in my bed. My heart stops when the stranger begins to walk past the door a fourth time. As I watch in disbelief, the figure stops in the middle of the doorway and begins to turn. I am flooded with complete terror as I watch this total stranger enter my room. His eyes are completely black and his skin is a deathly pale light brown. I attempt to scream but nothing comes out. I close my eyes, grip the covers tight, and begin to recite a prayer that my Grandma Mariana taught me when I was a child. Reciting the prayer before bedtime helped me conquer my fear of the dark and the boogieman. I open my eyes and he is still there staring at me with his menacing cold eyes. My panic intensifies and I hurriedly page the nurse and duck underneath the cover. Seconds seem like minutes as I wait anxiously for the outcome of the encounter. I can still feel the intimidating presence of the stranger. I know it's foolish to expect my hospital cover to ward off the weird gangly intruder but it's something that is inherently woven within the human psyche. There is no way possible that a piece of fabric can protect you from someone or something wishing to do harm. Coming to terms with this, I build up enough courage to peek out from underneath the cover. To my surprise, the man is gone.

"Yes Ms. Rhodes?" The nurse responds through the paging device.

"I need some assistance. Can you come here for a moment?" I respond as I look around the room in absolute disbelief.

"I will be there in one moment ma'am," she states before the line goes silent. Each second that goes by feels like an eternity. The nurse finally comes into the room. "Is everything okay?" She inquires with a weird concerned look on her face.

"Uh... yeah... well, not really. Can you tell me some of the side effects that are associated with the meds and testing I received?"

"What do you mean?" She questions with a puzzled expression. I'm not sure if I should divulge the true reason why I want to know. The last thing I need is for her to think I'm crazy and recommend that I be kept here even longer or try to pump me with more meds!

"I mean like does anything that's been administered to me

have hallucinogenic side effects?" I hope I explained it without coming off as a complete nut job.

"Uh give me a second," she says before glossing over my charts. "Well according to your charts, none of the meds administered are known to have hallucinogenic effects. Maybe it's just a mild case of PTS."

"What, post-traumatic stress?" I inquire as the notion starts to register in my head.

"Yes that's exactly what I'm referring to. I highly doubt that any of the meds or testing would have hallucinogenic effects. If you don't mind me asking, what exactly are you seeing or hearing?" I can't tell her what I was really seeing. It would sound completely absurd.

"Oh uh, I thought my uncle came to see me." I gush out hoping that it doesn't sound too bogus.

"Well you probably dreamt it because aside from your parents, no one else has been up here today."

"Maybe I was half sleep." Now I'm thinking it definitely has to be my mind playing tricks on me.

"Perhaps so," she responds as she starts to walk. Before she reaches the door, a doctor comes into the room.

"Ms. Rhodes, so far everything checks out ok. We can't find anything abnormal. We are still waiting for the rest of the test results to come back. They should be back by next Tuesday. You will receive a call notifying you once they come back. In the meantime, we are going to release you. Now if you start to feel any pain, dizziness, extreme fatigue, or anything else out of the norm, please call us immediately. In addition, I recommend taking a few days off from work. The daily stress of your job, may be a bit much for you to go right back to. Nurse Susan here will bring you your discharge paperwork once it's ready."

"Okay, I understand." I respond.

They leave the room and I start to get dressed. I can't wait to leave. I hate hospitals! Since I didn't drive, I'm going to need a ride. The first person I think of calling is my mom. I know her all too well. She is probably sitting at home worried waiting on my call. I should've relented and let her stay earlier. I call her cell phone. She answers on the first ring.

"Hey honey, is everything alright?"

"Yeah the doctor said that so far everything checked out

normal. I'm about to be discharged soon and I need a ride. Can you take me by my job so I can get my car? I can drive home from there."

"Are you sure that you're okay to drive?"

"Yes mom, and thanks. See you in a few okay?"

"Okay Tal," I hate when my mom calls me Tal. Her and my dad are the only ones that call me that, everyone else calls me Talia or Tally. I knew she'd be home waiting to hear from me. She has always been that way. She's never put work over me. When it comes to mothers, she's one of the greatest!

My mom makes it to the hospital in no time. I have all of my things together except for the discharge papers. My mom enters the room and gives me a super extra strength motherly hug.

"So are you all set to go?" My mom inquires after she releases me from her loving grip.

"Not yet, I'm still waiting on the discharge papers." I respond before putting on my jacket.

After waiting for over half an hour, the nurse finally comes in with the paperwork. I can hardly wait to leave. I'm literally ready to run out of the hospital. The sooner I leave the better I will feel. Hospitals have that critical effect on me.

"Sorry for the wait Ms. Rhodes we are short staffed today." The nurse says as she flips through the papers.

"It's okay, I'm just glad to finally be getting out of here." I respond. She goes over the paperwork, has me sign on a few lines, and then I'm all set. I don't know what to make of my health enigma. I speculate all of the things that could be going on with my brain. It could be a tumor, cancer, aneurisms, thinking about all of the possibilities will probably make me have another headache! I'm going be on pins and needles until I get the rest of the results.

The air outside of the hospital is buzzing with life. It has never smelled so good. I'm ecstatic to be finally leaving the sterilized purgatory. We get in my mom's car and head off to pick up Lindy. I wonder what Mr. Beck is going to say when I show back up to work. I'm hoping he won't send me back home to get more rest. Being idle at home will only make the time drag as I wait for the rest of the results. I need something to keep my mind off it.

"So what did the doctor say?" My mom asks as we enter onto the freeway.

"Well so far, they can't find anything. I have to wait for the rest of the results to come back."

"Okay well just don't let the wait drive you crazy. Make sure you find things to do to keep you occupied."

"I will. I'm hoping Mr. Beck doesn't tell me to stay home for a few days. I plan on going into work tomorrow."

"Tal honey, I don't think it's a good idea to go back to work quite so soon. You still have personal and sick time right?"

"Yes, plus I have a week of vacation left as well."

"Well I think you should call your boss and make arrangements."

"Okay mom," I retort as I reluctantly take out my phone and call Mr. Beck.

"Hello, thank you for calling Central Insurance. Kathy speaking how may I direct your call?"

"Hey Kathy its Talia, can you transfer me to Mr. Beck?"

"Talia, is everything alright? I heard about what happened and—"

"Yes, I'm alright."

"Okay that's good to hear. I'm transferring you right now."

"Thanks see you in a few days."

"Okay." The line transfers. Mr. Beck picks up.

"Hello, Dennis Beck speaking."

"Hey Mr. Beck,"

"Talia, is everything alright?"

"Yes, so far. I just got out of the hospital. The doctor recommends that I take a few more days off to recuperate."

"Okay take all the time you need, I heard it was pretty serious. Ryan from billing said you passed out in the lobby!"

"Yeah it was a bit intense. I've never had anything like that happen to me. They ran a bunch of test on me at the hospital. So far, the ones that came back were all negative. I'm still waiting on some of the results."

"Okay well just take a few more days off and keep me posted."

"I will Mr. Beck."

"Okay Talia, have a good day."

"You do the same." I respond before ending the call. "There, now are you happy?" I ask in a sarcastic tone as my mother smiles with approval.

"I just want to make sure that you're okay Tal."

"I know mom, I know." I respond as I smile back at her.

We arrive at my job. I kiss my mom and we say our goodbyes before I make my way into the garage to retrieve Lindy. I walk past the guard shack and see Bill the garage attendant doing what he does best, nothing. He's thoroughly engrossed in reading some random sports magazine. As I walk through the garage, I get this creepy nagging feeling that someone is watching me. I look over my shoulder and see nothing. I continue walking but I can't seem to shake it. I finally reach Lindy. As I grab the door handle, this weird sixth sense like sensation hits me. I turn my head slightly and see a blurry shadow from out of the corner of my eye. I quickly get in Lindy, start her up, and lock the doors. Either I'm hallucinating or something is actually following me! I get to the gate arm and bill takes his sweet time lifting it. I still feel the creepy feeling. It feels like whatever it is, is closing in on me. My heart beat speeds up as I continuously check the rearview and side mirrors.

As soon as the arm completely lifts, I speed out of the garage. The presence is following me. I plow through the streets sparing no expense on the gas. I look back again and see an old black car with tinted windows a few yards back. I stop and roll through a stop sign and nearly cause an accident as I increase the speed to lose the car tailing me. I slip through a few stoplights and check behind me again. Whew, the car is gone.

I finally make it home and somehow manage to park Lindy decently on the street before running into the house. The house is quiet. I figure that my mother probably stopped at the store before coming home. I run upstairs into my room, lock the door behind me, and hurriedly duck under my bed to retrieve my 9mm. I check the clip for bullets and get it ready. My father is pretty much against guns but Grandpa John always told me to keep one handy, which is exactly the reason that I avoided becoming a rape victim. I remember the lessons Grandpa John taught me about using one. I hear a car pull up outside. I cock my pistol and quietly creep up to the window. I take a quick peek outside and see the black car that was pursuing me parked a few houses down. On edge, I examine the surrounding area for anything or anyone else out of the norm. Thoughts of the creepy stranger from the hospital flash in my mind. Suddenly, noises coming from downstairs grab my attention. I go to my door with weapon in hand. Everything gets quiet. My panic increases as I silently wait with my finger lightly caressing the trigger. My heart is beating so fast that I swear it's skipping beats. The sounds of footfalls break the silence. They get closer and closer with every second that passes. I hear them stop outside my door. My doorknob starts to turn. I yank it open and aim.

"What the hell are you doing?" My mother yells with her eyes as wide as saucers.

"Oh shit! I'm sorry mom I thought that t-they were... there was someone following me!" I respond as the reality of the moment shocks a sense of rationality into me.

"Tal what are you talking about?"

"Here let me show you." I say I as reach out and attempt to grab her by the arm. She flinches back defensively. "Mom I'm not going to hurt you come on!" I reassure her as I make my way to the window. She slowly follows me.

"See look," I say as I point out the window.

"Um Tal, what am I supposed to be looking at?"

"There is a black car parked a few houses down!" I exclaim.

"Are you talking about the one that the old lady is getting into?" My mom inquires as she continues looking.

"Huh?" I say before taking a second look out of the window. I look and see an elderly woman closing the car door.

"Honey, are you sure you're okay?"

"I don't know, maybe it's the meds or the after effects of the headache." I speculate as I try to make sense of everything. "Mom I'm so sorry." I feel bad as the realization of what just happened, hits me.

"You need to get that gun out of my house!" She commands in a stern tone.

"Yes ma'am." I respond with my head down.

My mom leaves the room. I look down at the gun. "What the hell is wrong with me?" I question aloud as I stare at the weapon resting in my hand. I don't know if I'm losing it or what. I just pointed a loaded gun at my own mother! "I have to get rid of this." I mumble as I reach under the bed and grab the case that I use to house it. I remove the clip, clear the chamber, and use my pinky finger to check for a round. After confirming that both the chamber and barrel are empty, I put the gun back inside the case. I lock the case and leave the room with case in hand. I go outside and make my way to Lindy. As I get close to her, I click the button on my keyless entry mechanism. The trunk pops open. I remove my spare tire and put the case in the hollowed space beneath before replacing it. I close the trunk and look around at my surroundings. Everything looks normal. I feel another headache coming on. I head back into the house and go straight to the medicine cabinet. I pop two aspirin and make my way back to my bedroom. Once inside, I lock the door, strip out of my clothing, lie on the bed, and make myself comfortable.

I start to feel drowsy as I lay in my bed staring up at the ceiling. I try to clear my mind and get some rest but my brain just doesn't want to cooperate. Thoughts about my new house, Aiden, and the weird sixth sense swirl inside my head. After tossing about for a few, I finally manage to go to sleep.

CHAPTER 6

I open my eyes and see total darkness. I hear a voice calling me in the distance. The faint voice is that of a female. My eyes frantically search for the source of the sound but the vast darkness prevents me locating it. All of a sudden, everything illuminates and I realize that I'm standing in the middle of my grandmother's front yard. I look up at the sky and see a dark cluster of clouds forming. I hear the same female voice. This time the voice sounds like its chanting a spell. I feel myself lift into the air. I struggle to get back to the ground but it's useless. I feel motion sickness setting in as the supernatural wind current thrashes me about. In a state of panic, I start crying out to God. Suddenly, a deep voice erupts from the clouds. "Your God cannot save you!"

I jump up, feeling greatly relieved when I realize that I'm safe at home in my bed. Soaked in sweat, I scan around the room as my eyes adjust to my moon lit surroundings. Everything looks normal. I'm thankful that it was just a dream. It all seemed so real, the motion sickness, the howling of the wind, the ominous voices. I shiver at the thought of them. My nose catches onto the smell of brimstone. An overwhelming urge takes over and forces me to look at a particular section of the room. My vision captures what appears to be a man. I focus my eyes and realize that it's the same man from the hospital! I quickly reach over and tap the touch lamp on the nightstand. I look back in the direction of the man only to discover that no one is there, he's gone!

"What the fuck?" I think as I try to fathom what has just occurred. The smell of brimstone, the authentic look of the man, it had to have been real! I know I saw something! I throw on a pair of sleepers and a tank top and make a trip the bathroom. I splash my face with water several times to help shake off the grogginess. I feel sticky from all of the perspiration that occurred during my nap. I hate that "not so fresh" feeling. I decide to take a quick shower. I turn on the shower and grab my essentials before

disrobing and getting in. As the steaming hot water runs over my body, I think about all of the weird things that have happened as of late. A cold draft draws my attention away from my thoughts and focuses them on finding the source of it. It's not just a slightly cold draft. It's a bone chilling draft. It's cold enough that in spite of the hot rushing shower water, my nipples are getting hard and goose bumps are forming on my arms. I inspect the sliding shower doors. Everything appears to be in order. I try to ignore the draft, but it seems as if the cold intensifies.

"Let me hurry up and get out of here." I think as I grab my shower gel and scrunchie. After a haste scrubbing, I exit the shower. I'm in the middle of drying off when I notice something written on the fogged sliding shower door. "You will know," is the message scrawled on the foggy surface. An intense panic sweeps over me. Filled with dread, I rush back into my bedroom. With my heart beating like a rapid-fire drum solo, I waste no time getting dressed. *"Am I going insane?"* I wonder as I try to come to terms with the paranormal event. I need answers. I need to know that I'm not crazy. With courage intact, I return to bathroom. I step inside and my eyes instantly dart towards the mirror. I'm astonished with

my findings. The door is completely devoid of writing. The fog hasn't completely dissipated so there isn't a clear explanation for its disappearance. Unable to come up with an answer, I write it off as a figment of my imagination. The sudden emergence of my appetite steals my attention. With my stomach growling like a bear, I go down stairs to get something to satisfy my hunger. I step into the kitchen and see my parents sitting at the table. They have concerned looks on their faces.

"Have a seat," my father instructs. I halt my walk towards the refrigerator and do as instructed. My father searches for the right words to say before speaking. I already know the gist of what he is about to say. I know my mother told him about the gun and my paranoid episode. I see the anger in his eyes as we sit in silence. I can tell when my father is about to speak in a serious vein because he always twitches slightly before releasing his first words. "How is your head feeling Tal?" is the first thing he calmly asks. It completely throws me off. I was really expecting him to let me have it about the gun. I wonder if my mom told him exactly what happened, including the part where I aimed a loaded pistol at her. "I had a talk with your mom, she told me about what happened.

Now you know how I feel about guns, especially about having them in the house. You could've killed her!"

"Dad I'm sorry. I know your stance on guns and I understand you being upset, but someone was following me home! I swear they were! I have never felt a feeling like that before!"

"Okay so did you have any definite proof of it before you felt the need to arm yourself?"

"Well no but—"

"There is no but! I think the headache episode has a lot to do with it. Now if these types of things keep occurring, we might have to look into getting you professional help."

"Hold on wait, are you talking like a shrink or something, because if you are, I don't need that type of help!" I respond in a defensive tone. How could he even think to threaten anything like that? I feel my blood begin boil.

"Look you need to calm down all I'm saying is that we are concerned for your safety as well as ours. I don't think you're completely over the fact that you were almost victimized!" I knew my father was going to bring up the attempted rape. "Your mom is worried out of her mind over you; I'm worried about you. You're our only child. I'm proud of the woman that you have become. I just don't want any serious mishaps to occur that could affect your future. I love you Talia, we love you!" My father places his hand on my mom's hand to emphasize the "we" aspect of it. The sight of their affection calms me down. I love them too. I feel like crap because of what happened earlier.

"I'm sorry dad and I'm truly sorry mom. I already removed the gun from the house and if I feel any other symptoms or paranoia, I will definitely seek out help." We all take a brief moment to hug. I feel my mom's tears soaking into the shoulder area of my shirt. My parents mean everything to me. I'm the woman I am today mostly because of them.

After we smooth things over, my parents leave the kitchen and I prepare myself a bite to eat. I sit in silence as I eat my meal. My thoughts shift from the earlier incident to Aiden. I have really missed him. After eating, I decide to give him a call. The phone rings a few times before going to voicemail. I hang up and go back upstairs.

Once back in my room I grab my cable remote and begin watching an on demand episode of "The Walking Dead". As I fast forward past the opening credits, my cell phone begins to ring. I grab it off the nightstand and see Aiden's picture on the screen. Due to a recent accidental drop on pavement, my phone is currently less than fully functional, so in order to hold a conversation I have to use the speakerphone feature or my Bluetooth. I'm waiting for my free upgrade in December, so I have to deal with the slight inconvenience until then. I'm a bit frugal when it comes to anything other than fashion (splurging on looking good is my guilty pleasure). I slip on my earpiece before answering the call.

"Hey Aid," I utter as Rick kills a walker.

"Hey, I'm sorry I missed your call. What's up?"

"Do you feel like having company?" I ask in a straightforward manner.

"Um well it's kind of late notice but sure," he replies. Of course he would, I mean what guy other than a gay one would refuse. "What time did you have in mind?"

"How about in the next hour," I murmur while thinking of something cute and simple to put on.

"Sounds like a plan," Aiden responds.

"Okay," I mutter with half of my attention devoted to Rick and the gang. "I'll see you soon."

I wake up the next day to the sound of Aiden's soft snores. I love the way he looks when he's asleep. I'm hoping to hear something back from the hospital but it still might be too soon. In most cases, the wait is worse than the news. Aiden starts to stir a few minutes after I get out of bed.

"Good morning beautiful." He says as he looks at me with his gorgeous deep blues.

"Good morning." I reply. I'm glad I came over. I really needed him and not just for sex.

"So how are you feeling now?" He asks as he rises out of the bed.

"Well I'm feeling much better now. I'm glad I paid you a visit, I really needed someone to talk to."

"So do you really think someone was following you?"

"I'm not sure but I know I'm not crazy. I know what I felt and saw. I just can't believe that I pulled a gun on my mom!"

"Yeah that was pretty wild but it's not like you purposely

pulled it on her. You didn't know who or what was on the other side of the door before you opened it."

"Right, that's exactly how I felt about it, especially considering that fact that I, was almost raped a little over a year ago. My parents didn't see it that way though. My dad actually mentioned getting me help! He acts as if I have a history of mental illness or something and it's not even like that, it's just that things have been strange lately. The nightmares, the major headache, someone following me, I just can't put my finger on it!"

"Maybe something or someone is following you but it's not exactly what you think it is."

"What do you mean?"

"I mean maybe it's not an actual person, maybe it's a force. I know it sounds farfetched but it might even be a spirit. After my father died I... I saw something that I can't explain. I was never big on spirits and things of that nature but I think I saw my father. It happened about a week after his funeral. I was up by myself late at night watching reruns of a show that we used to watch together when I was a kid. As I'm watching this show with tears running down my face, the TV starts messing up. At first, I thought it was the cable signal screwing up but then I started to feel an extremely cold draft in the room. I looked away from the TV and laid my eyes on something that triggered instant fear. I saw a shadowy silhouette standing in the doorway of the living room! I didn't know whether to run or just stay still and hope that whatever it was would just go away. Just as I was making up my mind to run for the hills, a calm familiar feeling swept over me. Instantly, I knew without a doubt that the thing I was looking at was my father. I told Ashley about it the next day. She said that she'd had a similar incident in the basement. She was looking through some of our dad's old things when she looked up and saw a faint shadow in the shape of a man projected on the wall near the entrance way. There is definitely more to this life and the next, I think maybe you should dig a little deeper."

"You know what, maybe you're right. I know what I felt yesterday. I know it wasn't just my imagination. I know there is something following me but why? I mean why me and why now?

CHAPTER 7

Judgment day is here, the moment-of-truth has arrived. Today is the day that I will find out what's going on with me. The remaining test results have been a constant in my train of thought. Thankfully, I haven't had any more massive headaches. The worst part about the headache episode wasn't the headache itself; it was the loss of consciousness, the loss of control. It left me in a vulnerable state. I was unable to protect myself. That's the scariest feeling in the world and waking up in the hospital after the fact only made it worse.

I go through the same morning routine that I have become accustomed to, I'm glad to be returning to work. I get everything together and head out to face the day. I start Lindy and let her warm up while I get my playlist ready. I'm almost done with the list when my phone begins to ring. "Great there goes my list!" I mumble as I look at the number. It's unfamiliar to me. Figuring that it might be the hospital, I answer it.

"Hello?"

"Hello may I speak to Ms. Rhodes?"

"This is she."

"Ms. Rhodes, this is Kim from the lab. I have your results back."

"Okay great,"

"Yes it is. Everything came back negative. You have a perfect bill of health."

"Really, are you sure? Not one single thing?" I ask, shocked by the news.

"Everything is clean, no abnormalities present."

"How could I have a massive headache, lose consciousness, and still have a perfect bill of health?"

"I honestly don't know. I'm just conveying the results. If you have further concerns, I can transfer you to the scheduling desk and you can schedule an appointment with your primary care physician. Your PCP can then refer you to a specialist. Would you like me to transfer you?"

"Yes please."

"Okay Ms. Rhodes, I'm transferring you right now."

"Thank you."

"You're welcome, have a good day."

"You do the same."

Now I'm even more concerned. They can't find anything wrong, so what does this mean? I've lived almost twenty-five years with excellent health and then out of nowhere, I have a super migraine and pass out. There has to be something more. While processing the good but unexpected news, prerecorded messages begin playing on the line. I hate prerecorded messages! I don't know what's worse prerecorded messages or the crappy music that some business lines play while they have you on hold for an eternity!

"Hello?" A voice on the line says relieving my ears of prerecorded torture.

"Hello I was just transferred over from your lab department. I would like to schedule an appointment with Dr. Connors."

"Okay can I have your member ID number?"

"Yes hold on one second," I say before digging through my pocketbook for my medical card. "Okay the number is 14000-569-123."

"I got it. I'm speaking with Talia Rhodes correct?"

"Yes."

"Okay Ms. Rhodes for security purposes can I have your phone number and date of birth?"

"The phone number that should be listed in your system is 216-555-4347, and my date of birth is 06-12-87."

"Alright Ms. Rhodes the soonest openings that we have available are for next Thursday, October fourth. We have three available times 8am, 10am, and 3:30pm."

"I will take the eight o'clock appointment please. Thank you." I hear her typing in the information.

"Okay Ms. Rhodes I have you down for eight o'clock Thursday morning."

"Great. Thank you."

"You're welcome have a good day."

"You do the same." I hang up the line and enter the date in

into the scheduling app, before resuming the task of completing my playlist.

The drive to work isn't as annoying as usual. In spite of my health scare, I am in good spirits. The promotion, the new house, rekindling my relationship with Aiden, things are going pretty well. If I were a religious person, I would be praising God but since that's not the case, I will contribute it to luck and hard work. A nonreligious upbringing courtesy of mostly my father is to blame for my lack of faith in a higher power. My father says that religion is for the weak, for people that need a higher power to police and convict them. He says that those lacking self-control and good morals need it the most. Don't get me wrong, he believes that there is a God but he feels that he/she/or it allows people to make their own choices. He is a firm believer in free will. He believes that both God and the Devil live in us all and that it's up to us to make the right decisions. According to him, most people are afraid to admit their own shortcomings and are always looking for someone else to place the blame on. My mother has somewhat the same view, just not as extreme I suppose. I arrive at my job and find Kathy quite the opposite of her normal lively self. Her skin looks pale. Her blond locks are frazzled and dull. Her face looks drained and her eyes are heavy with worry. Something is definitely bothering her.

"Kathy is everything okay?"

"No not really, Tuna ran away."

"Oh wow really?"

"Yes. Yesterday when I got home after work, I went to fix Tuna her favorite dinner and she was gone! She would normally come out at the sound of the food cabinet door opening. I looked over the whole apartment and found nothing. Then like a bolt of lightning, I remembered that the maintenance man came to fix the garbage disposal. Tuna must've gotten out when he came in or maybe he left door open while he was servicing it. Needless to say, I called the leasing office and let them have it!"

"Okay well I hope you find her soon."

"Me too oh by the way Mr. Beck wants to see you."

"Is it anything good?"

"Not really. I don't think Jeff is going to be around too much longer."

"Oh geez thanks for the heads up."

I head straight for Mr. Beck's office. I can't believe Jeff. I told him to get his shit together! Now I might have to fire him! I knock on the door.

"Come in," Mr. Beck says before I step into his office. The look on Mr. Beck's face says trouble. He looks far from pleased.

"Hello Talia, close the door. I need to have a word with you." He says in a serious tone similar to one a parent might have after receiving a call from their child's school.

"Is everything okay sir?" I probe to get to the thick of it.

"No. There's no need to beat around the bush. Jeff has to go. I was waiting to see if the talk that you had with him might make him straighten out but it's obvious that he's too far gone in his bad habits to improve. I need you to tell him to clean out his desk, because he is done." Mr. Beck's words are along the lines of what I figured he was going to say. "Oh by the way is everything okay with you now? Are you having anymore health issues?"

"Everything is fine. I just got the last of the test results back this morning and I have a clean bill of health. I'm still not one hundred percent in agreement with the results so next Thursday before I come into work, I'm going to see my PCP and get a referral to see a specialist. I have to make sure. I don't want something popping up years after the fact."

"I understand. Make sure you keep me posted. If you feel any symptoms similar to the episode, let me know right away."

"Okay I will sir. Now it's time to go handle my Office Manager duties."

"That's what I like to hear!" Mr. Beck says as he gives his best effort at cracking a smile.

I leave his office and head right over to Jeff's cubicle. He's so preoccupied with looking at YouTube videos that he doesn't even notice me.

"Mmm hmm," I clear my throat to announce my presence. He quickly minimizes the screen and turns around.

"Hey Talia, uh it's not what you think… uh… I was just—" I cut off his weak explanation.

"Follow me to my office now!" I say in a firm tone. My adrenaline is pumping as we make the trek to the gallows. I have to show Mr. Beck that he definitely made the right choice in picking me for the promotion. We reach the office. I let Jeff go in first then

I close the door behind myself.

"Have a seat," I say in a cold emotionless manner. I feel a large lump forming in my throat as I build up the courage to complete my task.

"Look I'm cutting straight to the chase, we have already had a talk about you stepping it up and doing what you were hired to do. Mr. Beck is seriously on my back about you and now I swing by your cubicle and catch you watching YouTube videos? I mean really! I thought you said you going to straighten up?"

"I did, honestly Tal!"

"Don't call me that and if that's really the case, why did I catch you watching videos instead of working?"

"Look Talia it's like this, I need brief intermissions throughout the day to break the monotony of a typical work day and—"

"Enough!" I'm tired of playing with my food. It's time to finish my meal. "You can have all the intermissions you need, because from this day forward you're no longer an employee of this organization!" Wow, I can't believe how boss like I sound. I guess I am ready to be an Office Manager.

"So before when you were just one of us, one of the office

peons it wasn't a problem but now since you're a manager, it is huh? You're acting completely different. Now you're Ms. High and mighty! I mean, why couldn't you cover for me or at least put in a good word!" Jeff's fangs are drawn. He's hurting something bad. I can tell. He's only seeing it from his point of view, which I completely understand because if the shoe were on the other foot, I would more than likely have a similar reaction. He needs to understand that it's not personal it's only business. I search for the right words to say to cushion the blow, to detract from the harshness of the moment but it all escapes me. "So that's it I'm done?" He really wants to hear some something different and I desperately want to give him another chance, but I have to stay the course. I can't retract what I have already released into the universe. I mustn't let my emotions cloud my judgment. I have to finish this.

"Yes, and you can clear out your things by the end of the day." is the only response I can force from my lips. I feel emotionally anesthetized from the situation.

"Okay well since it's like that I'm not going to wait until the end of the day, I'll clear 'em out now!" Jeff says before storming out of my office and slamming the door behind him. The saying "It costs to be the boss," never rang as true as it does now. I can honestly say that I understand the meaning.

CHAPTER 8

"Duji you're such a bitch! I can't believe you just said that!" My favorite morning show "Rover's Morning Glory," broadcasts through the speakers inside Lindy as I weave in and out of the freeway lanes on the way to my doctor's appointment. I swear most of the people driving, drive as if they have no destination to reach. It seems like they're just coasting along until they eventually run out of gas or die, whichever comes first. During my morning commute, I often picture myself as a host on a radio show. I mean how cool would that be? To have a job where all you have to do is talk for five hours a day and have the rest of the day free to live. When I was a kid, I would use my little Sony recorder to make my own homemade shows. Amazingly, I still have both the recorder and the homemade recordings. Every so often, I take out those God-awful recordings and listen for the sake of nostalgia. There was a point in time where I seriously considered going to broadcasting school but my dad would not hear of it! He said that a career in radio is very fickle and women really don't excel in that field. He also said that if I wanted a career in broadcasting, I should set my sights higher like a news anchorwoman or something else of that caliber. The lack of support pretty much killed my dream. Regardless of the reoccurring "what if" that nags me every now and then I can honestly say that I am quite satisfied with my career choice. I have my own office, I make a nice salary, I have decent hours, and I don't have to slave or degrade myself to make a living. Lindy is exhibiting signs of wear and tear in the handling department. Her body is also showing indications of age. Dings, scratches, rust; she has accumulated her fair share of battle scars dealing with northeast Ohio's unpredictable weather. I know I should probably get a new car. I mean I could definitely afford it but it's not high on the list of priorities.

I reach my exit and am ecstatic to be finally getting off the freeway. The drive on the streets for the duration of the trip isn't as bad. I arrive with twenty something minutes to spare. My dad always says that, "a person who is late isn't a person about their business."

I enter the clinic and it's crowded with patients. "Oh boy," I mumble as I approach the help desk. The man behind it barely acknowledges my presence. "Good morning." I say in a slightly obnoxious manner.

"Hello, how may I help you?" He responds while giving me a "what the hell do you want?" look.

"I'm here to see Dr. Connors. I have an eight o'clock appointment." I can tell this guy probably doesn't have many friends. I'm surprised he even has a job dealing with the public. He seems like such a fucking prick!

"Okay and you are?"

"Talia Rhodes." I respond.

"Okay Ms. Rhodes. Take this form, fill it out, and bring it back up to the desk when you're finished." He says sharply as he slides a clipboard over the counter. "The medical staff, are in the middle of a meeting so be prepared to wait." Oh great I'm on time and I still have to wait!

I find the least occupied area in the waiting room and take a seat. I fill out the information and quickly return to the desk.

"Here, I'm finished." I state as I place the clipboard on the counter.

"Okay please have a seat and listen for your name." The prick responds as he grabs the clipboard from the counter. I walk back towards my seat only to find it taken. The person occupying it is an elderly woman. It rubs me the wrong way but I don't say a single word. I politely smile at her before going to find another seat. I find another seat nestled in the corner in between a heavyset woman and the window. It's definitely not as comfortable as my first seat but beggars can't be choosers. With a long wait ahead of me, I decide to make the best of it. I take out my phone and begin doing research on weird nightmares. The first thing I search for is reoccurring people in dreams.

After scrolling through numerous nonsensical explanations, I finally come across something that makes sense. According to the article, having a reoccurring person in your dreams can mean that the person dead or living is trying to contact you. The dead part sends a chill up my spine. *"What if the creepy brimstone and sulfur scented guy is dead? What is he trying to tell me? What if he's trying to tell me something important?"* I rack my brain thinking of what it could possibly be.

"Talia Rhodes?" A voice announces from the other side of the room.

"Yes?" I yell back as I get up from the seat and walk toward the voice. I see a nurse with a chart in her hand. "I'm Ms. Rhodes," I proclaim as I continue towards her.

"Okay Ms. Rhodes, follow me." I follow the nurse as she leads me from the waiting room to the examination area. We then go into an empty examination room.

"Okay Ms. Rhodes, do you mind if I call you Talia?"

"No, that's fine. Actually, I'd prefer it."

"Okay Talia, have a seat. I'm going to take your vitals, check your blood pressure, and ask you a few questions." She says before proceeding. She checks my heart beat with her stethoscope. Next, she straps the Velcro band of the blood pressure cuff around my arm and checks my blood pressure. I'm not a big fan of blood pressure devices. I don't like the way it feels when they squeeze my bicep. "Alright Talia, everything seems normal, so now I'm about to ask you a few questions, answer them as best you can okay?"

"I'm ready."

"Alright, have you ever been hospitalized for any serious injury?"

"Well except for a recent black out episode, no."

"Okay and do you know if there is a history of migraines, seizures, epilepsy, or mental illness in your family?"

"No not that I am aware of."

"Are you a smoker?"

"No."

"Do you drink, and if so do you do it obsessively?"

"I only drink socially,"

"Okay Talia I'm done. Put on one of those gowns," she points to a shelf near the examination table, "and the doctor will be in shortly to see you." The nurse leaves the room and my mind zones out as it always does when idle. It amazes me how some people can have careers in the medical field. I for one couldn't. Seeing blood, constantly being around the sick, and learning all of the medical terminology are all super cons in my book. That's why I majored in Business Administration and minored in Office Systems. It sounds like a lot but it's much simpler. It requires only basic algebra and zero science, which is probably why I took a liking to it. I was never a fan of either subject. Dr. Connors finally comes in to see me. She flips through the papers on the chart before speaking.

"So tell me what's going on with you Ms. Rhodes." She says as puts down the clipboard.

"Talia, just Talia… and to be quite honest with you, I'm not sure. Just recently, I had a massive headache and ended up blacking out because of it. I've never had anything like that happen before. I've also been getting a strange sense of being followed and I keep having these terrifying nightmares with the same reoccurring people and scenarios." I try to make sure I don't leave anything out. I need to get the right help.

"Wow, that's quite a lot Talia."

"Yes it is and that's why I need answers."

"Well I will certainly do my best to help you. Tell me about the headache episode."

"I was talking to a coworker and right after we finished the conversation, I started to feel this intense throbbing sensation accompanied by a loud ringing. It got so intense that I guess my system couldn't handle it and I ended up passing out."

"I see. Have you been under a lot of stress lately, at work, home, your private life?"

"Well... I just got a new promotion..." I try to think of everything that has been going on recently. "I recently reconnected with my high school sweetheart, I closed the deal on my new house, and like I stated earlier, I've been having nightmares."

"Okay tell me more about the nightmares." Dr. Connors says as she jots something down in her notes.

"Well in these nightmares, there are these shadow creatures with glowing red eyes and there's also this one guy that has features similar to my own."

"Okay well first tell me about the shadow creatures."

"Well, it's always four of them and one is always in the foreground while the others are in the background. The one in the foreground is the only one that speaks."

"Alright, so what does the one shadow person say?" The doctor asks as she continues jotting down notes.

"He says, "You will know,"." I respond as I study the doctor. I hope she doesn't think that I'm crazy. "Does any of this sound crazy to you? Do you think the feeling of being followed is linked to the dreams?" I ask while trying to come up with an answer as well.

"There could be a possible link, but I'm not a psychologist or psychiatrist so I don't want to assume anything. Another possibility is that the dreams, strange feelings, and headache episode, are a result of stress. Have you been getting enough sleep lately?"

"I've been getting rest, that's not the problem. Even when I have the nightmares, I'm still able to get sleep. Maybe it's the stress. The stress of the promotion, the new house, the nightmares—"

"Yes and I think that the strange feelings of being followed, could possibly be panic attacks. I definitely recommend seeing a psychiatrist and/or a psychologist. I can give you a referral before you leave. In the meantime, for your headaches I would suggest taking over the counter medication as needed like aspirin or something similar. For the panic attacks, I can prescribe you one of two different types of medication. We can go with a serotonin and norepinephrine reuptake inhibitor, also known as SNRIs. These medications are antidepressants. The other option is to try a Benzodiazepine. Benzodiazepines are mild sedatives that belong to a group of medicines called Central Nervous System Depressants. This would be my last choice though because Benzodiazepines may be habit-forming on either a mental or a physical level if taken for long periods of time or in high doses. The risk of addiction mostly depends on the person taking them. Benzodiazepines are often used in emergency rooms for treatment of signs and symptoms of panic attacks. Very few ER patients have become addicted. Do you want to give one of the medications a try?" I wait to answer, my brain is still trying to process the inordinate amount of information that the "oh see how much smarter I am than you," doctor has just spilled into my already complicated world.

"Given the choices, I think I will go with the non-habit forming one but before I commit to anything, what are the possible side effects of it?"

"I'm going to get to those but first keep in mind that the benefits of the medication are usually more important than any minor side effects. Also in most cases, side effects tend to go away after a few weeks of use." The way Dr. Connors is beating around the bush makes me consider not trying anything.

"I get that part but what are the side effects?"

"Well some of them are constipation, chronic cough, decrease in sexual desire or ability, dizziness, dry mouth, increased sweating, headache, nausea and loss of appetite, sleep problems, and weight loss." Damn, the side effects sound worse than the problem!

"Okay… how about I get back with you as far as the meds are concerned. I need some time to think about it." The last thing I need is drug issues to add to list of issues that I already face.

"Alright Talia well I still recommend seeing a psychologist. I can give you a referral," I really don't think I need to sit on a couch and have somebody pick my brain but seeing one might help me gain insight as to what's going on with my dreams.

"Okay I will take the referral to see the psychologist."

"Alright well I'm going to refer you to see Dr. Brooks. She is very effective at helping people deal with stress related issues. Just give her office a call and tell them I referred you. They should be able to get you in pretty soon."

"Okay thank you." I respond as I take the referral and leave the room.

I step back outside into the cold early October weather. I'm not so gung ho about Halloween this year. The nightmares and the being followed feeling already make it feel like it's here. I'm more so looking forward to Thanksgiving and Christmas. I wonder what I should get Aiden this year. It's been almost five years since I've gotten him a Christmas present. After school, I stayed on the West Coast for close to a year before returning home. Aiden briefly relocated from New York to New Jersey but ended up going back to the "Big Apple" for a couple of years before finally coming back here after the death of his father. Winter break of our first year of college was the last time we spent Christmas together. I went over to visit his family and then he left with me to visit mine. Back then, we tried to rekindle our relationship but the distance and the changes that we were going through wouldn't allow it. I guess it was all for the best because now I really appreciate him. I hope we can have a strong finish this time but who knows what the future holds. All that I can do is stay optimistic and try. I get into Lindy and start her up. I unlock my phone and place a call to Dr. Brooks' office.

"Hello Dr. Brooks' office Kelly speaking. How may I help you?"

"Hi Kelly my name is Talia Rhodes and I was calling to schedule an appointment. I have a referral from Dr. Connors."

"Okay give me a second. I have to check our system." She says before a brief silence. "The next available date I have is the fifteenth. Would you like to come in the morning, afternoon, or evening?"

"Evening, what's the latest time you have available?"

"We have a 5:30 available. Will that work for you?"

"Yes, that's perfect."

"Okay Ms. Rhodes I have you scheduled for Monday, October fifteenth at 5:30pm. Make sure you arrive fifteen minutes early to fill out paperwork, and bring two forms of ID, the referral, and your insurance card."

"Thank you, have a good day."

"You do the same."

Mondays after work on the freeway are always a challenge, that's why I left work almost an hour early. I should be able to make it with plenty of time to fill out paperwork. I felt a headache starting to brew earlier at work but a couple of aspirin helped keep it at bay. I keep having that weird creepy "someone is following me" feeling. I feel it starting to rear its ugly head as I exit the freeway.

Just as expected, I arrive at my destination with plenty of time to spare. I still have the creepy feeling lingering but I'm trying my best to ignore it. On the outside, the building is nondescript nothing really special or conspicuous about it. Attached to the front of it is a small sign that reads, "Brooks Counseling Services". I step inside. The decor definitely has a woman's touch written all over it. The walls of the waiting area are dark mauve with wine red accents. Several eye-catching paintings adorn them. Exotic plants rest in each of its corners. The reception desk is contemporarily up to date. Some random soft pop song that sounds somewhat familiar plays at a low level over the office's speaker system. I head over to the receptionist. She is a young brunette woman that appears to be around my age.

"Hi, I'm here for my 5:30 appointment." I state as I reach the desk and catch the attention of the receptionist.

"Hello, you must be Ms. Rhodes I'm Kelly. I was the one that set up your appointment." Kelly says in a courteous manner. "You're here pretty early Ms. Rhodes."

"Talia, just call me Talia. I didn't know being early was a bad thing."

"It's not a bad thing at all, I'm just surprised. Normally when I tell people to show up fifteen minutes early, they show up five minutes before their appointment. I'm glad you're not one of them."

"Well I'm glad that I stand out from the crowd." I respond.

"Take these papers and fill them out. Once you're done, bring them back up and the doctor may be able to get you in earlier."

"Okay great," I respond as I take the papers and find a seat. The paperwork takes no time to fill out. I return it to Kelly and go back to my seat.

"Talia Dr. Brooks is ready to see you," Kelly says before I'm even able to get comfortable in my chair. She leads me down a hall to the doctor's office. Dr. Brooks greets me at door. Dr. Brooks is a slim older female with short salt & pepper equally blended cropped hair. Her features have hints of Hispanic heritage. She has on a stylish pair of eyeglasses that complement the shape of her face. Her attire is chic and respectably casual. A large diamond ring adorns her wedding ring finger. She reminds me of one of the teachers I had back in college. Mrs. Watts was her name. I will never forget her. She really stayed on my case and pushed me when I thought about giving up.

"Hi you must be Ms. Rhodes. I'm Dr. Brooks." She says as she extends her hand.

"Hello Dr. Brooks," I respond as we shake hands. After the greeting, she welcomes me into her office.

Dr. Brooks' office is a soothing relaxed environment. Sounds of soft running water fill the air. Soft-lit florescent lighting gently illuminates the room. A sofa and a comfortable office chair rest in the center of the room. An ergonomic desk rests along the wall behind the chair and sofa. Potted plants are nestled in corners adjacent to one another. Calming and motivating pictures are intermingled along the walls. One particular picture really catches my eye. It has the silhouette of a man standing on the top of a mountain facing a sunrise backdrop. He has his arms raised in a manner similar to Sylvester Stallone once he reaches the top of the stairs in "Rocky". The slogan "peace is a state of mind" is in bold font across the middle of it. Underneath the picture is a fish tank populated with small exotic fish.

"So Talia, it's okay to call you Talia right?"

"Yes, actually I prefer it. I get sick of people calling me Ms. Rhodes it makes me feel old." I probably shouldn't have said that considering that she is definitely older. "I mean—"

"It's okay I understand. I was the same way when I was around your age. She says with a smile, showing her brilliantly white teeth. "According to the patient information, you're here today to talk about stress related issues, panic attacks, and a recent massive headache that resulted in loss of consciousness. Is that correct?" She says as she pushes her glasses up.

"Yes and like I told Dr. Connors, I'm not interested in taking any meds."

"I understand. Some of those medications have crazy side effects. But there is no need to worry about that I'm a psychologist, not a drug pusher!" She jokes as she flashes a warm smile. "That's a psychiatrist's job. I'm just a person that talks you through your problems. It's something that I've been doing for the past twenty years. I love it. I love talking to people and helping them, it gives me a sense of self satisfaction."

"Oh okay," I respond as I admire her enthusiasm for her profession.

"So where would you like to start?" She asks as she pulls a small notepad out of her suit coat.

"I guess we can start with the dreams." I answer as I adjust myself on the couch.

"Okay so tell me about them." She says as she writes notes on the pad.

"Well most of the time in these dreams, I'm paralyzed on my couch with these shadow men or rather creatures in front of me. I refer to them as creatures because they look far from human. They have piercing red eyes and a semitransparent appearance."

"Wow, they sound super creepy." Dr. Brooks comments.

"That's not the creepiest part. A strange man keeps reappearing in them too. There is something familiar about him but I just can't seem to put my finger on it.

"Really," she comments, briefly looking up while continuing to scribe.

"Yes and just recently, I had another strange dream where I opened my eyes and saw nothing but a black dark void. I could hear a voice calling out to me from somewhere within the darkness. I looked all around unable to see anything. Then all of a sudden, everything lit up and the voice stopped calling me. I was standing in the middle of my grandmother's front yard. A place I haven't been to in ages. The last time I visited my grandmother was when I was like five. While standing in the yard, I looked up at the sky and saw a bunch of dark clouds gathering. Then the voice from earlier started up again but this time, instead of calling out to me it sounded as if it was chanting a spell. As the voice continued to chant, I felt myself lift into the air. I tried my best to get back to the ground but I couldn't. Then some unknown force began to toss me around. After a while, I started to get motion sickness. In a state of desperation, I begin praying to God. While I was praying, a deep evil voice started to speak. It said, "That God cannot save you!" When I woke up, I looked around my room and in one of the corners, I saw the strange man from my previous nightmares standing there. There was also a strong odor of brimstone or some type of sulfur present as well."

"So you saw the guy in your room while you were awake?" Dr. Brooks asks while continuing in her notes.

"Yes. At first, I thought I was seeing things but the smell, that fiery smoky smell. It was so pungent that it was hard to mistake it for anything else. Also my parents don't smoke so that's why I'm positive that the smell is somehow linked to the guy."

"Okay let's go back to the part where you said that he looked like you. Let's just say that he is a real person, could it be possible that your subconscious is making a person from your past manifest into the present. For example, let's say that you have a cousin that you haven't seen since you were a kid. Even though you might forget about the person, your subconscious may still retain enough memory to make this person manifest through dreams and/or visions later in life."

"I get what you're saying. I guess that's possible. So do you think that could explain why I also saw him at the hospital the day after my blackout episode?"

"So you saw him again?" Dr. Brooks asks with her eyebrows raised.

"Yes and it was during daytime hours."

"So how did he look during the last appearance?" She asks. She has completely stopped writing and is anticipating an answer.

"Well he looked alive but not alive. He was solid and as clear as day but his eyes were completely black and his skin was a pale light brown color, very deathly looking."

"It sounds like he knows you and is trying to tell you something. If I we're you Talia, I would do some research into your family. Find out about your relatives and see if anybody matches or comes close to his appearance. Oh and I think your feelings of someone following you may be linked to him as well. I've heard of cases where a family member that is trying to contact a loved one has a desire and bond so strong that there is a psychic connection formed to where the one can feel the other's presence, even if they're not physically in the same place. I truly believe he is trying to contact you."

"Okay so what about the shadow creatures? What do you think the reason is that I'm having reoccurring dreams of them?"

"I wouldn't take the shadow men as literal interpretations. I think that they're a symbolic representation of some deep rooted issue that is bothering you."

"Do you mean like a traumatic experience or something?" I quiz as the attempted rape comes to mind.

"Yes, that's along the lines of what I'm referring to."

"Well I can only think of one traumatic experience and that would have to be the time that I was almost raped."

"Okay so tell me more about this attempted rape." Dr. Brooks says. I begin to feel uncomfortable. It's been over a year and I still have problems discussing it.

"Well I went to a bar and while I was out, I met this guy. He bought me a drink. We hit it off right away. He bought me another drink, and the next thing I remember is coming to in his apartment with him trying to remove my pants. If I didn't have my .22 caliber handgun, I would've become a victim. I definitely believe that I was roofied."

"So what happened while he was trying to remove your pants,

I mean how did the gun come into play?" Dr. Brooks' hand is moving rapidly as she scribbles on her pad.

"Um… well as he was struggling to remove my pants, I came to my senses. He removed one pants leg and I managed to kick him in the face. He recoiled and released his grip on my pants. I then scrambled around the room looking for my purse. I found it near my coat and shoes. I grabbed my purse and removed my gun. I turned just as he was lunging towards me and fired."

"Oh my God," Dr. Brooks stops writing and looks at me with a shocked expression on her face. "Did you kill him?" She asks in a low tone.

"No. The bullet grazed his head and gave me the opening I needed to gather my things and get the hell out there. After that, I've always kept some form of protection and I never accept drinks from strangers.

"Well I'm glad you were able to get away. I think that definitely has something do with the sensation of being followed and the panic episodes that you've been experiencing. What about the death of a loved one?" Dr. Brooks changes the subject which is exactly what I hoping would happen. The traumatic experience was life altering, which is probably why I felt so betrayed by Kenna. She took advantage of me just like the rapist attempted to.

"I lost both my grandparents on my mother's side of the family." I reply as my grandparents John and Mariana come to mind.

"So I take it you were pretty close to them huh?" Dr. Brooks is feverishly writing notes as we talk.

"Yes, I was. A part of me still feels empty. When they passed, it felt like pieces of me went with them."

"How long has it been since they passed?"

"Well my grandfather died first, about seven years ago and my grandmother died a few years later."

"Well based on that alone, I think that you may still be going through the grieving process."

"Really, I mean it's been years since they passed I should have gotten over it by now right? How can I still be grieving? I mean it's not like I stopped my whole life and just decided to stay in the house crying and balling my eyes out about it!"

"The grieving process takes a different amount of time for each and every individual. There isn't a set time or rule as to how long it should take you to process and move forward after the death of a loved one. It may last for weeks, months, even years after their death, and that's okay. You're supposed to be sad, especially if you shared a deep bond with them. The problem comes when your grief turns into depression and interferes with your life. You should still be able to function and engage in your normal, day-to-day activities. Now if you become so despondent that it interferes with your quality of life, then that would be an abnormal grieving process, it would no longer be considered grieving it would be depression. To me it seems that you are like most people, in the sense that you have worked through your grieving and adapted your life to the change. In the process, you probably pushed most of those intense emotions into your subconscious and now they're manifesting through your dreams.

"Okay I understand. That makes sense. So how do I get all of those repressed emotions out?" I inquire as I think of what Dr. Brooks has just explained.

"Well the first step is what you're doing today, which is talking about it. The next step is to acknowledge them. And the last step is to find a way to get closure."

CHAPTER 9

It's finally here, moving day. I'm officially a homeowner. Thanks to my father and mother, as well as Jessica, Aiden, and Ashley, the move is almost over in less than three hours. Even though I'm in good spirits about the move, a slight headache is dampening the occasion. The rest of the test results revealed nothing, which only leaves me in the dark as to why I keep getting them, or what is triggering them.

"We're almost done." I say enthusiastically trying to keep up a front of wellness, while the throbbing of the headache increases. I under estimated the amount of stuff that needed to be moved, I should've gotten the twenty-four footer instead of the seventeen. Oh well, I'm glad it only took two loads. "Just this last load left and then we can crack open the twelve pack." I say aloud jokingly, well aware of the fact that most of us don't drink beer. I haven't had a sip of it in almost four years. Diane, my friend from college used to throw 'em back like a contestant in a competition.

After seeing her piss on herself, use a towel to wipe it up, and then use that same towel to wipe her face after she threw up, I decided to reduce my own consumption. Although what really made slowdown was this one time when one of my ex-boyfriend's got so drunk that he mistakenly used an ashtray on my dresser as a urinal. Those experiences along with being roofied, has made me keep my alcohol intake down to a minimum. The last time I consumed any was the night I reconnected with Aiden and before that the night with Kenna, which was a bad idea on my part. One thing that I definitely will never use again is weed. I absolutely hate it! The times I've tried it never resulted in good experiences. I get overly paranoid, emotional, and unmotivated on the stuff.

We finish the move and everyone is in good spirits. I order a few pizzas and beverages. Jessica's husband comes to pick her up and stays for a few. The house feels warmer than it did previously.

After an hour or so of hanging out, everyone has left except Aiden. I'm still hard at work arranging the last of the furniture when he catches my attention. I feel him creep up behind me. He places a soft warm kiss on my neck and whispers, "Hey Talia, how about you stop working hard straightening up the house and let me work on you?" I turn around to give him my full attention. He catches me off guard. He has stripped off everything but his boxer briefs. "I saved the best for you," he says as he places my hand on the rim of his underwear. I am beside myself. His rippling hard body and large bulge are too tempting to resist. Within seconds, we are completely naked.

After a long sensuous series of kisses, Aiden picks me up, props me on his shoulders, and begins pleasuring me. His passionate kisses, force me to release sensuous moans of pleasure. He continues feasting on my bountiful love as I dig my fingers into his dark full mane. My legs begin to twitch and my abdominal muscles tighten. I'm hot and ready. I throb in anticipation of the main event. Aiden stops and slowly removes me from off his solid muscular shoulders and places me on the plush carpet. "Turn around and get on your knees." He commands. His authoritative voice and demeanor sends my arousal into overdrive. I quickly

obey. He uses his fingers to part me and slowly slides himself

inside. His first series of thrusts produce a mix of pain and

pleasure, more so the latter. I vocalize my approval erotically. He

continues giving me what I need. He tames my savage pent up

beast with his hard thick love. I feel my paradise melting around

him as he labors inside. He's rough yet gentle. He switches speeds

randomly; this makes me melt even more. He maintains his

stamina like an adult film star. I feel friction on my knees as I

moan loudly. *"I hope my knees don't get carpet burn."* is the

thought that whispers in the back of my mind. I want to release so

bad. It's a burning desire that ravages my entire being. I want to

give in but I resist and force it back. I'm greedy. I want as much

raw passion as he is willing to give. His love goes deeper and

harder. I desperately grab at the plush carpet as he pounds my

world. I continue to resist the climax, steadily losing ground. My

body starts to shake uncontrollably. I'm ready to explode. In the

blink of an eye, it happens. I let out a loud yell as I reach the

climax zone. The chain reaction of my eruption forces Aiden to

climax as well. We collapse to floor. It feels like I'm floating on clouds. I roll over to face my champion lover.

"I've loved you forever." I utter as I look into his eyes.

"I love you too Talia," he says before placing his lips on mine. The kiss is electrifying. I feel a slight chill enter into the room.

"Are you cold?" I ask while looking around trying to figure out where the draft is coming from.

"Yeah a little bit. I wonder where it's coming from." Aiden responds.

"I don't know," I murmur as I try to pinpoint the source of the cold air. A sudden bump from outside makes me jump.

"Are you okay? Aiden asks with a concerned expression.

"Did you hear that?" I whisper with wide eyes.

"Hear what?"

"The bumping sound from outside," I answer as I slowly rise from off the floor.

"Babes I don't hear anything." Aiden says as he follows suit. The sounds persist but Aiden is seemingly oblivious to them. I walk across the room and notice that it is substantially colder on one side of the room, the side closest to the weird picture. As I stare up at the eerie artwork, a dreadful creepy feeling emerges.

"I'm throwing this creepy shit out on trash day," I mumble as I continue looking. The picture is very unsettling. It has an ominous cloudy backdrop and a crowd of faceless people with a man in front of them. The man is the only one that has a face and he seems to be staring directly at me. I want to stop looking at it but I'm powerless to do so. It's affecting me deeply I want it out of my house immediately.

"Hey," I feel Aiden's strong hand grab my shoulder, "What's with you honey?" He asks. I turn to face him.

"This picture has to go tonight!" I state before turning and grabbing the edges of it. As I attempt to take the picture off the wall, I feel a sharp sting on one of my fingers I quickly retract my hand and look at it. I see a small red line forming. "Shit!" I say aloud as I examine the wound. Thankfully, it doesn't appear to be deep.

"Are you ok?" Aiden asks.

"I cut myself on this damn picture!" I say in an agitated tone.

"Here let me do it. He says as he steps forward. He grabs the picture, and removes it with little resistance. "Where do you want me to put it?" Aiden asks.

"Just throw it out back." I respond.

After taking a shower and bandaging my wound. We decide to retire for the night. The combination of warmth from Aiden's body and one of my favorite comforters, allows drowsiness to overtake me. As my conscious slips away, my mind travels to the land of dreams. I crossover into the dream realm and arrive in the midst of wild raging debauchery. Loud heavy drums resound in the distance as naked and semi-naked bodies dance and grind erotically against each other. "Why are we here," I murmur as I turn to Aiden. He looks at me with a weird blank expression before raising his arm and pointing. I look in the given direction and see Kenna completely exposed walking over from across room. I look down at my own body and notice that I too am completely in the buff. I turn back towards Aiden only to see that he is gone. I spin back around and come face to face with Kenna.

"Remember that night?" She says before surprising me with a deep long passionate kiss. The kiss is shocking, yet arousing at the same time. "This is what you want." She says seductively as she draws back.

"Where are we?" I ask aloud as Kenna slowly backs away. As she backs away, my eyes take notice of the somber-faced man from my visions and previous dreams. He looks a little different this time. His eyes are glowing red and he has on a dark crimson robe, with an upside down star embroidered on the chest area. "Who the hell would wear that?" I say aloud, not really caring who hears my remark. The man moves closer but doesn't appear to walk, he sort of glides across the floor towards me. I want to run but my body refuses to move. Panicked, I look around and notice all of the once exposed partiers are draped in similar dark robes. Within seconds, the man is right in front of me! The drums have ceased and the attention of the partygoers is now focused on him.

"You will know!" He proclaims in a commanding ominous voice.

"Hey babe, wake up," I wake up in bed with Aiden lying next to me.

"Hey Aiden, what happened? How did we end up in bed?" I ask in a puzzled tone.

"Huh? What are you talking about?" Aiden asks.

"Oh nothing," I respond as I realize that the raunchy gathering was only a dream. "I was just having a bad dream." I utter as I fight back a yawn.

"We have a problem," Aiden says in a serious tone.

"Huh, what's the problem" I respond.

"Well, I want to spend the day with my girlfriend but I promised my sister I would help her today." He says with a sly smile.

"Oh so we're an item again?" I ask jokingly.

"Only if you're willing to give us a second chance," he responds.

"Um I don't know… just playing. Of course, I'm willing to give it a go. Third time's the charm." I say before reaching over and planting a kiss on him.

After breakfast, Aiden leaves and I decide to get ready. In the middle of brushing my brushing teeth, I notice a blurry image move in the hallway. "What the…" I mumble as I stop what I'm doing and shift my full attention to the doorway. I quickly shut off the water and creep into the hallway. The temperature in the hall is drastically different. There is a distinct chill. I can see my breath. I hear noises from downstairs and decide to have a look. "Aiden," I call out softly as I reach the top of the stairs. The noises persist as I cautiously extend my foot. As I step on the first stair, they seem to increase. Something doesn't feel right. Going with my gut instinct, I halt my journey down the stairs and swiftly creep into my bedroom to retrieve my pistol. With weapon in hand, I resume my trek down the stairs. Adrenaline surges through my veins, as I get closer to my destination. As I reach the first floor, the noises stop. I inspect the living room and find everything in order. The dining room is in order as well. When I step inside the kitchen, I immediately notice that the back door is wide open. "What the hell?" I utter as my brain processes the conundrum I now face. Before I get a chance to examine the door, the sound of footsteps coming from the front of the house interrupts my investigation. Going off pure instinct, I rush to the source of the sound.

Once in front, my eyes instinctively dart towards the same strange man from "Tasty Bones" standing off in the distance. We lock eyes for a brief moment. I feel the malevolence in his cold hard stare. Something inside urges me to confront him. I raise my weapon and start walking towards him. To my surprise, he starts shaking his head and walking backwards. He then turns and goes into a full sprint. I'm determined to find out who he is and what he wants so I quicken my pace. I'm gaining ground on him or so I think. He turns a corner, I follow suit only to find that he is gone! *"Where did he go?"* I'm racking my brain trying to figure out the answer. I was only like three yards behind him, so unless he is some sort of illusionist, I don't know how he pulled off the vanishing act. His mysterious escape is frustrating to say the least. I return home frustrated and a little on edge. My hair is wild and sweat produced by the brief unsuccessful chase covers my forehead.

As I step inside the living room, my eyes lock onto something that stops me dead in my tracks. The creepy picture is back in the same spot on the wall! I am beyond puzzled. I don't know what to think but one thing is for certain, it has to go! I find a pair of gloves to put on before trying to remove it. I learned my lesson from the last time. I take the picture down and rest it against the wall before beginning a thorough search of the house. I carefully inspect each room making sure not to miss anything. As I continue going through the house, I return to the upstairs bathroom and an instant chill slaps my senses. It is extremely cold. I can't figure out the source of the coldness. I look around the room, analyzing every square inch. I try to come up with a possible explanation as to why it is so cold. I continue surveying the room. I notice a section on the medicine cabinet mirror is foggy and has an inscription scribbled on it. "You will know," is what the mysterious writing says. Now I am pissed. I pull out my phone and angrily dial Mr. Reynolds. The phone begins to ring. I think of all the things I am going to say to him while waiting for him to answer. *"How the hell could he sell me a place like this?"* I wonder as my temper rises with each second that goes by.

"Hello this is realtor Reynolds how may I help you?" A voice on the line says before I start laying in on him.

"Mr. Reynolds this is Talia Rhodes, we really need to talk about this house. I don't think you were all the way honest about the history of it. I just moved in and a few strange things have already taken place. I have no explanation for them so you need to tell me the truth, the whole truth!" I say in a demanding voice.

"For one, who the hell is the creepy guy stalking me and why does the house have so many cold spots?"

"Um…" Mr. Reynolds goes silent on the other end. "You have a stalker? What does he look like?" He asks in a serious tone.

"He is a white man, possible early thirties, with jet black hair, grey eyes, and pale luminous skin." I answer.

"Well I can't recall ever running into someone in that neighborhood that fits that description Ms. Rhodes and as far as the drafts are concerned, that house was completely renovated before being placed on the market and every square inch of it was inspected by my company. Furthermore, I have fully disclosed the history of the house to you but if you need further confirmation, I would be more than willing to go down to city hall with you and look through the records." Mr. Reynolds says. His response helps to calm me down slightly but it still doesn't resolve the matter. I sit idle on the phone as I give a trip to city hall consideration. "Are you still there Ms. Rhodes?" Mr. Reynolds asks, grabbing my attention.

"Uh yes, I don't think a trip to city hall will be necessary." I respond.

"Okay well I don't mean to rush you off the phone, but I'm in the middle of a meeting. Is there anything that you need ask?"

"Yes, just answer this one question before you get off the phone?"

"Sure Ms. Rhodes, shoot." Mr. Reynolds replies.

"Can you tell me where the picture in the living room is from? I mean do you know who the artist is and who originally brought it to the house?"

Mr. Reynolds thinks before responding. "If I'm not mistaken, the picture is a piece inspired by a song from an eighties musician. I believe the last owner is the one responsible for bringing it. According to him, the musician died while on the verge of stardom. I'm not sure, if the guy painted it himself or if he acquired it and how. Maybe if you search the web, you'll find more info on it."

"Okay well thanks for your time. Have a good day." I hang up the phone, grab the painting, and head back outside. I pop the trunk and throw the picture inside. I want to call the police but what could I possibly tell them, someone broke in and put a painting back up on my wall? They would probably think that I'm insane. I decide to take matters into my own hands.

I look up a few home security places and make some calls. After making contact with several, I finally get lucky with one that schedules me for same day service. That's a miracle considering its Saturday. Next, I begin looking for a guard dog. I remember Jessica telling me about an animal shelter where her husband got their dog. It's in a neighboring city about twenty minutes from my house. I'm familiar with the place. I recall seeing it once or twice.

I arrive at the pound in no time. As per a sign posted out front, I drive around to the back of the building and park near the customer entrance. I step inside. The smell of wet dog, mixed with special pet food, and that weird indescribable scent that is present in all animal facilities greets me. I make my way up to the desk where I see a couple of employees stationed. One is deeply enthralled in paperwork and doesn't notice anything outside of it. The other one greets me with a courteous smile.

"Hi how can I help you today?" She asks while still keeping a smile.

"Hi, I'm here to look at your dogs." I respond.

"Okay just take one of those forms and fill it out. I will gladly show you the ones we have available." She says while directing my attention to the stack of forms neatly resting next to her on the counter. I take one as she hands me a clipboard with a pen attached to it. I find a seat and fill out all of the necessary information. I complete the form and return to the desk with the finished paperwork in hand. I give it to the attendant and she thumbs through it. Once she checks it, she writes something on the front of it and shifts her attention back to me.

"Okay Ms. Rhodes let's go find you a pet." She says as she gets up from the desk.

"Just call me Talia." I add as usual.

"You got it." She replies.

I follow her through a set of double doors leading into a hallway. We walk down the hall past various rooms. The telltale barking lets me know we're getting close to the dogs.

"Diana you have a call on extension 267" a voice announces over the intercom system.

"Talia, will you excuse me for a few minutes? I have to take that. If you want to look at the available dogs while you wait, go through the second set of double doors at the end of this hall. I'll be there shortly."

"Okay," I respond before Diana leaves. I continue walking down the hall. I walk through the second set of double doors and enter into the dog kennel area. It has quite a few different dogs. For the most part, I'm not impressed with their selection. Most of the dogs look like mutts and strays picked up off the streets or dropped off on the kennel's doorstep. They have a few Lab mixes, some Sheppard/Dobermans, and some others whose features aren't as distinguishable. I continue looking through the dogs hoping to find one suitable to my liking. As I'm nearing the end of the selection, I notice the one I want.

According to the label on the cage, the dog's name is Max and he is a husky/wolf mix. His off-white and black coat is brilliant, and his grayish blue eyes are some of the coolest I've ever seen. He looks at me as I approach his cage. Surprisingly, he doesn't bark. I put my hand up to his cage. He sniffs and then he starts to lick my fingers. I know right away that he is the one I want to take home. Diana comes into the room. She sees me by Max and walks over.

"So I see you found one you like," she states as she looks down at Max.

"Yeah, I think I want him," I respond as I too look at him.

"Okay well let me give you a little background on him. He is two years old. He's been here for about two months. They picked him up on Chevy Boulevard. He didn't have a tag or a collar and no one has come forward claiming ownership, so if you want him he's yours. All of his shots are up to date and he is neutered. For you to get him today the only things we need from you are, an ID, a seventy-five dollar adoption fee, and if you rent we need approval from the landlord stating that you are allowed to have animals on the premises."

"I don't rent, I just bought a house." I state proudly.

"Okay well I need proof of residency. Do you have any with you right now?"

"I might have something in my car," I reply.

"Alright well, just give me your ID and I will get the process started while you go and have a look.

"Okay." I respond before reaching into my purse to retrieve

my wallet.

As we return to the entrance lobby, I locate my ID. "Here you go." I say as I hand her my driver's license. Diana takes it and heads to the copier.

"I'll be right back. Give me a few minutes okay?" I state as she places the license on the scanner portion of the copier.

"Sure. I will be preparing the rest of the paperwork needed for Max until you get back." She responds.

I quickly go out to my car and check in my glove compartment. I find some paperwork that will suffice, and return to Diana at the desk. She takes the paperwork over to a copy machine and makes copies of it.

"Can I use my debit card?" I ask as she updates the files in the computer system.

"Yes but we prefer check or cash payments. You will be charged an additional fee for a card payment." She responds

"Okay I'll write a check instead. Who should I make it out to?"

"You can make it out to Ohio Protective Animal Services or OPAS for short." I fill out the check and give it to her. She takes it, makes a copy of it as well, and finishes the process. After she's done, she pages someone to bring Max up front. A few minutes later, a man comes through the double doors with Max on a leash. He also has a small box under his arm. He gives me the leash's handle and box before returning through the double doors. "The box that he just gave you contains a few of Max's things. It should contain, his favorite chew toy, a blanket that he enjoys sleeping with, some of the food that we've been feeding him, and a couple other goodies."

"Okay thank you," I respond, as I get ready to leave.

"No, thank you for giving Max a good home," She says with a smile.

I leave the shelter with Max. I open the back passenger door to put him into the car and he won't go. He begins growling at the car. When I close the door, he stops. I open it up again and grab his box of belongings. I dig into the box and find some dog treats. I take out a few and place them on the seat to coax him into getting in. The plan is unsuccessful. He doesn't budge an inch. He just sits and growls. I can't figure out what the problem is. After several failed attempts, I close the back door and open up the front passenger door instead. To my surprise, he stops growling and hops in. I then load his things into Lindy, rev her up, and begin to head home. As I'm driving, I turn through the radio stations. Unable to find anything worth listening to, I plug in my phone and put on a playlist.

CHAPTER 10

I arrive home with time to spare before my appointed security installation. I pull Lindy into the driveway and proceed to get Max out of the car. At first, he's cooperating with me but as we get closer to the house, he begins acting weird. As we approach the front porch, he starts to pull back. I lightly tug at the leash to coax him into following but he is being stubborn. After enduring a brief bout of tug of war, I manage to get him in the house. I look around the house to make sure everything is the same as I left it. I don't see anything out of the ordinary, so I continue getting Max settled in. He slowly starts to get relaxed in his new surroundings. While Max is adjusting, I resume organizing my house. I knock out the rest of the living room, dining room, and kitchen in no time.

After double-checking my work, I let Max out into the backyard and proceed up the stairs to start on the second floor. The ringing of the doorbell stops me halfway up. Thinking it's the scheduled serviceman, I rush back down to answer the door. To my surprise, no one is there. *"That's odd."* I think as I step out to begin searching the perimeter. My search is unsuccessful. With no explanation present, I write it off as some dumb kid playing around or a neighbor's doorbell frequency crossing with mine. As I return to the front of the house, my eyes take notice of a white envelope left on the welcome mat. I pick up the mysterious parcel and take it inside with me. Upon taking a closer look, I notice that the strange mail has Elizabeth written on it.

"Who the hell left this?" I murmur as I open it. There is an old folded piece of loose-leaf paper in it. As I'm removing the paper, another piece of paper falls out of it. I bend down to grab the fallen item as I unfold the letter and begin to read:

"May 22, 1988

Dear Elizabeth,

Hello, I know you. I have seen you in my dreams. I hope to see you in person one day but that may not be possible. My time on this earth is short. Everything that I have hoped and dreamed for is now in jeopardy. My enemies conspire against me. They pray and lust for my demise. Ignorance clouds their judgment. All praises are due to the great Lucifer. My work will continue and its legacy will flourish. In time, you will discover the truth. Once the guardians feel you are ready for it, it will spring forth and the knowledge of your true existence will consume you. You are my flesh and blood. I will return to reclaim all that belongs to me.

Honor you always

M-T-R"

I finish reading the letter, totally confused and freaked out at the same time. *"Who the hell is Elizabeth?"* I wonder as I look at the other piece of paper that fell out of the letter. It's a cut out newspaper article from October 21, of the same year. The headline reads, ASPIRING MUSICIAN DIES IN TRAGIC FREAK ACCIDENT.

The article talks about how some rocker on the verge of stardom died in a fire that started in his studio apartment. According to the article, a spark from a cigarette ignited an open container of paint. The musician Michael Theodore Rosette, who went by the name Armichael, was a recent transplant to the New York scene by way of Cleveland, Ohio. The article goes on to state that his music was unique and reminiscent of his idol, Jimi Hendrix. There is also a picture accompanying the article. I look at the picture and immediately recognize Armichael as the man from my visions and nightmares!

I study the picture a little harder and notice the creepy painting that I now have in my trunk is on the wall in the background! I finish reading the article and put both papers back in the envelope. As I'm putting them back in, my fingers feel a small solid object inside of it. The object is a guitar pick. I grab it out of the envelope and study it. One side has a symbol that looks like two hands holding something. The opposite side has the initials M-T-R inscribed on it. For some strange reason I am drawn to it. Something about it feels familiar, like a warm memory. After reading the letter and newspaper article, I feel compelled to retrieve the creepy painting from Lindy's trunk. As I'm walking to Lindy, I see a C.T.S. security van driving up the street towards my house. *"Maybe I should see how much it would cost to get some surveillance cameras setup?"* I think as the van draws near. Within seconds, the van pulls up into my driveway. I can hear classic 80's rock resonating from the vehicle as the driver parks. The singer howls like a banshee on meth. The van makes a complete stop. The music ceases along with the low rumble of the engine. To my surprise a black man that appears to be in his early 30's hops out of the vehicle, which is somewhat of a surprise considering the type of music. I was expecting to see someone quite different.

"Hello. I have a 2 o'clock appointment scheduled for a Ms. Rhodes." The man says as walks over towards me.

"Hi, I'm Ms. Rhodes." I respond.

"I'm Chuck, and I will be your expert installer today. If you have any questions, feel free to ask." Chuck says before looking down at the paperwork on his clipboard. "It says here that you want the basic installation package."

"Yes and I'd also like to know how much it would cost to setup a surveillance system in addition to the basic service."

"Well ma'am—" I interject.

"Talia, just call me Talia." I state before allowing him to continue. It sounds weird having an older person call me ma'am.

"Well Talia, we have a few different packages. The first one, the traditional package requires you to have some type of DVR at your home, unless you want us to monitor video for you, which is usually the most expensive plan. Very few residential customers go that route. The next one is the pulse package. This plan enables you to view feed from the cameras live over the internet from any device, ranging from your smart phone, laptop, or even your tablet. The cameras also have motion analytics that allow users to create motion-activated clips and send it to themselves or others. The system can also store it remotely. The cameras range from $33.60-$36.48 apiece. The service itself is $39.99 a month, with discounted equipment and a suite of other interactive services like remote arm/disarm, free apps, and even text and email notifications. The last one is similar to the pulse, but it combines parts of both packages, for $55.99 a month."

I think about the options before responding. "Okay well I think I want to go with the pulse package."

"Alright, just give me a few minutes. I have to notify the office and get clearance and processing for the add-on service." Chuck contacts the office and they authorize him to add the additional service. "Okay Talia I got the approval. Give me a few minutes to get started. I have to grab all of the equipment out of the van and run a few lines," Chuck says before going back to his van. Within minutes, he begins the instillation. While he's installing the system, I check on Max in the backyard and resume arranging the house. I'm just about finished arranging when my phone starts to ring. I pick it up and I see a contact on the screen that I haven't seen in a while, it's Kenna. I tap the answer icon.

"Hello Talia?"

"Yes, hey Kenna what's up?" I ask as I mentally speculate the reason for the call.

"Um… I was wondering… are you going to be free later to hang out? You said that we were still friends so—"

"I'm in the middle of something, hold on for a sec." I respond while thinking of what to say. I weigh my options and decide that it wouldn't hurt for us to hang out. I mean besides, we're still friends so why not?

"Kenna, are you still there?"

"Yes," she says in a sweet bubbly voice.

"So… what did you have in mind?" I ask while finishing the last box of things to put away.

"How about we grab a bite to eat and do some karaoke?"

"Okay sure. Are we meeting somewhere, am I picking you up, or what?"

"Well I was figuring we can take one car to save on time and gas." She says.

"Okay well I can pick you up around seven. I'm getting a security system installed right now and finishing up the rest of the stuff around my house."

"I still haven't seen your new place yet. How about I come to your house, you give me a tour, and we take your car?" I can hear the seduction in her voice. Regardless of how much she tries to mask it. I know what she wants and to be quite honest, part of me wants it too. At the same time, I'm thinking about Aiden. I'm mentally reliving our most recent night of passion. I can still smell his scent and feel his skin against mine. Everything about him is still fresh to my senses. I have the urge to decline the get together but the weird longing for Kenna prevails.

"Okay sure. Are you ready to take my address?" I respond. Damn I'm weak. I hope it doesn't come back to bite me.

"Yes I'm ready." She responds.

"My address is 5525 Hope drive. It's located in West Shore Village."

"I'm saving it in my GPS. See you at seven."

"Alright," I respond before hanging up.

Within two hours, the security instillation is complete. "Okay Talia it's set to go. Now all you have to do is log onto the system using your phone and follow the instructions to synchronize it. Once it's synchronized, you will be able to monitor your house at any time. You can go on vacation in Hawaii and still be able to keep an eye on it!" Chuck directs me through the set up process and within minutes, my phoned is synched and ready. "Alright Talia you're activated and protected. The last thing I need is for you to sign these forms." Chuck says as he hands me a pen and gets his paperwork together. I sign all the forms and he rips off the customer copies from each of them. "Here you go Talia." He says as he hands me the copies. "Now if you have any problems, call the number on the top of the first page I gave you and customer service will assist you. If it's a service issue, they will send out someone within forty-eight hours."

"Okay thank you." I respond barely able to concentrate. Thoughts of Kenna consume my train of thought. I feel a tingle as brief glimpses of her naked body flash in my head.

"You're welcome ma—I mean Talia. Have a good day." Chuck says as he shakes my hand and leaves.

After Chuck leaves, I remember the painting in the trunk. I want to throw away but something tells me that I should hold on to it, especially since it has a connection to Armichael. I retrieve the creepy artwork, and rush back to the house. Once inside, my mind goes to work thinking of a place to store it. I definitely want it somewhere where I won't have to see it constantly but I also want the location to be convenient if ever I would need to retrieve it quickly. *"I can put it in the basement."* is the thought that wins the final say in regards to the location of the painting. With painting in hand, I quickly dash into the basement. I hastily rest it against one of the walls before returning upstairs. Basements give me the creeps.

Once I reach the kitchen, I decide to bring Max in. I call him back inside and settle down on the couch to watch TV.

I'm in the middle of watching "The-40-Year-Old Virgin", when a strange noise coming from the basement catches my ear. I mute the TV and listen. Something is definitely down there. I put the movie on pause and head down the stairs to find the source. The noise gets louder and more distinct as I draw closer. It sounds like scratching accompanied by heavy shuffling. An overwhelming feeling of dread sweeps over me as my foot lands on the last step. *"My I shouldn't do this."* is the thought released by my conscience. I do a double take when I notice the painting is no longer resting against the wall where I left it. Part of me wants to turn back around. The other part of me is curiously intrigued and wants to continue. I build up my nerves by convincing myself that it was probably Max's doing. I continue to walk further into the basement.

"Max," I call out. The noise stops. I hear another noise overhead, the sound of something running over carpet. "Max," I call out again. Max responds with a bark at the top of the stairs. The noise in the basement starts up again. My rational mind urges me not to continue. I do the exact opposite. I throw caution to the wind and go further into the basement.

I reach the other side of the basement and see the painting resting face down in front of the storage room near the laundry area. I pick up the painting and place it aside. *"What am I doing?"* I wonder as I realize that the strange noise is originating from the room. "I must see this through." I murmur before forcing myself to enter the room. Once inside, I see another door leading to a smaller room. *"I don't remember this being here?"* I think as I move towards the mysterious room. There is no mistaking it. Whatever is responsible for the noise is inside. "Here goes nothing." I utter as I extend my hand to open the door. It shakes like a nicotine addict jonesing for a fix. I try to control the shaking. I manage to wrap my fingers around the knob and twist. The door won't open. It appears to be locked from the inside. I tug on it a little harder but to no avail. The noises persist. I give the knob a full twist and yank as hard as I can. The door still won't budge. I'm determined to get in the room. I continue yanking on the door. After many failed attempts, I stop trying to open it and begin searching for something to break the knob off. I search frantically throughout the house. I manage to mess up some of the areas that I just straightened up, in my search for a tool. After looking for what seems like an eternity, I finally find a hammer. I rush back to the basement with hammer in hand. I give the doorknob several hard whacks. The last whack sends it falling to the basement floor. The door slowly creaks open. The room is dark. I use the light from my cell phone to illuminate it. I look around the room. There is no sign of life in it. I don't know what to think. I question if my mind is playing tricks on me as I continue exploring the room. In the midst of walking through it, my foot bumps into something. I look down and see an old storage case of some sort. I attempt to lift it up, and loosened layers of dust choke my breathing. I let a series of violent coughs before dropping the case. After regaining my composure, I briefly look for the source of the noise. *"Maybe a critter got into the basement?"* I think as a try to deduce a logical explanation. Unable to find the source, I pick the case up and exit the room. With the old case in tow, I head back upstairs.

When I get back upstairs, I step into the kitchen and stop dead in my tracks. All of the cabinet doors and drawers are partially open. The shock from the sight makes my body involuntarily jump. Max is frozen in a statuesque pose staring and growling at one of the corners in the kitchen. From what my eyes can detect, nothing is there. I walk over to the area in which he is staring. It is ice cold. I place the case from the basement down on the kitchen table and pull out my phone. I figure if I log onto to the surveillance site, I should be able to find out who or what is behind it. I type in my access code and begin searching through the footage. I am able to see everything from the past hour up until the present. I fast-forward through most of the captured film and stop right at the point when Max enters the kitchen. I watch in utter disbelief as an unseen force opens cabinets and drawers in a synchronized pattern leading to the corner that I found Max growling at when I returned from the basement. I don't believe in ghosts so it does little to frighten me. This is my house so I'm going to handle things my way. I close all of the cabinets and drawers, and place the contents of the trunk on the table. The spread varies from old records and CDs to worn notebooks. It also has a portfolio that contains random sketches. Most of them are just basic artwork. Some are of various pieces of fruit, buildings, and naked people posed in typical art poses. I continue flipping through the sketches when one of them catches my eye. My fingers freeze as my full focus is drawn to a specific sketch. I feel my mouth gape open as my shock level rises. The sketch on the paper is Armichael! At that moment, my phone rings. I pick it up and Kenna is on the other end.

"Hey Talia I'm pulling up now."

CHAPTER 11

As of late, I've been hanging out with Kenna on a regular basis. Aiden has been mega busy with work so we haven't been spending much time together. I don't know what I'm doing. I have a mixture of conflicting emotions. Kenna is giving me the companionship that I need and in some aspects, substituting for him. There is still a strong sense of attraction between us. I have tried my best to keep it platonic and avoid doing things that I will regret but every time I'm around her, I find it harder to resist. Even though she says she respects my relationship with Aiden, she still drops subtle flirtatious hints. Those hints give confirmation to my suspicions. She is coming back over tonight. The last time I invited her over, we almost crossed the line. If it happens again, I don't know if I will be as strong as I was before. Honestly, I don't know if I'm willing to stop it.

On a lighter note, all of the weird occurrences have ceased. I have even stopped having crazy dreams. It seems as if finding the case in the basement had something to do with it. I'm still perplexed as to why the previous owner had a sketch of Armichael. He looks so familiar but I can't figure out why. Some of his features are similar to my own but I can't seem to come up with an explanation that satisfies the mystery. I have become obsessed with making a connection to him. I refuse to let it remain a cold case. I'm also curious about the identity of the Elizabeth that the twenty plus year old handwritten letter was addressed to.

The desire to solve these mysteries has reached an all-time high. My burning curiosity finally gets the best of me. While sitting in the living room flipping through some channels on TV, an idea pops in my head. *"Maybe I should search to find some type of family tree for Armichael."* I turn off the TV and go to my computer desk. I boot up my laptop and anxiously wait for it to load. It finally loads and I punch in my short but effective password. After it grants me access, I click on the internet shortcut and begin my search. The first search engine that I try yields too many varying results. Most of the results are links to Armichael's music and unverified wiki pages. I don't trust those types of pages; most times their sources are unreliable. I search further. I go through every single search engine that I can think of. The only things that I come up with are more links to his music, information on his death, and images of the crime scene. I'm just about to give up when I come across something different. A fashion designer named Armichael is the first link that really gets my attention. I click on the link and begin to read.

"The renowned fashion designer known as Armichael Thomas, has left an indelible mark on the fashion world. His uncanny eye for fashion and marketing genius has helped him evolve from top designer to full-fledged mogul. His business savvy rivals his keen eye for fashion..." blah, blah, blah, it's apparent that whoever wrote this piece has a serious penchant for brown nosing. I close out of the link and do an additional search. My

search drums up a recent interview. I put two & two together and figure that since it is recent, he obviously isn't dead. Intrigued by the renowned legend, I click on the link and it loads up a video. In the interview, he talks about his influences.

Interviewer: so Mr. Thomas, where did you come up with the name Armichael? What does it mean?

Armichael: well of course, it's apparent that Armichael isn't my birth name. Actually, it's my way of paying homage to one of the greatest musicians ever. The man was a genius cut down before his time.

Interviewer: according to sources, you guys were close. How did you guys meet?

Armichael: I met the original Armichael back when I was a kid struggling to get my foot in the door. We were in different fields, but the artistic passion was the same. He took me under his wing and taught me how to broaden my artistic vision. He was definitely an artist before his time. People were hailing him as the next Jimi Hendrix...

A slight chill in the room interrupts my viewing. I glance at the temperature on the thermostat. Out of nowhere, I hear a loud thud in the kitchen. It makes me jump out of my seat. Max, who was just asleep on the floor next to the sofa, is now in an alert fierce stance. His tail is hung low. The fur on the back of his neck is standing up. His fangs are bared and ready. His ears are arched forward. It's clear that whatever is in the dining room or kitchen has agitated him. I don't believe in ghosts so I muster up the courage to find out the source of the sound. Max growls as he begins pacing back and forth. I look around for a blunt object to take with me. I end up grabbing the closest thing to me, a tennis racket. I slowly tip toe into the dining room. It is eerily silent. I don't find anything out of place, so I continue onward. I struggle to keep myself from shaking with fear as I slowly enter the kitchen. I notice all of the cabinet doors and drawers are partially open just like last time but this time the oven and refrigerator doors are ajar as well. When I turn to look at the table, I am shocked to find a strange book resting on top of it. I walk over to pick up the book. It looks very old and worn. The front cover is faded and hard to read. I attempt to wipe it, hoping that my efforts will produce some sort of legibility. My efforts yield little result. Most of the wording is missing.

"What the fuck is this?" I say aloud. I immediately take out my phone and log into the security feed. It takes a few minutes to find the right camera. I go back to the past ten minutes. Minutes into the footage, I feel my eyes widen as I watch what looks like video from a magic show. The refrigerator opens, and is followed by the oven and then the cabinet doors and drawers. While all of this is going on, the book appears out of thin air and hovers through the kitchen before finally descending onto the kitchen table. I'm so engrossed in the video feed, that the sound of the ringing doorbell makes me jump. I almost forgot that Kenna was coming over. I rush to close everything up in the kitchen and throw the book in one of the drawers.

"Hold on a second!" I yell as I make my way back into the living room. I walk into the vestibule and look through the peephole. Just as I thought, Kenna is patiently waiting on the other side of the door. I open the door and she gracefully switches inside. A sweet seductive smell follows her. Her long flowing hair is neatly curled. Her makeup is flawless. Her green eyes are like radiant emeralds of lust.

"I stopped by a red box and grabbed a couple of movies," she says as she hands me the movies and takes off her jacket. Her outfit is quite an attention getter. She is obviously over dressed and too made up for watching movies. I know what she wants. I know what she craves. I feel something come over me. I'm not going to hold back. If she wants another night of passion, I will be more than willing to give it to her.

"Sit down and make yourself comfortable. I'm about to go pop some popcorn and grab some candy and drinks. What would you like?" I ask while checking out every inch of her beauty.

"Uh a soda will be fine I guess, cherry if you got any." She responds with a warm cute smile.

"Okay." I respond as I smile back. I feel the attraction. It's like a pot of boiling rice, the hot white foamy froth almost running over the top, the steam of anticipation. I go into the kitchen. Max begins pawing at the back door. I open it and he runs off into the recesses of the fenced in backyard. I fill his bowls up with water and food before setting them out on the back porch and closing the door. I grab a bag of popcorn from out of the cabinet, put it in the microwave, and set it to pop. I make sure to put it on for only two minutes and fifteen seconds. I've learned from experience, that this is the perfect amount of time to get the most popped kernels without burning a single piece. The preset function always seems to overcook it. I get the drinks and candy together and suddenly, I feel compelled to take the book out of the drawer. Led by compulsion, I pick up the book. I browse through a little bit of it while the sound of kernels popping and the smell of fresh hot buttery goodness fill the air. When I get to the middle of the book, a piece of paper tucked in between the pages gets my attention. I open it up to reveal a hand written note:

"Why do you feel a moral obligation to do right? Why can't you have what you want and not have to feel like you owe something to someone? You fight against your nature, against the natural order of things; you strive to be morally correct but what is morally correct? I feel it is morally correct to get all that your heart so desires. Do all that is right and pleasing in your eyes. God is in each & every one of us. Therefore, we are all gods of our own destiny!"

The written words on the note speak to me. They ring so true. It feels like something is watching me. It's as if it knows my thoughts. It seems aware of Kenna's intentions as well.

"Why should you always play it safe?" It inquires in a deep seducing feminine voice. *"Give in to your repressed nature."* It further coaxes. *"Didn't you enjoy the last time?"*

"Yes." I respond bashfully, unsure of whom I am answering to. I can feel the blood rushing to my cheeks as I entertain the thought.

"Are you having the sex you want to have, or are you holding back, not fully expressing your deepest desires?" The mysterious voice asks causing me to blush even more and reminisce about the night with Kenna. I'm ready to accept it. I now understand. A strong sense of confidence overtakes me. Enough playing around, I'm going to give her exactly what she needs. I surge with confidence and desire as I return to the living room with goodies in hand.

"I love the smell of popcorn!" Kenna says in an enthusiastic manner. I turn on the TV and pop in the first DVD my hand touches. The movie happens to be "Love and Other Drugs". We barely make it through the film before the undeniable power of lust takes over. Kenna begins rubbing my upper thigh through my sleeper pants. My conscience comes in to play.

"What would Aiden think?" It whispers as it attempts to be the voice of reason.

"Whoa, what are you doing?" I ask as I fight to keep my level of arousal down. Her hand service is steadily increasing it. I feel myself awakening in places that should be reserved only for my lover. The tingle has manifested

"I'm just rubbing you, relax. It's not like I put your nipple in my mouth." She says in a humorous tone with a naughty look in her eyes. I know that forcing her hand off me would be the right thing to do but it feels far too good. I love when my upper thighs are rubbed.

"You know my situation," I protest with my mouth while my lack of action speaks differently.

"I know your situation but do you really know your situation? I mean c'mon, if you truly were committed Aiden, would I be here right now? Besides, it's not really like you're cheating, I mean we're both women for Christ's sake!" Kenna says while she continues rubbing me. The truth of the statement stings like a punch to the nose. I shove her hand away from me. I feel like such a mess of contradiction. She's right and I know it. If I really had a problem with that night, why would I allow her over to watch movies? The two of us alone in my house watching movies doesn't seem logical given our history together. Maybe I'm sending mixed signals or maybe we really want the same thing and I need to come to terms with it.

After a moment of debate, my curiosity gets the best of me. I look over and see the intensely lustful expression on Kenna's face. It makes me fall even deeper into the pit of hot warm emotion. I stop thinking. I give in and let my lascivious nature take over. I grab Kenna and in one swift motion, place a sweet, passionate, lust infused kiss on her warm, soft, succulent lips. She responds by applying equal passion. It is at this moment, that I realize we've fallen overboard. We are drowning in a sea of lust and deep carnal desire. We begin tugging at one another's clothing, trying hard to remove them while sustaining the moment. We run neck and neck like contestants racing to see who can undress the other first.

We stare at each other with the fires of lust in our eyes. I motion her down to the floor before I ferociously begin kissing and nibbling on her soft supple frame. I start at her neck and work my way down. I feel the movements of her body on my lips. I hear her soft moans as my tongue lightly trashes over her creamy smooth landscape. I can feel her anticipation building as I move closer and closer to her sweet wet jackpot. I place a series of teasing kisses on and around her stomach. She squirms with excitement.

"Oh yeah," Kenna moans as I continue my titillating foreplay.

"You're all mine tonight. I'm going to do any and everything I want to you and you're going to lay here and take it all. Do you understand me?" I say in a bossy manner.

"Yes," she utters in a breathy tone. I can tell that the way I'm talking to her is driving her past wild. I resume kissing on her body. My lips finally arrive at the gates of heaven. Her labia, is moist with lustful juices. I caress it with sensuous tender kisses. I spread it apart with my fingertips as my tongue begins dancing on her clitoris. The pleasure is intense. She digs her fingers into my hair. I continue satisfying her. Her moans get louder as my tongue glides back and forth. I alternate to up and down motions. I increase the speed and it puts her into overdrive. "Ooh fuck!" She screams while pulling at me, motioning my head up from between her legs.

"I knew you'd give in." She says in a super seductive tone.

"Be careful what you wish for…" I retort before continuing to lose myself in the moment of sultry lust. I feel her legs starting to shake.

"Ooh baby I'm almost there, I'm about to cum!" She says as I feel her grip tighten. "Oh shit!" She exclaims as she releases.

The room is silent as we lay both staring at the ceiling and thinking about what has just transpired. *"What have I done?"* I ponder as I keep my focus on the ceiling. I try hard not to look at Kenna.

"I hope you realize that we can't do this again." I say aloud with my eyes still fixed on the ceiling. The statement is a pathetically weak restriction that holds little merit. My actions have overshadowed my words, and spoken amplified decibels louder. It's like comparing an announcement projected through a bullhorn to a slight whisper toned afterthought. It loses even more ground because I recall myself saying something similar after the night she betrayed me, the night she took me to a level that I wasn't prepared to handle. After a few seconds of silence, Kenna responds.

"I figured you would say that." She says while she turns and adjusts her body towards me. "It's not as deep as you think it is. Most men would revel in the fact that their girlfriend is adventurously bisexual." She places her hand on my chest. I turn to face her.

"So where do you want to go from here?" I ask as I look into her jade eyes, trying to find a single inkling of doubt.

"All I know is that I want you Talia. I don't care about you having him. I've been having these dreams about it. I mean about all of us, you, me, and him. In the dreams, there is a man that looks like you telling me we're destined to be together."

I feel my heart drop into stomach in response to what Kenna has just said. I can't believe it. Are having similar dreams? Could she be referring to Armichael?

"Okay so if it's our destiny to be together, how do you suppose I go about telling Aiden?"

"You don't tell him. We tell him." Kenna's response is weird but exactly what I need to hear.

"Fair enough, now I think it's time you return the favor." I murmur as images of her pleasuring me appear in my head.

"That's what I like to hear." Kenna retorts while positioning her smiling face between my legs.

Kenna and I sensuously connect as if it's the last time we will be together. She gives me soft euphoric passion, and I give her my all. Seconds melt into minutes, and minutes into hours, we climax consecutively. She enjoys every moment of it. I think the idea of sharing me, only turns her on more. We continue going until we both drift off into a well-needed slumber.

CHAPTER 12

"Talia, how could you? How could you betray me like this? How could you betray our family?" My father asks as he stands at the foot of the bed covered in blood. I lay in bed confused as to why he is in such a state and how he has gotten into my house. I look in the corner and see Armichael. He has a weird indescribable grin on his face. I look in the doorway and see three dark shadow figures standing in it. I look down and notice myself covered in blood and a bloody knife next to me on the bed. *"What the hell?"* I think as I'm trying to compute the information my retinas are receiving. Then, as if things weren't weird enough, my long lost grandmother emerges from the closet. She looks long and hard at me in unison with everyone else in the room. She opens her mouth. Bees and other flying insects begin swarming out of it. "I'm not dead!" She yells in an ominous tone. The room starts spinning. Everyone it begins to stretch and distort like reflections in a funhouse mirror.

A warm wet sensation on my clitoris awakens me from my nightmare. I open my eyes to Kenna giving me oral pleasure. "Good morning Talia." She says as she pauses and flashes a naughty smile before resuming.

"Hell of a way to wake to up! I wish every morning was like this!" I state as she continues servicing me.

"I'm gonna keep going until you explode." She says before getting even more into it. Her wonderfully brilliant talent, forces me to squirm and release soft moans. It's unexpected, which makes it even more pleasurable. The element of surprise has taken the experience to an entirely different level.

As I'm nearing my peak, Kenna cups my left breast. Her soft but firm grip intensifies my climax. The release causes seizure like tremors to travel throughout my body. My reaction is the reward earned by her warm pleasing tongue. She comes up for air after completion. I give her a passionate French kiss as my way of saying thank you.

"Talia,"

"Yes?" I respond.

"I… I think I love you." Kenna says as she looks at me with a green-eyed gaze. I pause unsure of what to say in response. Then, like an act of divine intervention, words find their way into my thoughts.

"I honor you Kenna," is my response. She looks at me in a puzzled manner.

"Okay, what does that mean?" She asks.

"Well, I feel that people use the term love too loosely. When I say I honor you, it means I recognize your place in my life. It also means I respect what you are to me and give you merit for your position, which is now right by my side." I have no idea where the explanation came from but I can see it working its magic. Her puzzled look changes to a smile almost instantly.

"Well Talia if that's the case, I honor you too," she responds.

"How about I show you how much I honor you, by fixing you my grandfather's world famous breakfast?" I ask as she gives me her full attention. I have her well past smitten with me. I can tell that she hopes whatever we have works. In some weird way, I'm hoping the same thing.

After taking a shower together, I fix breakfast and we enjoy it, as well as each other's company. Once we've finished breakfast, we continue our movie date from the night before. In the middle of last film, Aiden calls. I feel nervousness set in as I stare at the phone's screen.

"Go ahead. You know you want to answer it." Kenna remarks with a humorous expression.

"I'll be right back." I respond before putting the film on pause and exiting the room. I grab my Bluetooth and answer the call. "Hello?"

"Hey honey. Have you been thinking about me?" Aiden's voice is strong and appealing.

"Yes I have, I've been thinking about a lot of things." I state in a hushed manner.

"Is everything okay?" He inquires, obviously detecting a difference in my tone.

"Yeah, I'm fine... just a little sleepy." is my false response. I hope it suffices.

"Are you sure?" He asks. I guess the answer didn't appease his inquisitiveness. I hate when people ask a question and can't accept the answer.

"Positive," I articulate in a slightly irritated tone.

"Okay well anyway, I just got back in town from my business trip and—" I cut him off.

"So when are you coming by to see me? I haven't seen you in a while. I thought you vanished off the face of the earth!"

"Ha, ha very funny Talia," He responds. "Actually, I was thinking about stopping by today and you could've stopped by to see me as well ya' know."

"Yeah, whenever you're there Mr. Career man. Every time I call you you're out and about and I don't like visiting people unless I know they're home."

"Fair enough, so how about today?"

"I don't think today would be a good day. I have a lot on my agenda. Working full time during the week gives me little free time for handling errands, um how about tomorrow?"

"Okay sure I guess. That was weird."

"What was weird?"

"How you made a big deal about not seeing me lately and then I offered to see you today and you blew me off."

"No it's not like that. It's just that you need understand that not everything revolves around your schedule. I have a life and a career too!

"I understand that but—"

"Obviously you don't but anyway, Kenna and I have some girl things to do so I'll call you when I get back in." I hang up the phone quickly. No good bye, no I love you, just a swift impersonal disconnect. Sure, I feel remorseful about it but I'm stuck in an odd position. Making him feel bad about his lack time for me is a temporary diversion from the more serious issue.

"What's this?" Kenna asks, as she holds up the book that I found the night before.

"I'm not sure. I found it yesterday." I reply.

"Well I've been checking it out and there is some pretty interesting stuff in here," she says as she hands it to me.

"Yeah it's definitely an eye catcher." I respond in a slightly sarcastic tone as I take the book from her.

"So, I take it you're waiting to tell him?" Kenna asks as she looks at me with her bright inquisitive green eyes.

"Yeah I'm gonna wait for the right time, I still don't know how I feel about the whole situation. What if he doesn't go along with it, I mean... what if after hearing it, he wants nothing to do with me?"

Kenna grabs my hand. "Where's your confidence? Are you serious? Our situation is every man's dream! If I'm on board with it, he will be too. Trust me I know. Why wouldn't he be onboard for something that will fulfill his deep desires as well as yours?" A lot of what Kenna says rings true in a weird demented way. The note and the voice from last night come to mind.

"Okay well he's coming over tomorrow so I want you to come over too." I start to feel a strong assurance rising from within.

"Well if that's the case, I might as well spend the night again." She says.

"Alright well I'm done with movies. I need to get out and clear my head. How about we do a little shopping?" I haven't been out shopping in ages. I'm long overdue.

"You read my mind." Kenna states with a smile.

"How's Crocker Park sound?"

"That's fine; they have a few stores I wouldn't mind checking out."

The drive to the shopping plaza is brief. We arrive at our destination with plenty of time to shop and goof off. We check out pretty much all of the clothing stores from H&M to urban outfitters. We also visit Arhaus furniture and bed bath & beyond. We visit the last two stores mainly because Kenna thinks that my home décor could use an update. She called the look of my house "retro". After she convinces me to buy a few items to spruce things up, we finish our shopping excursion and get back on the road.

"Hey Talia, since we're out do you mind if we stop to visit some of my friends?" Kenna asks as we leave out of the shopping plaza

"Um sure, I don't see why not." I respond. "So where do these friends of yours stay?" I ask as we pull up to a red light.

"Just give me second." Kenna says as she begins dialing on her cell phone. "Doug, hey it's Kenna—are you guys still meeting—okay well I'm bringing a friend—alright we'll be there in a few."

"So what's going on?" I ask, as the light turns green.

"We are going to meet them at "Pappy's Place" in the next half hour." Kenna says as she starts thumbing through the contacts on her phone.

"What kind of friends are we meeting?" I ask while trying to keep my eye on the road.

"If told you, I would have to kill you!" She jokes, "Just kidding. They're a cool bunch. You'll like them." She reassures

Within twenty minutes, we pull up to "Pappy's Place", a bar and grill located in Westlake. We step inside and Kenna leads me over to a section that has two large tables placed together to accommodate a party of about ten. Most of the people seated in the section look like average everyday people. My eyes stop and focus on this one particular member, the creepy man that has been following me!

"You know him?" I ask Kenna as I stare at him.

"Him, oh yeah that's Doug. You look like you've seen him before."

"Yeah remember that day at work when he was getting off the elevator?"

"No not really, are you sure that that was him?" She asks with a fuzzy expression on her face.

"Yes and he's the same guy that I saw on my date with Aiden, and the same one that broke into my house!" I reply in an agitated manner as I survey the rest of the people. As we get closer our eyes lock. It's definitely him. He has the same look as the other times that I've seen him. I need answers. We reach the tables. Kenna starts the introduction.

"Hey everybody—"

"Why have you been following me?" I ask Doug loudly, stopping Kenna mid-sentence. Doug stops chewing his food and speaks.

"Hello my name is Doug and I'm not following you. I've been keeping an eye on you."

"Uh okay…" I respond, confused by his response.

"Come on let's have a seat. You're starting to bring unwanted attention to us." Kenna says as she grabs my hand and leads me to a seat on the opposite end.

"Look Talia, there's a reason I wanted you to come here with me. There's a lot of stuff that you need to know. They need to enlighten you."

"Okay what are you talking about?" I respond as I look at the other people seated next to us.

"You need to know the truth. Things in your life are not what they seem."

"Are you going to tell me what's going on, or are you going to keep speaking in riddles?" I ask with a slight hint of irritation in my tone.

"Let me introduce you to everyone," Kenna says as she ignores my inquisition. She stands up. "They already know who you are, so I will introduce them to you."

"How do they know me?" I ask.

"You will soon find out." She says in a low voice before getting their attention. "Hello everyone, I'm quite sure you already know who Talia is, so now I need you to kindly introduce yourselves to her." The first person that speaks is a blond haired man seated across from me. He is a tall thin white male with bleach blond spiky hair and a pale complexion.

"Hey Talia I'm Drake," he says as he extends his hand. I extend mine as well. We shake and then he returns to his seat. The next person that speaks is a slender black woman with a British accent.

"Hello Talia, the name's Sophie. Nice meeting you," I shake her hand as well. The rest of the group introduce themselves as well. Bobby is a weird Indian guy with thick-rimmed glasses and off kilter jokes, Jacob, is a youthful dark haired evenly tan man with a serious demeanor. Cathy is a leggy racially mixed woman, with an accent that I can't quite seem to put my finger on, and Nadine is a foxy Italian with cold blue eyes and dark hair with streaks of blue blended in. David is an older huskier Hispanic man with a long scar on the side of his face. Rochelle is a petite woman with short cut hair and soft light brown skin. She is the warmest of the bunch. Joe is a heavyset white guy with a ponytail, and sweaty palms. I will try to avoid shaking his hand in the future, and lastly, I meet Isaac. He is a fit well-built coffee colored man with a friendly smile and a fierce presence.

"Okay now can anyone tell me how everybody here knows me?" I ask aloud hoping, for some sort of answer. Doug looks at me and speaks.

"We know you because we are meant to know you. Someone very dear to you is trying to make contact. Let me ask you something Talia. Have you ever wondered about these religions? Let's take for example Christianity. Have you ever wondered why in order to become a Christian, you have to deny yourself of your natural thinking? You have to constantly repent and hope that you don't die in your sins or you won't make it into those pearly gates. On top of that, the only way to make it in is by believing in the Son of God. Even if you live a good life, you still won't make it in because of that one little stipulation. Now do you think that's fair?"

"No not really," I respond.

"Exactly, I mean think about it, why is it so bad to think about sex outside of the realm of marriage; or if you have ambition, that's not aligned with bible teaching then it's considered sinful or selfish. The Bible itself is one big contradiction. It says that it's wrong to kill, but David killed Goliath and went down in history as a great hero. If you want to know the truth, we're offering it to you." Doug says in a passionate manner. Something about his words ring true.

"Okay so what should we believe?" I ask with interest clearly apparent in my voice. Doug gets up, walks over to me, and hands me a business card.

"Come to our service Wednesday night at nine for your answer." I look at the card. It has the same weird symbol that's engraved on the guitar pick with the words "Hands of Aka Manah" written under it.

"Did you leave a letter at my house?" I ask as I tuck the card inside of my pocket.

"What letter?" He responds with a genuine clueless expression. I wonder if he's playing stupid or if he really doesn't know anything about it. I want to probe for more answers but something tells me that now is not the right time.

"Never mind," I utter before Doug walks away and returns to his seat. The rest of the meeting goes smooth. I actually find myself warming up to the strange bunch of folks that are Kenna's "friends". After the meeting, we head back to my place. My thoughts are running circles in my head. So many things have been happening lately. It no longer seems like my life. As we're driving in the car, I feel compelled to talk to Kenna about her group.

"Hey Kenna, how long have you been in this group, club, or whatever it is that you consider it?"

"Well I've known a few of the members for years, since high school. I joined a few months back. I respect the things that they stand for. As a child, I hated when my grandmother would force me to go to church. All of the love and pie in the sky sermons, mixed in with the fire and brimstone preaching. It's just one big contradiction! I mean, how can a God that loves us so much, punish us so harshly when we stray away from the path?" I've never seen this side of Kenna. It turns me on much more than her looks. It's refreshing to hear her speak her mind.

"You know what, I agree with you. I was never a big fan of Christianity, Catholicism, or any other religion for that matter. Most of them use fear to keep believers converted. First, they reel you in with love. Then, they keep you in with fear. I've always thought that laying hands, catching the Holy Spirit, and visions of "The Virgin Mary" were simply illusions. Parts of one big smoke and mirrors act."

We arrive back at my house. As soon as we step in, a weird

odor hits us. "What is that smell?" Kenna asks as she scrunches up her face.

"I don't know." I reply. The smell is weird yet familiar at the same time. I step into the living room, and freeze dead in my tracks. The creepy picture is back up on the wall! I get closer and notice that a black smudge is next to it. It appears to be a partial handprint.

"What's wrong Talia?" Kenna asks.

"Something is different," I state as I log into the security feed. "Look Kenna, there have been some things going on lately that I can't explain." I look at the feed and I can't believe what I'm seeing. "Here look at this," I say to Kenna before showing her the surveillance footage.

"What the fuck?" Kenna says exactly what I'm thinking. I can't even begin to explain how the creepy picture that I put in the basement magically floated upstairs and placed itself back on the wall! I search for a way to say what I suspect is going on.

"I don't believe in ghosts but I can't physically explain what's going on. Cold spots, noises, floating objects, strange dreams, I can't think of anything else that can explain it." Kenna has an expression of total shock on her face.

"So when did all of these things start up?" She asks as she takes a seat on the couch.

"Well, I think it all started in my dreams. Before I moved into this house, I was having dreams about it. In this one reoccurring dream, there are these weird shadow creatures with red piercing eyes and Armichael is there as well."

"You're talking about the fashion mogul right?" Kenna asks.

"No, I did some research and found out that he got his name from this other guy, a musician on the verge of stardom that died in some type of freak fire. "Hold on wait a second." I go to my computer desk and grab the newspaper clipping. "See, this is the guy." I say as I hand it to Kenna. Her jaw drops open.

"Whoa, this is getting creepy!" She says as she examines the article. "This… is the same guy from my dreams!" She announces.

"So what do you think is going on?" I ask.

"I think we need to get some professionals involved. You know like on the movies. Ghost hunting experts or something." Kenna says.

"So you really think its ghosts?" I try to keep a straight face as

I say it. I can't explain it but just the thought of ghost hunters or paranormal investigators, whatever you want to call them setting up their little gadgets around my house, and chasing footsteps and orbs is quite comical. Although having a priest come and exercise the demon or entity would be even funnier.

"Do you mind if I take another look at the book you found?" Kenna asks as she hands me back the newspaper clipping.

"Be my guest," I respond before going in the kitchen to retrieve it. I fetch the book and return to the living room. I hand the book to Kenna. She takes a few moments to sift through it. Kenna stops and looks directly at me.

"I knew I've seen this book before. I just couldn't remember where I saw it. I think that whatever you're dealing with is trying to communicate with you. You really need to come to our next meeting. Maybe it will give you some answers."

CHAPTER 13

I wake up and immediately begin thinking about what I have to do today. Kenna slumbers peacefully next to me. Seeing her gives me confidence. I pray that my new situation doesn't hurt Aiden. I hope for the best as I get up and get ready to face the day. I know it's supposed to be wrong, but why don't I feel guilty? How can I just continue doing what I'm doing and not feel remorse? Am I crazy? Am I losing my mind? I love hanging out and being intimate with both of them. They each give me something that the other can't. It might sound a little unsavory, hell maybe even self-centered but they're both far too good to let go. I've thought about what Mrs. Daniels and Ashley might say if they knew. I've also thought about what my mother and father would say. These thoughts quickly lose merit when I return to the realization that this is my life, not theirs and after today, Aiden will have the choice to either stay involved or part ways. I suppose that I've gone too far to turn back now. Aiden will be here shortly and I have to lay it on the line. I refuse to live a lie. I'm not going to be one of those people who have to constantly lie and keep up a juggling act, so I'm just going to go through with it.

I get into the shower. It wakes up all of my senses. I feel my pores open up. The rushing water helps to clear my mind. It relaxes me. A voice in the distance interrupts my moment of tranquility. I hear the voice again. It sounds like one I've heard before but I can't recall from where. I shut off the water and wait in silence to hear it again. After a few moments of being lost in anticipation, I hear it. It sounds like someone calling me. I wrap a towel around myself and slowly make my way out of the bathroom. I creep past the bedroom and see Kenna still asleep in bed. Knowing it's not her sends a sense of dread coursing throughout my body. I feel the adrenaline building up as my heart beat increases. I go from room to room expecting, or rather hoping to see someone, to prove my sanity to myself. I manage to make my way to the basement and not find a single thing! As I head back upstairs, I see Kenna at the top of the stairs.

"Hey Talia I was looking for you, did you turn down the heat?"

"No. I just got out of the shower." I respond.

"Well when I woke up, it was freezing cold in the bedroom."

"I don't know why it's so cold up there; the temperature is on seventy-six. I noticed it on the way back up from the basement." I go into the bedroom to feel it for myself. I enter the room and immediately notice the drastic difference in temperature. The bedroom is so cold that I can see my breath. I step back out into the hallway and the temperature is warm. Something is very wrong. I rush back into the room, grab my phone, and punch in my code to check the surveillance footage. I look at footage from the time I leave the room until the time Kenna wakes up. At first, there appears to be a glitch on the footage but as I continue to look, I notice that what I'm seeing isn't a glitch at all. I'm seeing what appears to be a shadowy being. The way it moves is similar to that of a person. It moves around the whole room. It looks like it's searching for something. I see it leave out of the room. I switch the camera footage to the hallway camera. I spot the figure move down the hallway. The figure vanishes seconds before I see myself emerge out of the bathroom and creep past the bedroom. I put two & two together, and assume that the shadow man was probably the one calling out for me.

"Damn," Kenna says as she glances over my shoulder at the footage.

"You know you could've asked to see it instead of standing on your tip toes," I say in a slightly sharp manner.

"I'm sorry, it's a habit I guess," she responds.

"So what do you think it is?"

"Uh it looks like a shadow person from off one of those ghost shows."

"You are really serious about this ghost stuff huh?"

"I'm just saying Talia. The evidence points to it so what else could it be?"

"I'm not sure but I will deal with this after we deal with Aiden."

"Fair enough, you're lucky that I don't scare easy, or I would've run out of here at the first sign of anything paranormal!"

"I know. Now hurry up and get ready for breakfast. I'm cooking French toast and I don't want it to get cold!"

The sound of the doorbell echoes through the house as we finish eating breakfast. "Aiden came earlier than I expected," I state before putting my fork down on the nearly finished plate. I slowly walk to the door, the whole time I'm fighting myself, trying to shake the fear that is starting to build inside of me. I pause, take a deep breath, click the locks, and twist the knob. The door opens to reveal Aiden and his usual gorgeous smile.

"Come in," I say as I step aside and allow him to enter. I want to beat around the bush but something inside urges me to get straight to the point.

"Aiden I have something to tell you," I blurt out as I think of the next thing to say. Right as I'm about to continue speaking, Kenna enters into the room.

"Hey Kenna," Aiden says in a friendly manner accompanied by a slight wave.

"Hello Aiden. It's good to see you again." Kenna responds with a sultry tone and a look that oozes attraction. "We all need to sit down and discuss a few things." She says as she strolls over to where we are.

"Talia, what's going on," Aiden questions with a puzzled expression on his face.

"Well Aiden, things are different now… I'm different…" I can't seem to find the right way to say what's on my mind.

"What do you mean?" He questions.

"Um… well… Kenna and I are more than just friends, we're involved" I feel a huge weight lift off me as I release the information, Aiden's face freezes in disbelief.

"Yeah," Kenna chimes in as she grabs my arm and stands next to me. The look on Aiden's face is one of confusion. He pauses for a moment and looks down.

"So let me get this right, you called me over here not to show me how much you love me, or even to show how much you've missed me; you called me over here to tell me that you and her," he pauses and points at Kenna, "are fucking?" I instinctively grab Aiden.

"Calm down it's not like that." I state as I try to keep things from going sour.

"Okay so what is it like?" He asks as the veins in his face begin to show.

"It's like we're not really fucking—" before I can finish my sloppy explanation, Kenna interjects.

"Yeah, it's not fucking it's just getting to know each other, expressing our feelings for each other on a physical level. Kenna says before grabbing Aiden by the hand. Aiden has an extremely crazed look in his eyes, like that of a wounded animal backed into a corner. "I'm not trying to take Talia from you; I want to share her with you." She proclaims in a calm almost serene manner.

"Are you crazy? Do you really think I want to share anything with you?" Aiden questions with a red hue starting to invade his face. "She's cheating with you! Any physical intimacy with another person outside of your relationship is considered that! It doesn't matter if it's not with another man!" Aiden turns his attention towards me. "How could you do this to me and expect me to accept it?" Tears start to form in his eyes.

I watch in disbelief as Kenna slowly attempts to embrace him. Aiden fights it at first but then surrenders to it. It's like watching a lion tamer. She uses some weird unknown force to calm him.

Aiden cries on her shoulder, while she gently rubs his back and continues holding him. While comforting him, she motions me over. At first, I'm apprehensive but I slowly find myself drawing closer. She grabs my arm and places it around herself; I cautiously place the other one around Aiden. We all hug for a few moments before continuing the conversation.

"Talia, what am I supposed to tell my mom, what am I supposed to tell Ashley? Oh mom well see Talia's other partner, Kenna said that she doesn't mind sharing her; Ashley it's okay maybe you will find one like that too, somebody to share!" Aiden expresses his legitimate concerns.

"Why do you have to tell them anything? We are all adults. This is your life to live not theirs." I say with a confident, absolute tone. I look over at Kenna and see her smiling ear to ear. "Basically what I'm saying is that we can handle this on our own. We can show them how this can turn into a happy-ending. All I'm saying is, let's try something different." Aiden stands in silence as he thinks about what I have just said. Kenna is giddy with delight. She appears to be enjoying every moment of it.

"Talia, I'm not that kind of man. I can't accept the fact that, the person I'm committed to is openly cheating on me! I won't allow it!" Aiden breaks away from us. "I... I can't deal with this right now, I have to go." He says as he walks toward the front door.

"Aiden wait," I try to stop him.

"Talia we're done! Get out of my way, I'm ready to leave!" He proclaims as he shoves me aside. As I make one last attempt to stop him, Kenna intervenes.

"No, let him go he will be back," she says as she grabs my hand.

"I hope your right," I respond as I watch the love of my life walk out the door.

CHAPTER 14

I pull into the front parking lot of an old strip of inconspicuous office spaces and storefronts. The buildings look abandoned. I glance down at the address on the business card, and check the address in the GPS device to make sure it's correct. "It's definitely the place." I mumble to myself as I look for any signs of life. If I recall correctly from my teenage years of working at Marc's (a chain of grocery stores in Ohio), strip plazas always have back entrances to all of the separate suites. I began driving around back. I reach the back parking lot and see several cars parked. I recognize Kenna's car and I park close to it. I step out of my car and begin walking. I see a light lit up above one of the entrances. I go to the door and pull the handle. To my surprise, it's locked. I'm about to take out my phone and text Kenna when the door next to where I'm standing opens. Drake emerges from the entrance with a cigarette in his hand.

"Hey, I see you came. It just started." He says before placing the cigarette in his mouth and lighting it.

"Oh, okay thanks." I respond in a puzzled manner as I go inside. I step inside of a small corridor. Everything is dim except a bright light illuminating from a room at the end of the hall. As I get closer, I begin to hear familiar voices. I can hear Sophie and Doug talking. I reach the doorway and enter the room. I see a larger group than before at "Pappy's Bread". It has to be at least fifty or more. The walls are decorated with various ominous symbols. The only two that I recognize are the upside down crosses and pentagrams. The floor looks like a life size chessboard. Candles rest on ancient looking gothic holders throughout the room. In the front of the room, a large stage intimidates the rest of the room for space. An altar stands on top of it with more candles neatly placed on it. A huge triangle symbol like the one on a dollar bill hangs in the background like a sales banner at a department store. Doug stands in front of it draped in some type of weird modern day druid garb. Sophie is by his side dressed in something similar. I guess Drake was right; I arrived right on time for the beginning of service. Something inside of me is on the alert. I have an unsettling feeling about being here. It feels like I'm in one of those Hollywood horror movies. You know the type that involves devil worshippers, kidnapped virgins, and blood sacrifices. I'm so waiting to see them bring out a bound and gagged virgin for the slaughter. My level of open mindedness is at a minimum. Blame it on the media and entertainment industry. Doug steps to the center of the stage and begins to speak.

"Brothers and sisters, I honor you all as we gather in the house of truth. God dwells in us so we are all gods and goddesses in our own right. We are creators of our own destinies. The enlightened among mortal men, as followers of the truth it is our responsibility to bring the truth to all who want to know and accept it. The masses are brainwashed with false teachings and kept enslaved by fear. They tell us that if we do not accept Jesus as our lord and savior, then we cannot receive the gift of heaven. They tell us that we have to believe in Allah or the Virgin Mary. They tell us that Lucifer is evil. They tell us that no matter how morally upstanding we are, if we don't accept Jesus we will surely burn in hell. Because according to what a man of their so-called God told me, deeds will not get you into heaven. Well do you know what I say to them? I tell them to keep their God and their heaven. We want our paradise now! This world is ours to rule my siblings! We are the followers of the truth! The true religion is no religion! The truth is a way of life! The truth is to no longer deny your flesh but embrace it. Embrace our true nature!"

Cheers erupt throughout the room. I can feel the fires of passion resonating. It's quite apparent that Doug has a significant amount of pull within this group. I wander if he's the leader. He leaves the stage accompanied by Sophie. Another oddly attractive dark haired woman meets them and the three of them go into another room. I look around the room as the members await the next part of service. Drake enters the room with a scent of cigarettes slightly masked by cologne accompanying him. He goes straight to the stage. He grabs a microphone and begins to speak.

"Brothers and sisters, it is now time for indulgence. All those wishing to participate, please step forward." Several men and women go up to the stage. My eyes connect with Kenna's eyes.

She knows that I am totally lost as to what is going on now. She makes her way over to me through the rows of various other members.

"Okay can you tell me what's about to happen now?" I ask in an almost whisper as Kenna moves next to me.

"This is the part where we embrace our flesh," she responds before grabbing me by the hand. "Come on follow me." She says as she leads me to the front of the room.

"Whoa hold on, I don't—" I try to project my reservations.

"Come on, don't you trust me?" She says as she continues to lead me further up front. Doug, Sophie, and their companion emerge from the room completely disrobed! Two other members emerge as well pushing out carts full of weird-shaped chalices. They begin dispensing them to all of the other members on stage. I hesitantly take one that is handed to me. I look inside of the chalice. It is filled with a deep, reddish liquid. After everyone has received a chalice, Doug steps on the stage and makes an announcement.

"Brothers and sisters let us now partake in our desires as one big family." I look around at everyone quickly devouring the dark liquid.

"Go ahead Talia drink it." Kenna says as she nudges me. She drinks hers with no hesitation. I place the chalice to my lips, and take a small sip. The liquid's sweet tangy warm flavor surprises my taste buds. I slowly start to drink more of it. Before I know it, the chalice is empty. I glance around at all of the other people on the stage and notice that they are all disrobing. As I'm distracted by what's going on around me, I feel a tug on my belt buckle. I look down and see Kenna naked on her knees undoing my pants. I make a weak attempt to stop her. She gets more aggressive. She successfully unfastens my pants and forcefully pulls them down. Once they are down, she begins servicing me. As she is servicing me, Doug's other companion, the dark haired woman, catches my attention. Something about her is different from the others on the stage.

Everything begins to look strange around me. I look back at Doug's companion and am startled to see two piercing red eyes staring back at me! I turn and look down at Kenna. She briefly stops giving me cunnilingus and looks up; her eyes are completely black! It looks as if she's possessed. I feel possessed. I feel my body moving in ways I don't want it to. It's as if I'm in some sort of trance. I feel myself taking off my clothes. A strange heat engulfs my being. I stop Kenna mid pleasuring session and force her onto the floor. I spread her legs and return the favor. The companion laughs in wicked delight. I feel her getting closer as I continue. Kenna howls in pleasure as I intensify the oral pleasure she is receiving. She writhes and twitches unnaturally. We are all possessed. The strange drink has made us regress to our primal nature. Kenna releases a low-pitched growl as she reaches the point of climax. Instead of slowing down, I continue at a more intense pace. The only reason I stop is because a slight tension begins building in my head. The tension is soon accompanied by throbbing and ringing. They rapidly escalate to overwhelming levels. I grab my head as I fight to keep from slipping away. My efforts are unsuccessful. My awareness fades.

"Beep, beep, beep…"

The sound of the alarm wakes me up. I'm in my bed. *"How the hell did I get home?"* I muse as I get my bearings. The sound of running water catches my attention. I get up and go into the hallway. The sound gets louder as I get closer to the bathroom. Someone is taking a shower. I open the door and see the body frame of a female behind the shower curtain. I reach for the curtain. Before I can get a grip on it, the person inside the shower pulls it back. It's Kenna.

"I was wondering when you were going to wake up. We do have jobs to go to sleepy head." She jokes as she turns off the water. She looks extra perky.

"How did we get here?" I ask.

"We drove remember? I followed you home because you said that you wanted to carpool to work in the morning."

"I did?" This is all news to my ears. I don't remember telling her anything.

"Of course you did Talia."

"Oh okay," I respond. I don't remember anything after the wild exhibition session.

"So do you do that type of thing often?" I ask as I hand her a towel.

"No. That was the first time that I've participated. I normally just stay in the audience and watch."

"Okay so what made you want to do it last night?"

"Well if you really must know, you made me do it."

"Huh," I utter confused by her response.

"It's just something about you Talia. I want to do and share everything with you. I'm yours and I just want to show you." Our lips lock in a moment of passion. I feel her energy.

"If you keep this up, I might have to move you in." I joke as I start to get in the shower. "I will be out in a few."

"Okay. I'll whip up a little breakfast," Kenna says before heading out of the bathroom.

I turn on the warm water and let it spray all over me. It feels soothing; it helps to wake me up. I still feel remnants from last night. I think about Aiden. I haven't heard from him since he stormed out. I want break down and hound him all day until he gives in but I don't want to seem weak to Kenna. I know in my heart of hearts, that I don't love her but for some strange reason, I need her in my life. I need what she brings into it. I need the excitement and intensity.

I step out of the shower feeling a little better. I dry off and get dressed before making my way downstairs. Kenna greets me with a breakfast of turkey bacon, biscuits, and eggs.

"Hurry up and eat before it gets cold." She says as I sit down and get ready to feast. I quickly devour my breakfast and we head off to work.

The ride to work starts in silence. For some reason, I neglected to turn on the radio or boot up a playlist. My brain is sifting through a million thoughts and I'm sure Kenna's is doing the same. Remnants of the indulgence session linger in my mind as I try to come to terms with the new direction in which my life is headed.

"So would you ever really consider living together?" Kenna inquires, interrupting the silence of the trip. I pause for a moment and ponder the idea.

"What about your lease?" I ask while stopping at a light.

"Well it's almost up so that's not a factor. The joke you made earlier really made me consider it so I want to know how you honestly feel about it." In all honesty, I wouldn't mind having Kenna move in. It would be nice to have someone else around to witness the crazy stuff that's been going on at the house. It would be nice but at the same time, I don't think it would be right. She's in a weird group that freaks me out! It also bothers me that I can't account for the hours after the indulgence session. I wonder if the drink that we consumed had something to do with it.

"Do you know what was in that stuff that we drank last night?" I ask abruptly changing the course of the conversation.

"I'm not sure. I was told that it was sacred, a gift from Aka Manah." Kenna replies.

"Okay so who is Aka Manah?" I ask as we pull into the parking garage.

"Do you remember the lady that accompanied Doug and Sophie on stage last night?"

"Are you talking about the one that got naked with them?"

"Yeah her, she is known as Amy. She is the one that prepares the drinks under the divine direction of Aka Manah. She is aka Manah's mistress."

"So what is Aka Manah?"

"According to the book of truth, he's the gate keeper to the throne of Lucifer. Doug can explain it better than me. He talked to you after service last night. You don't remember the long conversation you guys had?"

"To be honest with you Kenna, I don't recall anything after being on stage. I was surprised when I woke up in my own bed!"

"Well I remember everything. Right after indulgence, Doug ended the service. Then Doug, Sophie, Amy, you, and I went back to his private area. You were talking to Doug. I was sitting next to you. You told him that you were interested in joining. He was telling you about the calling over your life. He told you that when the time was right your purpose and real identity would be revealed. He said that Aka Manah has placed a certain task upon you. He said it was in your bloodline. He told you that someone in your family is trying to reach out to you, someone from your past. You told him that you already knew who it was. Then Amy got up and touched your forehead and you started speaking in some weird language. It was like… it was you but not you."

"Oh okay...?" Now I'm even more puzzled than I was before I opened my mouth.

"Let me call Doug and see if we can meet up with him later. You can get more answers from him."

I park Lindy and we start walking towards the elevator. As we are nearing the elevator, I hear someone calling me from behind. I recognize the voice and it makes me avoid responding to it. As the elevator opens, I feel a tap on my shoulder. I turn and just as I expected, it's Shane.

"Hey Talia, didn't you hear me calling you?" He asks with a stupid expression on his face. "Hello Kenna," he says in a condescending tone.

"Shane." Kenna responds in a flippant manner.

"So I guess you guys are carpooling now huh?" He asks as a way of desperately trying to fish for information.

"Well actually, we are now officially an item." Kenna states boldly.

"Yeah," I chime in. The expression on his face is priceless. To add insult to injury, Kenna places a sensuous kiss on my lips.

"Uh you guys go ahead and take the elevator. I gotta go back to my car to get something." Shane says before walking away.

"Fucking prick good riddance." I think as we step onto the elevator. Times like these only make me like her more. As the elevator door closes, I grab Kenna into my arms and deliver a sweet long fire filled kiss.

I step into my department and see Kathy at the front desk. "Good morning Kathy." I say as I approach her desk.

"Good morning Talia. How are you doing today?"

"I'm doing pretty good this morning, how are you?"

"I'm great, actually."

"That's good to hear. So did you ever find Tuna?"

"Yup, I found her. After tearing apart my apartment, giving both the property manager and the maintenance man an earful, and going door to door on my floor; I ended up finding her in my spare room closet! She was taking a nap underneath my summer clothes. I completely overlooked that area."

"Well I'm glad that you found her."

"I am too, have a good day Talia and thanks for being concerned."

"You're welcome. I'll catch you later."

The whole time I'm at work, my mind mills over the night before, Aiden, Kenna, and Aka Manah. I have to concentrate extra hard to block them out to get any done. The clock on my computer screen is my worst enemy. I find myself constantly checking it and counting down the hours until my day is over. I'm anticipating meeting up with Doug and getting some answers.

"I deny God and all religion

I curse, blaspheme, and provoke false gods with all despite,

I give my faith to Lucifer, and do his work through my hands.

I am an offspring of Lucifer.

I pledge to enlighten others in the ways of truth."

"Do you understand what this means?" Doug asks before grabbing his cup of tea and taking a sip.

"I think it's basically saying that we should reject the traditional teachings of religion and embrace our needs. It's also saying worship the devil right?"

"Yes that is exactly what its saying. As offspring of Lucifer, we are predestined for a greater purpose, a greater truth. As a child, I was taught to fear Satan. Everything wrong and evil was blamed on him. I was instilled with hate for him and everything he represents, but now my eyes are open to the truth. Isaac will tell you, go ahead Isaac tell her your story."

"Well, I was raised up in a traditional black Baptist church. You know the type where the preacher goes into rhythmic rants, and people catch the "Holy Ghost" and dance around wildly or pass out. I had a brother a few years older than me. We were close. Due to our closeness, he revealed his homosexuality to me before he mentioned a word of it to anyone else, including our parents. I always knew there was something different about him, so when he came out, it wasn't a big surprise. Our parents on the other hand, became angry and very displeased. They tried to keep it a secret from all of their church friends but it still got out. Members of our community ostracized him. They harassed him and called him all types of ignorant hateful things. It was terrible. I tried to be there for him as much as I could but I guess it wasn't enough. Especially with him having to deal with hate and disdain everywhere he went. There's a stigma in the black community, a closed-minded view of the world in which we live in. The type of music we listen to, the way we dress, the way we socialize.

As a kid in school, I was picked on for liking Rock-n-Roll quote UN quote, "White Music", or "Devil's Music", as some call it. I couldn't help what I liked. It was like, if you weren't listening to Rap, R&B, Hip-hop, or Gospel, there was something wrong with you. I had it bad but nowhere near as bad as my brother did. It got so bad that he couldn't take it anymore. I will never forget one of the last conversations we had. I came home from tutoring and found him in the upstairs hallway crying. When I asked what was wrong, he told me that our parents threatened to kick him out. He said earlier that week, my father gave him an ultimatum. He told him that if he didn't go back to being normal by the end of the week, he would have to find somewhere else to live. We had the conversation on Wednesday of the week of the ultimatum. That Friday was to be his last day if he didn't conform. Now here's what I don't get. If a person is born a certain way, how can they change the way they were born? The ultimatum only made things worse. The next day, the eve of the last day, he came home reeking of alcohol and marijuana. Our parents were attending a night revival service and I had just gotten home from band practice. His speech was slurred and he was ranting like a crazy man. He was saying things like God hated him and he was destined to go to hell. He was rambling on about ending it all. Tears were streaming down his face. I kept trying to talk him out of it... I guess I didn't try hard enough. He took me being concern the wrong way and we ended up getting into a big argument. Tempers flared and then pride and anger took over. We both said some nasty things to one another before he stormed out of the house.

Later that night I was awakened out of my sleep by a presence in my bedroom. My brother was standing near the doorway. I called out to him but he didn't respond. He just kept staring at me. Something didn't seem right. As I began to get out of bed, he raised his finger towards me and spoke. He said, "Find the truth before it is too late." Then he quickly walked out of the bedroom. I followed him. However, when I reached the hallway... he was gone! At the time, I had no idea what he was talking about, I figured he was probably still drunk and high so I disregarded it and went back to sleep. The next day I woke up to the sound of my mother crying. It turns out that my brother died the night before shortly after our argument. After he left the house, he attempted to rob a local convenient store. I guess with him on the verge of being homeless, the alcohol, drugs, and desperation got the best of him. During a botched robbery attempt, he ended up shooting the store clerk twice before taking a bullet to the chest. He was found a few blocks away. He bled out and died alone. I think him visiting me after death was his way of letting me know that the religion our parents brought us up in was false. It was because of their lack of understanding and compassion that my brother ended up doing what he did. After his death, I grew distant and started to hate them. Shortly after graduating from high school, I left home and haven't been back since." Doug waits for Isaac to finish before speaking.

"See Talia, that's the type of thing that we are trying to get people away from. The hate, the contradictions, for them to say that they worship a God of love is contradictive in itself. Any religion that has scriptures telling slaves to obey their masters is definitely a religion I want nothing to do with, Isaac was the one that enlightened me to the truth. I was just a street punk with no direction. He showed me the way and I ran with it, and that's what I'm offering to you. Join us." Isaac's story was moving but I'm still not completely convinced that their way of life is for me. I don't hate God and I certainly don't love the Devil, I'm neutral, indifferent.

"No offense, but I'm not sure if I'm ready for it. To be quite truthful I'm still trying to remember parts of last night. I don't want to make blacking out a habit." I state, clearly making my apprehensive feelings known.

"See that's the beauty of it Talia, you don't have to do anything that you're not comfortable with. Our way is a way of complete freedom. The only reason we're offering it so passionately is because it is destined for you, you were chosen. It is in your blood. Someone in your lineage preordained it." The way that Doug is talking, makes it seem more like a prearranged marriage than a religious choice.

"Okay so who exactly is responsible for preordaining it?" My mind scrolls its memory index of family members. I draw a blank as to who could be the guilty culprit.

"I am not privy to that information. The revelation of the person's identity is only for you to know. In order to receive the knowledge you must exit this room and go into the last room on the left. The message will be waiting for you."

"Okay so what will I be looking for; a piece of paper, writing on the wall, a recording?"

"All messages will be delivered in a suitable form for the receiver. Trust me, you will know the message when it's delivered; it will be uniquely catered to you."

"Alright gotcha," I respond as I reluctantly get up and leave the room. Nervousness sets in as I make my way down the hall. I feel like a kid on Christmas Eve waiting to open a nicely wrapped present. Staring at the outer wrapping and wondering what could be inside. Shaking the gift and trying to decipher the sound. That is the best way to describe the anticipation building from within. I reach the door. I hesitantly grab the doorknob, twist, and open it. The room is lit dimly and has a crisp chill. I slowly step inside. Once I'm completely in, the door closes behind me. I turn around and see Amy in a semi see through robe. She smiles at me and touches my face. Her hand is ice cold. The touch sends an electric surge through me. An image of my grandmother flashes in my head. I jump back startled, not sure of what just happened.

"Don't be afraid of me Elizabeth." Amy says in a soothing voice. She draws me in close to her. She rubs my face again. I give in to the electrifying currents. They flow through my body, releasing a warm heating sensation. More images start to flash in my mind, images from my childhood, images of Armichael, images of my grandmother, and images of them together. The manner in which they are together doesn't seem romantic or sensual. It is akin to how a mother and child would interact with one another. The images then change and show my grandmother arguing with my father. They then fast forward and show her being drugged and placed behind the wheel of a car by him. Those images are then replaced by images of the same car careening off the road. Next, they show her in some type of hospital or medical building. I see her stuck in a room bandaged and bruised, with a dazed look in her eyes. The final set of images show an older version of her, in a place inhabited by other elderly people. The word Lakewood and a building are the last images that I see. I snap out of the trance like state and realize that I am in a janitorial closet by myself. Amy is nowhere to be found. I leave the room disoriented and confused, unsure if Amy was actually there, or if I was simply hallucinating. I make my way down the hall back to where the others are. *"My grandmother is alive?"* I chew over the revelation as I reach the door. Everyone simultaneously looks at me as I enter the room.

"Did you receive your message?" Doug inquires aloud, while Kenna and Isaac are probably asking the same thing mentally.

"Yes, I got my message. Kenna come on let's get out of here!" I rush over to grab her. She reluctantly gets up and follows.

"What the hell is wrong with you?" She asks as I rush down the hall with her not far behind.

"I will tell you when we get to the car." I respond as I continue towards the exit. We get to Lindy and I crank her up with no hesitation. I speed out of the parking lot.

"Now do you mind telling me what the hell is going on?" Kenna probes as I drive at a breakneck speed wishing I were already home.

"I don't know what type of weird cult you're in but I want no part of it! I saw something that I shouldn't have. The message that I received was a load of bullshit and that Amy lady, thing, or whatever, is fucking strange!" I'm still outraged with what I saw. *"There is no possible way that my dad would commit such an atrocious act. I've lived with the man my whole life so I of all people would know! I mean he's my father for God's sake!"* I interrupt my thoughts to finish my statement. "I think you should stop associating with them too!" I lay my feelings on the line, not holding anything back. Kenna doesn't respond. She just sits in silence. I guess she's searching for the right thing to say or the best way to say it. She finally breaks her silence.

"Talia, I was the same way. You're just a little freaked out right now because it's something you're not used to trust me. When I was first exposed to the truth, I was freaked out and paranoid for like a whole week. I don't know what the message was, but if you want to share it with me, I'm all ears. Once you start to fully understand it, everything will be fine." Kenna says as she places her hand on my thigh.

"Look Kenna, I get what you're saying and if you're into that type of thing, that's fine. Me on the other hand, I don't want anything to do with it. Even if I told you what I saw, you wouldn't understand. So basically what I'm saying is that if you're going to stay in that cult, I think that it's best for us to go our separate ways." Kenna removes her hand and her face begins to show traces of anger.

"You can drop me off at home and bring my stuff to work

tomorrow." She says coldly as she turns her head to face the window. The rest of the ride is silent. I pull up to her apartment. She quickly gets out without even turning back to acknowledge me, no good-bye not even a simple wave.

CHAPTER 15

The wet gloomy weather appropriately matches my dismal mood perfectly. It's like God or whatever force in charge, knows the funk that I am weathering. The drive to work is shitty. It's just the latest addition to the cruel running joke that my life has become. Things have been sucking a lot lately. I haven't heard from Aiden since the big disclosure and Kenna has been giving me the cold shoulder as well. I just can't seem to win. Now don't get me wrong. She still speaks to me, just not outside of work and when she does, she coldly calls me Ms. Rhodes. Just recently, when we were alone in the break room, I wanted to say something but my pride kept me from doing so. It's keeping me from giving in and waving the white flag. I know I should probably be the bigger person but I'm not too fond of her association with that cult of devil worshipers.

I arrive to work later than usual and my favorite parking spot isn't available. "That's just great," I huff. I end up having to park in a space farthest from the elevators. As I begin my trek, I step on an uneven section of pavement and it breaks one of my heels. "Shit" I mumble as I fight against gravity to keep my balance. *"Now I'll have to wear my running shoes all day."* I think as I return to the car to retrieve them. Breaking the heel was so disheartening due to the fact that the pair was one of my favorites. I loved the way they accentuated my legs and gave my rear an extra oomph of fullness. After changing my shoes and walking all the way to the elevators at the other end of the garage, I realize that I left my papers on my desk at home. "Fuck" I mumble as I press the elevator call button. I'm pissed because I printed out the latest version and neglected to save it to my email or SkyDrive. Now I'll have to work on an older version and try to remember all of the updates and changes. To make matters worse, I feel a headache starting to brew.

After waiting forever in the parking garage, an elevator finally arrives. The door opens to reveal Kenna. She steps out of the elevator and stops right in front of me. Feeling self-conscious about my footwear, I try to avoid direct eye contact. I'm ready to put the drama to rest. Before I can even start to repair our relationship, she makes the first move.

"Look Talia," she says throwing me off completely. She hasn't called me that since the fallout. "I'm not willing to give up on us. We need to work this out." She finishes.

"Okay so what do you propose we do?" I ask as a deep longing from within rises to the surface.

"I know that you're not comfortable with the way things are but I really want to be with you Talia. I know that the group I'm involved with makes you uncomfortable and if you will just give them an honest chance—" I cut her off before she can finish.

"Kenna I miss you, I really do, but I'm not too sure about your lifestyle. It completely goes against my beliefs. My parents will definitely not understand or accept it. I'm still trying to figure out how to tell them about us!" It feels good to get that load of burden off my chest.

"Why are you worried about what they think? We are the main ones that you should be concerned with." Kenna says.

"Okay maybe you're right but this isn't your everyday situation. When they find out that I have a relationship with another woman, they're going to disown me!"

"It doesn't matter Talia, you're a grown woman. This is your life, your destiny, we're all human, and no one is perfect. I'm pretty sure they have done things that they will never tell you about, they are not as perfect as they appear," the look in her eyes, the passion in her statement, touches a truth from deep within. "There are a lot of things that you don't know about your parents. You really need to give the group a chance." I don't know what to say. Something inside of me senses that she knows more than she is willing to admit. I really need to find a way to get it out of her but first we have to patch things up.

"Alright well I'm ready to put all of the nonsense behind us. I need you with me. I need us." I say before laying a sweet kiss on her longing lips. She draws closer to me and reciprocates an equal amount of passion. Sidetracked by the moment, I forget about the elevator. I shift my focus towards it just as the doors are closing. "See what you made me do? Now I have to wait another thirty minutes for it to come back down." I joke as I press the call button to summon the elevator back to the garage.

"Well now I'm here to wait with you." Kenna responds. We have a laugh about it before I escort her to her car. We make it back to the elevator just as it reaches the garage. Once inside, we laugh and chat like schoolgirls for the duration of the ride. We reach our floor and quickly revert to "at work" mode. We both take one last look at each other before heading in opposite directions towards our respective departments.

I enter the office and begin my tardy walk of shame. Kathy is hard at work transferring calls and handling outgoing mail, Jessica is discreetly watching highlights of "Mob Wives". She's taking a brief break from her work but unlike Jeff, she always gets it done so there's no reason to raise a stink. It's just another day at the office, I wonder if my grandmother was actually into black magic. I also ponder what her and my father fell out over. What could be so bad that it would keep someone away from his or her family for close to two decades? Maybe my father really did try to kill her. That could be the reason why she stayed away but I just can't see my father doing something so heinous. I really need to get some answers. I need to go back to that group. While in deep thought, I receive a call on my office extension.

"Hello this is Talia speaking, may I help you?"

"Hey T, its Kathy Mr. Beck needs to see you right away."

"Okay I'm on my way."

I step into Mr. Beck's office. He doesn't look like he's in the best of moods.

"Hey Mr. Beck, you wanted to see me?" I inquire as I prepare for the worst.

"Yes I did Talia. I'm having a problem and I'm going to need your help. Shane's been messing up a lot lately. Remember the special project that I had him working on?"

"I remember it, the one that you wanted me to stay on him about."

"Right, well thanks to you he got it in on time but he completely screwed it up! Thank God, we caught it before sending it over to the client or the new account would definitely have been in jeopardy. Given your knowledge and track record, I should have had you handle the project instead. Well anyway, I need you to relieve him of his position."

"Okay so let me get this right, you want me to fire Shane?" I'm surprised and delighted at the same time. How I feel about Shane is the closest I've come to hating someone since high school. Mr. Beck is giving me his head on a silver platter. I try to contain my joy as he continues to talk.

"Yes that's what I need you to do as my Office Manager, fire him!" The look on his face is dead serious.

"Um… well… okay, when do I have to do it?"

"I need it done as soon as possible."

"Okay, I'll get right on it." I say as I head out of the room. I feel my face muscles forming a smile as I exit. I leave Mr. Beck's office and go straight to my target: adios Shane! I reach Shane's office. I'm so excited and nervous that I fail to knock before entering.

"Shane, I need to have a word with you," I request in a professional tone.

"Uh yeah sure Talia, you know you could've knocked." He

says in an irritated manner. His attitude only gives me more motivation. I close the door. I want to have some decency about it. No one else needs to hear what we are discussing. Even though I don't like the guy, I don't want to embarrass him. Firing him is enough of a treat for me. It's just as Grandma Mariana always said, *"Too much icing on a cake is bad for you."* I don't pull any punches; I go straight for the kill.

"Alright look Shane, your performance hasn't been satisfactory."

"What do you mean?" He asks with a puzzled look on his face.

"You really messed up on the special project that Mr. Beck assigned to you. If we didn't catch the errors in time, it could have cost the company the entire account. And in conjunction with other things, it means that we're going to have to let you go." I state leaving no need for further explanation. Shane looks at me as if I'm playing a cruel joke.

"You've got to be kidding me right?" He says with a slight laugh.

"No, you're fired."

"How am I fired and who the fuck are you to fire me?" He gets up from his desk. I can tell by his reaction that I just ignited his fire. I take a deep breath before responding.

"Well as the Office Manager, I'm letting you go."

"You're letting me go? You must be fucking kidding me! Where the fuck is Mr. Beck?" He says as he storms past me and heads out of the room. I have to intercept him. If it looks like I can't handle Shane, my recently acquired position might be in jeopardy. I rush quickly behind him trying everything short of physically grabbing him. I see Kathy in the hallway as we head towards Mr. Beck's office.

"Kathy, call security now!" I command as we briefly cross paths.

"Okay Talia,"

With no other option left to stop him, I grab Shane by the shoulder. "Hold—" before I can finish my sentence, Shane turns around and takes a swing at me. Thanks to my reflexes, the intended punch narrowly misses my face. Things have just deteriorated; I ready myself as Shane goes into a full rage. He follows up his punch with a fast openhanded blow. The force of the smack throws me off balance.

"You fucking carpet munching cunt!" He yells furiously. I'm in complete shock that a man has just struck me. My face stings and my eyes water as I recoil from the blow. My knees buckle and I fall to the floor. Shane, pleased with his handy work, let's out a cruel laugh and then continues to Mr. Beck's office. As Shane walks away, other office staff members begin to gather around me

"Are you alright?" One of them asks as they help me to my feet.

"I'm fine." I respond feeling more embarrassed than hurt. The sounds of an argument ensuing down the hall, is a telltale sign that Shane has reached Mr. Beck's office. I slowly rise up from the floor and look around at the now gawking audience of Central Insurance employees drawn away from their mundane work activities by the allure of drama. "Go back to work everyone," I instruct, with the side of my face still tingling from the brutal smack. I make my way down the hall towards Mr. Beck's office, hoping all the while that I don't become a witness to a murder. I hear the sound of rapid footfalls approaching from behind. I turn and see three security guards rushing towards the scene. I step aside, in hopes that they will give the Neanderthal brute exactly what he deserves.

"Are you okay?" One of them stops and asks with a concerned look. I guess he noticed me rubbing my face.

"I'm okay just a little dinged up." I respond while still rubbing my bruise

"Is he armed?"

"Not that I know of,"

"Okay stay here," the man commands in a serious tone before rejoining his comrades. They reach the office and burst inside just as Shane flips over Mr. Beck's desk. One of the security men reacts by spraying Shane directly in the face with pepper spray. Shane cups his eyes and screams in pain as the men rush in and subdue him. The look on Mr. Beck's face is one of pure terror. It's a safe bet to assume that he wasn't expecting Shane's postal reaction. Once they have Shane subdued, the men drag him out of the office.

"Bitch it's not over!" He threatens as security manhandles him away. Mr. Beck approaches me with the look of a man on the verge of peeing his pants.

"Are you alright?" He asks as he places his hand on my shoulder.

"I'm okay." I respond.

"Are you sure?"

"Yes I'll live." I state as I continue rubbing my throbbing face.

"If you need the rest of the day off, I will still pay you for it without you having to use any of your PTO. I just want to make sure that you're okay. As a matter of fact, you can take a few extra days off as well."

"I only need the rest of the day off. I'll be fine." I respond. Mr. Beck is desperately trying to sweeten the deal and cover his own ass. If I weren't dedicated to my career, I would definitely play my hand right and get a few perks.

As I make my way out of the department, I run into Kenna. "Is everything okay? I heard that Shane went ballistic and attacked you. I saw security escorting him out."

"Yeah I'm okay. I'm a trooper."

"Well trooper, I think I need to come over later and tend to your wounds."

"That sounds nice. Wait, don't you have that group meeting

tonight?"

"Yes my "cult" is having a meeting," she says as she uses air quotations. We both laugh at how absurd it sounds now in hindsight of the makeup.

"Well how about I give it another chance."

"You mean—"

"Yes, I want to give it another try."

"Okay great! How about I pick you up around eight?"

"Perfect. That will give me enough time to rest and clear my head. I'm headed home now."

"Shouldn't you go to the hospital or the police station?" Kenna inquires with a worried expression.

"No not really, he only managed to smack me, I should be fine." I let a little bit of confidence seep out to put her at ease.

"Okay. I will see you later." Kenna says before giving me a quick discrete kiss on the cheek. I'm angry that I let that asshole get the best of me. If I were a man, I would've really let him have it. I should press charges just to add insult to injury. I would definitely have a case and witnesses to boot. I don't know. I mean I really hate that fucking guy but I hate courtrooms even more.

Watching countless court shows has really left a lasting impression on me. I'm just grateful that I won't have to deal with him at work anymore.

I get home with just enough time to get ready and fix a bite to eat before Kenna arrives. I get in and head straight to the shower. I have to clean the filth of the day off before I feel comfortable.

Once in the shower, I feel the headache starting to subside. I close my eyes as the hot water massages my bruised face and opens my pores. The moment of relaxation is interrupted by a weird sensation on my back. I open my eyes and turn to see Amy in the shower with me!

"Wh—"

"Shhh," she says as she puts her finger on my lips. She then starts rubbing my chest. Her hand is a stark contrast to the hot water. She moves in closer. I feel her lips press up against mine. My head begins throbbing and my ears start to ring. I feel my conscious slipping. Everything goes dark.

I awake to the chimes of the doorbell. It takes me a few

minutes to realize where I am. I'm fully dressed and sitting on my couch.

"What the fuck?" I murmur as I try to wrap my mind around what has occurred. The last thing I remember is being in the shower and Amy appearing out of nowhere. A vibrating sensation in my pocket lets me know where my phone is. I pull it out and see Kenna's picture on the screen. I quickly answer it. "Hold on, I'm coming right now." I utter as I get up and open the door.

"It's about time you answered. I've been calling and ringing the doorbell like crazy!" Kenna says as she smiles at me.

"I'm sorry, I must have fallen asleep. What time is it?" Kenna quickly glances at her phone before responding.

"Um it's ten till eight,"

"Really, wow." I feel like an alien abduction victim trying to account for the last few hours.

"Is everything alright?" She asks in a puzzled tone.

"Well no not really," I respond.

"What's wrong?"

"I don't know. Earlier while I was taking a shower, Amy appeared.

"You mean in the shower with you?" Kenna asks.

"Yes. She appeared out of thin air, then she kissed me and I blacked out. I woke up on my couch fully dressed and I have no recollection of how I got there or how I got dressed!" Kenna doesn't say anything. She just looks at me with an astonished expression. "What? You don't have anything to say?" I ask, as a worrisome feeling starts to bubble.

"You've been chosen."

"What are you talking about?"

"You have received a divine touch, Amy has chosen you."

"Whoa. What?"

"You have been chosen babe. Doug will tell you all about it. Come on let's go."

"Okay." I respond. I feel like I have no other choice. The headaches, nightmares, and weird occurrences have led me down the road of desperation. I need answers and I fear that acting as if nothing strange is happening will only make things worse. Before leaving, I make sure to grab the weird old book.

While in the car heading towards our destination, my phone

vibrates. I take it out and see that I have received a text message from Aiden. I'm surprised to say the least.

"Hey Aiden just texted me," I say aloud as I quickly open up the message.

"He's ready," Kenna responds as she continues to drive to our destination.

"I'm ready to talk☺," is what the text message reads.

"How did you know?" I ask as I look up from the phone screen.

"Intuition, besides it's better to share you than not have you at all. I told you, having a woman that's into other women is every man's fantasy."

"I guess… or maybe it's love." I reply.

"It could be, only time will tell what his true intentions are." She says with a weird smile. "I hope you're ready for him." I'm not sure what she means by her statement but she hasn't steered me wrong yet, so maybe I should open up more and truly accept what she has to offer. Perhaps I should give loving her a try as well. Kenna is everything one could hope for in a companion. I really admire her "grab life by the balls" mentality. I remember the first time we went out together. She was such a firecracker. Her ginger hair matches her personality perfectly. I think I really am starting to love her. However, it's a different kind of love. It's not that sappy fairytale bullshit. It's more like... I recognize the qualities in her that boost me. She adds something to me but I can't quite put my finger on it. As Kenna continues to drive, I open up the weird book and begin to read this one particular passage:

Revelation of truth

Wherefore, it is true that my knowledge encompasses the truth of all that is. My wisdom is an ever-flowing stream that quenches all who thirst. It satisfies the appetite of the passionate and comforts the spirits of the weary. The manifestation of my descent is clear unto you. All fully within my strength, not that of the false gods; wherefore I am he that men come to with their rightful worship, not the false gods or their books, that are wrongly written; I come to you in a dream, as a whisper in the wind; as a fleeting vision. The time is near, my slain children will be avenged, and I will smite all false gods.

As I'm reading the passage, I feel a headache starting to rear its ugly head. We arrive at the meeting ahead of schedule. The lot is packed with more vehicles than the previous service. The headache is still lurking in the recesses of my brain.

"Is everything alright?" Kenna inquires as she takes notice of me rubbing my temples.

"Uh yeah I'm alright. I just feel another headache starting up."

"Talia," Kenna grabs my hand and shifts my full attention to her.

"Huh?"

"Are you sure that you're alright?"

"Yes, I'm okay trust me."

"Okay I'm just making sure before we go in. I don't want you passing out again or not remembering significant chunks of time."

"I know, thank you for caring."

"You're welcome now let's hurry up and get inside. I've got a surprise for you."

We rush to get inside. Kenna burst through the door with me trailing not far behind. In our haste, we almost have a head on collision with David.

"Whoa, chicas what are you doing?" He asks in an intense

tone.

"Sorry about that David, have you seen Doug?" Kenna asks.

"Yeah he's in the back room. Be more careful in the future."

"We will thanks," she responds before we continue on our way.

"That's the room that he is normally in before service." Kenna blurts as we approach a door with weird writing on it. She knocks on the door and barely waits for a response before opening it. Kenna opens the door and I see Doug in what appears to be some type of deep meditation.

"WH—sorry," Kenna say as we are stopped dead in our tracks by the sight.

"Don't be, it's okay come in. I have a few things to discuss with the both of you." Doug says as he gets up from his meditation. "You have some questions for me?"

"Well yeah, how did you know?" I ask, completely astonished by his statement. I was actually just thinking about the weird occurrences that have been happening at my house.

"You want to know about some scientifically unexplainable things that have been occurring in your life," he responds as he looks intensely at the both of us.

"Yes. There have been a lot of strange things going on that I have no explanation for." I take out the weird old book. "Have you ever seen this book before?" I ask as I hand it over to him.

"Yes… I have seen this book before. I used to own a copy of it years ago. It helped me find the truth. Prior to meeting Isaac, I would often frequent this used bookstore and kill time browsing through its assortment of tomes. I was particularly fond of the older ones. They seemed to have a sense of richness about them, which books at the time were lacking. Anyway, one day I'm in the store perusing through books and what not, when the owner gets my attention. He hands me this book and tells me that I must take charge over it and ensure that it gets into the right hands.

Now at the time, I thought he was wacked out on something or needed to be committed to some type of mental asylum. He said that I would hold on to it for twelve years before leaving it for its rightful owner. He gave it to me without charging me a single red cent! I hung onto it and eventually started reading it. It really put me on the right path. I met Isaac shortly thereafter and the truth exploded into my life." Doug takes a closer examination of the book. He flips towards the back of it as if he's looking for something specific. His eyes light up as he reaches a particular section of it. "As a matter of fact, it looks exactly like the copy I used to have." He states as he closes the book. "But anyway I don't want to get too deep into this conversation. Let's save it for another time. So you're considering joining us then correct?" Doug asks as he shoots a quick glance towards Kenna. She must have informed him of my renewed interest.

"Yes I am, but I don't know—"

"I don't think that you are ready. I still hear doubt in your voice. You will join eventually, just not tonight. There is no pressure." Doug gets up and moves toward the door. "Service is about to begin. Follow me." He instructs before going out of the door. We leave the room and go down the hall toward the main event room. As we walk down the hall, I decide to text Aiden back. I retrieve my phone from my pocket while I continue walking.

"I love you and I'm ready for you to come back ttyl☺," I quickly text into my device. I'm relieved and elated to have him back in the fold. I press send and shove the phone back into my pocket.

Once we reach the main ceremony section, I feel a weird surge of energy. "Find a seat, we will be out shortly" Doug says before ushering us through a set of double doors. We emerge from the doors and enter into a room packed full of people. The people are as diverse as the colors of a rainbow. So many different types of people from different walks of life all gathered for a common cause, the truth. I see several people that look familiar. Some of them are of importance. I immediately notice a few professional athletes among the gathered. Doug and Isaac step out on the stage. I do a double take as I recognize the mayor of the city on the stage to the left of them. I recognize him because of recent stories in the news. Isaac is standing on the stage before the altar, draped in dark attire. The air is ominously thick with anticipation.

"Good evening brothers and sisters, we are all gathered here to get reacquainted and stand united as one big family of truth." He says in a loud booming voice. Clapping and cheers erupt from the crowd. The energy is starting to build. My head begins to throb and the ringing starts up as well. I'm starting to see the big picture. I don't want to be like my parents. I need to express myself freely, even if that means further exploring my sexuality beyond the limits set by my upbringing. If I'm gay, I'm gay. If I'm bi, I'm bi. It doesn't matter. I matter, my happiness matters. I want to live a life without shame, an existence based on truth. I shouldn't care what my parents or anyone thinks if it means depriving myself of things I'm destined to have and experience. I feel my phone vibrate as I listen to Isaac ignite the fires of the crowd. I look down at it and see my father's number. I immediately press the ignore button. Now is definitely not the time to talk to him.

A big blue flame manifesting on the stage catches my attention. Smoke quickly gathers around the powerful wonder of fire. It is far different from any other flame that I have laid eyes on. It is controlled and self-contained. The flame's appearance stops Isaac's passionate rally. The room goes silent. Then suddenly, like a work of fiction brought to life, Amy emerges from it! She is cloaked in a dark red robe. Her eyes are ablaze with excitement. Everyone looks on in amazement as the flame and smoke dissipates and reveals her complete form. She is beautiful but dangerous. I find myself oddly attracted to her. It's as if I'm under her spell. I'm dumbfounded as to how she emerged out of the fire unscathed. It is even more shocking than her appearance in my shower. It goes against the laws of nature. It's not humanly possible! Everyone around me bows. I attempt to move but my body won't cooperate. I try to look away and regain control over myself but I'm stuck in a trance like state. I feel myself moving closer to her. The throbbing and ringing intensifies significantly but the state that I am in has rendered me numb. After fighting briefly against the mysterious force controlling me, I snap out of the numbing daze and find myself on the stage in front of Amy. The pupils of her eyes glow bright red with delight as she looks at me. Our minds become one *"Join us."* She persuasively communicates to me without the use of speech. I am indeed chosen by her; I am chosen by the truth.

"Amy has chosen you Talia." Isaac proclaims in a hushed tone.

"You will become one of us. It is your destiny." Amy says in a dark enticing voice. She stretches out her hand. Her fingertips touch my forehead and the electrifying chill of her touch surges into me. Everything starts to spin. I get dizzy and pass out.

CHAPTER 16

I'm back home and yet again, I'm not quite sure how I got here. Kenna is next to me in bed. Fierce howling winds force the tips of a tree branch to scrape along the outer surface of my bedroom window. I begin lightly tapping Kenna in an effort to wake her. After a few attempts, I am successful.

"Hey, what did you wake me up for?" She asks groggily.

"How did we get here?" I question with my finger pointing down to emphasize the point.

"Are you serious?"

"Yes."

"So you mean to tell me that you don't remember coming back in my car?"

"No, I don't." I murmur as I rack my brain trying to recall anything after Amy.

"You drove. Please tell me you remember that."

"Not really but did you notice anything different about me after we saw Amy?"

"Um I'm not sure what you mean. You acted like yourself, only you were more confident, it was as if you finally knew and accepted your destiny. You were so sexy last night I couldn't resist. I couldn't stop myself from giving you my all. The way you handled me was so... so... I can't even put it into words!" Kenna states as she smiles naughtily. I smile back still unsure of last night's events but all the while, relieved to be back home safe.

"I'm sorry for waking you up I remember now." I falsely respond before kissing her and rolling back over. I don't remember shit and I probably never will remember last night. I glance at the clock. I still have at least forty-five more minutes to rest before getting up to face the day. I want to continue pondering over the issue but my urge for more rest is stronger. Within, a matter of minutes, I feel myself slowly starting to dose off.

A couple of taps from Kenna saves me from being late for work. "Babe you're going to be late and your phone keeps going off." She says as she hands me my phone. I swipe it unlocked and notice multiple text messages. I check the first message and I'm taken aback by it.

"You will pay soon enough!"

"What the fuck," I murmur as I scroll down and see the same message multiple times. "Look at this!" I say before handing back it to Kenna. She reads it in amazement.

"Wow, somebody really has it out for you. Maybe you should take it to the police." She says as she returns it to me.

"I'm not worried about them. It's probably just some asshole with the wrong number." I reply as I hop out of bed. Besides, I've got bigger things to worry about, like finding out if the vision I received from Amy is true."

"So you don't think it's Shane?" Kenna asks as she follows me out of the bedroom.

"I doubt it. I think we're even after the smack he laid on me yesterday. If he's going to go after anyone, it would probably be Mr. Beck."

I take a quick shower and grab a breakfast snack before seeing Kenna off. I finish getting ready and head out shortly after. For some strange reason, I feel compelled to take a different way to work. As I'm driving, I take notice of an assisted living facility. After slowing down and taking another glance, it starts coming back to me. I realize where I've seen it before. It's the same place from the vision! I look for cops before performing a U-turn.

I pull into the parking lot and park in the first open space. Right before I get out of Lindy, it hits me. *"What is my grandmother's full name?"* I scroll through my phone and text my mom. I dare not text my father, especially not after the vision from Amy. I want to believe with every fiber of my being that it's not true but I would hate to chance it. My mom responds back with the name Cecilia Elizabeth Rosette. Armed with the information, I head inside. As I step inside of the building, the permeating stench of the elderly hits me like a wall of cold reality. I hope to God I don't end up in one. The people in them seem so miserable. It's like the last pit stop for the unwanted. It seems like some of the people at these places are thrown away and forgotten. My nose adjusts to the odor as I make my way to the main desk. I reach the desk and see an attractive mocha colored woman going through paperwork. I feel pity for her. She has to deal with the smell day in and day out.

"Hi may I help you?" She asks, clearly picking up on the lost look on my face.

"Hello, I'm here to see... Cecilia Elizabeth Rosette..." is my shaky response, I'm still unsure about the name. She types in the information and begins searching for the match. After a few seconds, she pauses and looks up at me.

"So far I don't see a Rosette in our system but I have one other section to look through so hold tight." She continues her search. "Sorry ma'am but according to our records we don't have anyone by that name in any part of this facility." Her answer gives me more of reason not to believe the things shown to me in the vision. I feel like leaving, but an overwhelming urge for the truth takes over.

"Rose Elizabeth" is the named whispered into my mind from an unknown source. I'm reluctant to repeat it aloud. I don't know if I really want to know the truth. I'm definitely second guessing my

reason for coming here in the first place. *"You must,"* the disembodied voice says. I'm seriously starting to question my sanity as well. I dare not ask if the attendant heard it because I already know what her answer would be.

"Okay well do you see anyone by the name Rose Elizabeth?" I ask reluctantly. She begins another search through the database. "I'm here to see my long lost grandmother. I haven't seen her since I was six…" I start to lay on the sob story.

"Ms.—"

"Talia, just call me Talia. Ms. or ma'am is too impersonal and it makes me sound old." I say with a slight giggle.

"Okay Talia well I've found someone by the name of Rose Elizabeth. I don't normally do this but due to the nature of your situation, I can escort you to her room after you sign in and show me a current form of identification." She says with a slight smile.

"Okay, I definitely appreciate it." I respond before digging in my purse for my wallet. While I search for my ID, the attendant picks up her phone and makes a call.

"Hey Darius, it's Simone, do you mind watching the front desk? I have to escort someone to see a resident—you can? Okay great. Thank you." She hangs up the phone. "Just give me a minute Talia," she says as she places the receiver back on its base.

"Okay," I shoot back before handing her my driver's license. "So how long have you been working here? I ask as I sign my name on the visitor log

"I've been here about six months." She responds. I want to ask her how she has managed to tolerate the weird smells for so long. That's somewhat of a godly feat. I probably would have quit after receiving my first paycheck! I am in the middle of picturing myself in her shoes when a heavyset man enters the room.

"Thanks D," Simone says to Darius as she gets up from the desk.

"You could've just asked me to take her," he responds as he looks over at me. Something about the manner in which he looks at me is quite unsettling. He stares at me long and hard, like I'm a piece of meat and he's a hungry loin in a cage. Darius allows Simone to come from around the desk before taking her place. "Don't take too long." He says as he takes his perverted glare off me and redirects it to Simone. She takes notice of him checking her out and releases a fake giggle. I know the giggle all too well because I've done it before when I was approached by a guy that I wasn't particularly attracted to.

"Mmm hmm," is how she brushes off his comment. "Follow me." She says as she turns her attention towards me. I can feel Darius' eyes follow us as we walk out of the room. He seems like the type that would stand outside of a woman's window and masturbate while watching her undress. Simone leads me out of the entrance lobby and down a long corridor that connects to another section of the building. We arrive on the other side and travel past a series of rooms, most of which have open doors. I take brief glimpses into each of the rooms that we pass. Quite a few of them house lonely souls with their eyes glued to the news or some other form of daytime television.

As we travel further down the hall, my ears detect someone humming a vaguely familiar melody. The faint melody triggers regressed memories that I wasn't even aware of having. It invites me to it like an old friend, images of watching people holding hands in a circle while chanting the elusive melody emerges in my brain. I feel goose bumps forming on my skin as Simone stops in front of the one particular room from which the humming is originating.

"She should be in here," she says as she grabs the chart from the cubby attached to the wall near the door. She verifies the paperwork, before shepherding me inside. I enter the room and almost immediately recognize the person inhabiting it. It is without a doubt my grandmother.

"This is her," I proclaim as I take in the magnitude of the moment. She looks just like the images from the vision.

"Are you sure it's her?" Simone asks as we move closer towards the elderly woman.

"Yes I'm positive." I respond as a feeling of relief sweeps over me. I'm not crazy. The vision is real. "Grandma…?" I utter as I draw closer to her. She slowly turns. At first, she has a look of confusion. Then it hits her. She remembers who I am.

"Yes Talia. I've been waiting for you. Oh my, you look so much like your father. C'mere and give me a hug." She says with a slight Haitian accent. I walk over to her. As we embrace, she whispers into my ear, "We need to talk," in a serious tone.

"Okay," I gush, hardly able to contain my excitement. I can't believe that the vision is true. It feels surreal. I haven't seen her in nearly twenty years. It's like seeing a ghost.

"How… why are you here?" The question spills out of my mouth. I study her carefully, still in disbelief that she is actually sitting in front of me.

"I'm here because of you. I've been here for a long while waitin' for you. There is a lot that you need to know. Excuse me miss do you mind, we need to talk about some private family matters." My grandmother says to Simone.

"Okay, I'll be right outside Talia." Simone announces before quickly exiting the room.

"Now my child, I'm going to get straight to the point, Corvis isn't your father." I'm left speechless by my grandmother's revelation. "I know what you're thinking, but you have to trust me on this. He is an evil deceitful man. He killed your real father and has been pretending to be something he is not ever since!" I'm past confused. I study her face for a hint of deceit, some ounce of falsehood. She has to be lying!

"Okay so what are you saying? Who is my real father and why did Corvis, kill him?"

"The man that you know as your father killed him long ago

before you were born and your whore of a mother helped feed you one big lie. Corvis is really your uncle and your real father was Michael Theodore Rosette." The information hits me like a combo from a prizefighter, hard, fast, and highly effective. The wind is figuratively knocked right out of me. Michael Theodore Rosette, M-T-R, Armichael is my real father!

"Hold on, so you're telling me that the man I know as my father, Corvis Michael Rhodes killed my real father, Armichael the musician?"

"That's not Corvis' real name and yes, I think that about sums it up."

"So what is his real name?" I ask while desperately trying to come to terms with the disclosure.

"His real name is Corvis Remi Rosette. He's from bad seed. He was conceived out of evil. The bastard was always jealous of Michael. He hated him to the core. I found out about the murder years ago and threatened to expose him. He put poison in my veins and tried to kill me. By the grace of Amy, I survived." The look in her eyes is dead serious.

"You know Amy?" I ask, surprised by the coincidence.

"Yes, she is our family's guardian spirit. Everyone that dedicates their life to the true God has a guardian assigned to their family. She must have come to you already eh?"

"Yes, she gave me a vision… of you. She let me know that you were still alive. So Corvis was responsible for the fire?"

"Yes but the fire didn't kill Michael. He was dead before the first flame was lit. Your real father was on the verge of super stardom. He mastered the art of intertwining the family's blessing into his musical gift and Corvis, his bastard half-brother grew outrageously jealous because of it. The authorities labeled it as a freak accident but Michael came to me in a dream and showed me the truth. That bastard poisoned him!" Tears start to form in my grandmother's eyes. "For years I've wanted desperately to put a hex on 'em but forces beyond my control would not allow it. He has the blessing that was bestowed to your father shortly before my husband's death. If I were to kill Corvis, the blessing would leave our bloodline. That is why you are the one that has to put an end to his evil."

"Huh me, why me, I mean, how…" I'm so overwhelmed. I can barely get out my complete thought.

"Only the first born from the next generation can reclaim the blessing and set things right."

"What do you mean by set things right?" I don't like where our conversation is headed.

"You have to kill him. It is your destiny my dear child. An eye for an eye, blood for blood, you must avenge your father's death and take back the blessing of power that is rightfully yours."

"So you're saying that I have to kill my father, I mean Corvis?"

"Yes, it is the only way. You must give in to your true self."

"I-I don't know if I can do that…and what is my true self?" She sounds completely insane! She wants me to risk going to jail for the rest of my life in order to restore a power that I'm not even sure exists!

"It is the person that you're destined to be. It is the reason why you suffer."

"What do you mean?"

"I know all about what ails you. The nightmares, the headaches, periods of unaccounted for time, the unexplained ghostly phenomena—"

"H-how do you know about these things?" I ask, clearly shocked by her knowledge of what has been occurring.

"These are all signs of your true self. Both your real father and I experienced them before making the transition. You were never meant to live a normal life. You must give in to it. It wants to avenge your father and reclaim the power. The more you resist, the longer you will suffer." As if on cue, I start to feel another headache brewing. I think it's time to leave. It's all too much to digest.

"Look grandma, it's great seeing you again but this is all too much for me to handle." I turn to leave.

"Wait," my grandmother grabs my hand. I see the sad desperation in her eyes. "One last thing, you must listen to me," she says in a low whisper "someone wants you dead!"

CHAPTER 17

I get to work with minutes left to spare. Being late is one of my major pet peeves. It's like my father... wait... no, he isn't my father. He's a fake calculating murderous asshole! I mean that's how I should feel but I don't! My father has only done right by me. Don't get me wrong, I want to believe that my grandmother is telling the truth, but her claims are downright horrendous. I mean sure they correspond with the vision but it can't be true! Armichael is not my father and Corvis is not a killer! He's as law abiding as they come! He got on my case once for taking a piece of candy from the grocery store. He drives the speed limit one hundred percent of the time and he donates to charities! I can't handle the way things are going. I don't want all of these sudden changes in my life. My life was just fine last month. I want to go back to that; I want things to go back to how they were! I don't want it to be any other way! I don't want to find my true self, and I don't want to spend the rest of my life looking over my shoulder because someone wants to kill me! I just wish all of these problems would leave me alone!

Sitting in my office, I reflect more on my life and recent choices. I look at an old office picture with all of the staff, Jeff and Shane included. Maybe I could've done things differently. Maybe I should've really given Shane a chance. I mean, perhaps I should've gotten to know him better. Who knows, if things would've started out differently, we probably could have been just fine and Jeff... I still can't believe that I ended up being the one that fired him. Now he's just a memory lost in the past, like the acquaintances before him. That's the funny thing about life, everything changes; nothing is ever constant. I don't know, maybe I should contact a few of my associates and see what they're up to. Half of them are probably married with a kid or two, who knows? Maybe I should have done the same. Perhaps I should break things off Kenna and go back to how it was with just Aiden. I've really let my lust make a mess of things. I mean think about it, what person in their right mind would honestly accept sharing their significant other? I think I'm going crazy. I'm finding it harder to hold on to what is supposed to be my life. Everything is ruined!

A call on my cell phone interrupts my reflective pity party. I look at the screen and see a restricted number. I contemplate pressing the ignore button and going on about my day, but the curiosity from within wins over. I receive the call. I wait to speak. I just sit and listen to whoever is on the other end of the line. From what I can decipher, it sounds like someone is breathing heavy with a television on in the background. The lack of conversation is irritating me more and more by the second. The irritation finally gets the best of me.

"Hello," I harshly verbalize expecting to get some type of response. At first, there is nothing. Then a voice emerges.

"Your time is almost up!" The mystery caller says in an off kilt fashion. It makes me think about the warning from my grandmother. I'm irritated with it all. I feel anger starting to rise.

"You know what, I don't have time for assholes that want to

sit at home and play on my phone, so if you're going to do something to me, bring it or shut the fuck up and quit contacting me!" I don't even wait for a response. I hang up the phone and return to my work.

I manage to get everything on my "to do" list done before lunch, which is perfect because I plan on going out for bite to eat. I make my way out of the office and see Kenna coming down the hall.

"Hey" I say as I greet her with a forced smile.

"Hey Tally," she says as she stops in front of me. "Is everything alright?" She asks as she examines my face. "You look a little under the weather." She adds.

"I'm okay... no actually I'm not. Can we talk in private?" I murmur while I think of a place to go for privacy.

"Sure," she responds.

"Since I'm going out to lunch, how about we talk in my car?"

"Okay."

We get to Lindy and the nervousness sets in. Then it hits me, her scent is different.

"Are you wearing a different perfume?" I ask as a means of stalling while I figure out the best way to say what's on my mind.

"Yeah, I decided to change things up."

"Oh okay well anyway I've been thinking… are we really ready to be out in the open?" I discharge my thought.

"Um I don't know, what do you mean by ready? We're not children, we're adults so if not now, when?" She responds with a slight hint of defensiveness.

"I mean with everything that's going on, I'm not sure if it's the best thing. I feel like I'm being selfish." She takes a moment to think before responding. I take it as my queue to keep talking. "I never told you about the message I received did I?"

"No, you haven't told me anything about it."

"Well, I did as Doug instructed. I went into a closet and Amy was there. She touched my face and all of these images started flashing before my eyes. The vision showed me exactly what happened to my grandmother and where she currently stays. Earlier today for some strange reason, I had an irresistible inclination to take a different route to work. I ended up taking the back streets most of the way. As I was driving, I saw the exact building from the vision. To make a long story short, my grandmother was there just as the vision had showed me. Now here's the kicker, she told me that my father is not my real father. He is actually my uncle."

"What?"

"But wait there's more. My real father is the guy from both of our dreams

"You mean…"

"Yeah that guy. He was a musician on the verge of success when he was killed. My uncle poisoned him and made it look like an accident. According to my grandmother, he murdered my father out of jealousy and hate. When she threatened to expose him, he drugged her and tried to kill her as well. Obviously, she survived but she was never the same. She is terrified of my uncle. She has been in hiding under an alias name for almost the last twenty years because of it."

"So why didn't she go to the cops?" Kenna asks.

"She didn't tell the police because she didn't have any substantial proof and she wants the family blessing to be restored, which can be done by me avenging my father's death. An eye for an eye, blood for blood, I don't know what to think, feel, or do. How do I avenge somebody that I never knew? How do I kill the man that raised me to avenge a man that until recently I never even knew existed! I'm sorry for laying all of this on you but I don't have anyone else to turn to. I didn't even tell Aiden. That's why I feel that I am definitely in over my head. I'm involved with two people at the same time, I have a dead dude that's supposed to be my father haunting me, and I keep having these unbearable headaches!" I feel tears start to trickle from my eyes. It's amazing how I went from trying to break up with Kenna, to revealing all of my problems to her. As the tears continue to fall, Kenna leans over and embraces me.

For the rest of the day, my thoughts are consumed with the choices that I have to make. On my way home, I have a festering thought of escaping it all. The festering thought is trying it's damndest to sell me on what it's offering. The sales pitch is exactly what I'm looking for, a way to get away from it all. My mind begins to fancy images of me offing myself. A scenario of me taking out my 9mm and ending it all keeps popping up in my train of thought like an annoying song. You know, the type of song where you hear it so much that you find yourself singing it and eventually liking it. Life has become too wild and unpredictable. It's funny how things can change so drastically in such a short amount of time.

Once I get home, I rush into the house. I fumble with the alarm a few times before finally disabling it. I run up stairs and go straight into my hiding place. I grab the case that contains the pistol. I remove the pistol and stare at it. I have contemplative thoughts about going through with it, "The Unpardonable Sin". *"What if the God that they preach about in the Christian and Catholic churches is real? If I go through with killing myself, according to them, I'm leaving one hell for another!"* I'm really tripping. I've lived my entire life without ever even once, considering the rules ordained by those religions. That stuff is all fairytale, smoke, and mirrors. I've come too far to puss out now. I take the clip out and load the deadly instrument. I make sure the safety is off and position the barrel of the gun to the base of my temple. I steady my nerves as I wrap my finger around the trigger. I take a deep breath and squeeze. CLICK, nothing I try it again CLICK, still no boom. Pissed off by the failed attempts, I continuously start pulling the trigger. CLICK, CLICK, CLICK, still nothing happens! I remove the gun from my head and aim it at the floor. I squeeze the trigger, BOOM. A loud thunderous force erupts from the barrel and rattles my eardrums.

"What the fuck?" I murmur as I look down through the gun smoke at the newly made hole. I hold it back up to my head and pull the trigger yet again, click, nothing. Once again, the gun fails me. "Fuck this," I grunt as I make a dash towards the kitchen. If a gun doesn't work, a knife will certainly get the job done. I enter the kitchen and grab the handle to the drawer that houses the knives. I pull, but the drawer won't budge. I add a little more strength into the next tug and still nothing. I use all of my strength with repeated tugs on the handle but still no progress. On the last tug, the handle breaks free sending me falling to the floor while the drawer is still sealed shut by some unknown intervening force. "Fuck!" I scream as I fling the drawer handle across the room. "Why won't you leave me alone? It's my life. If I want to end it, it's my choice not yours!" I yell like a mad raving lunatic at some invisible being that doesn't respond. Another great idea pops in my head. I race upstairs into the bathroom. *"I can overdose and still get the job done!"* I think as I enter the room. I open the medicine cabinet only to find that it is completely empty! Every single bottle of medication has been removed! Not one single cold tablet is left! Frustrated and desperate, I leave to check in my bedroom. I tear the room apart searching on and around the dresser, nightstand, and in all of the drawers. My efforts yield nothing but a mess that I will have to clean up later if I can't find a way to complete the intended deed. I hear sirens from outside. *"Shit! One of my neighbors must've heard the gunshot and called the cops. That's what I get for living in a well to do neighborhood."* I think as I rush down the stairs. The sirens get louder. I grab my phone and swipe the password. I then log into the security system. I see a cop car pull into my driveway. It's a good thing that my firearm is registered and I'm licensed to carry it. I will just tell them I was getting ready to clean it and it accidentally discharged. It's better than telling them *"Oh I was trying to kill myself but the ghost of my father intervened."* That would probably get me committed to the crazy farm!

KNOCK, KNOCK, KNOCK, loud solid knocks erupt from the other side of the front door. I hastily get myself together before calmly walk up to it. I look into the peephole and see two officers on the other side of the door. I take a deep breath before opening it.

"May I help you officers?" I utter with the doorknob clutched in my sweaty palm. It is a female and male cop duo. A TV cop drama instantly comes to mind at the sight of them.

"Hello ma'am, one of your neighbors called in. There was a report of gunshots." The female officer says as she keeps a steady sharp gaze on me. Cops are trained that way. If they notice the slightest hint of awkward behavior, they're on you like flies on a hot pile of shit in eighty-five degree weather.

"Oh I'm sorry about that. I was getting ready to clean my gun and it accidentally discharged."

"Okay well may we come in?" She asks clearly doubting my explanation. That's her cop instinct telling her to cross all t's and dot all i's. In most cases, a healthy dose of suspicion can make the difference between life and death. Especially when dealing with real criminals.

"Sure," I answer back as I cordially invite them in. "See I was over here by my couch about to clean it when my dog Max startled me." The lie effortlessly spills out of mouth. "Max, come here boy!" I call Max as a means of further substantiating my claim. He bashfully comes into the room with a chew toy clutched in his mouth.

"So you're sure that that's all that happened?" The male partner inquires.

"Yes, that is all that happened. I got startled by Max as I was in the process of cleaning my gun."

"Okay well do you have the proper registration for the weapon?"

"Yes I do, give me a moment to retrieve it please. Thank you." I rush upstairs and go into my important document cabinet. I recover the needed paper work and return downstairs.

"Here you go," I say as I hand over the papers. They both gloss over the documentation before handing it back.

"Be more careful in the future." The male cop instructs, with a hint of apprehension in his eyes. He may have his doubts about my account of how the incident occurred but what can he do? I provided a solid explanation and appropriate documentation.

"You have a nice night Ms.," the female officer says.

"You both do the same, and please be safe out in those crazy streets." As I show them out, the female officer takes one last look back before hesitantly exiting.

CHAPTER 18

It's now or never. I try to contain my anger as I ring the doorbell. "Hold on I'm coming." My mother yells as I take in the cold autumn air. There is no easy way to go about this, so I just have to get straight to the point. The door opens and as always, my mom greets me with a warm smile. "Hi honey, haven't heard from you in while." She gushes as she attempts to hug me.

"Yeah I've been busy." I respond as I give her a loose forced one back. I wonder how much of the truth she knows about her husband. "Is dad here?" I ask in a low subtle tone, as I step into the house.

"Um not yet why?" She responds with a puzzled expression.

"I really need to talk to you alone, it's important."

"Okay, is everything alright?"

"Not really I want to talk to you first before I talk to him."

"Alright, well let's go into the kitchen." I follow her into the kitchen. I'm really making an effort to hide my anger.

"Okay Tal, so what's on your mind?"

"I know you love me and that's why I need you to be honest with me." I state as I figure out the best way to continue. "If you knew something that was very important, would you tell me the complete truth, or would you lie and try to cover it up?" There, I got it out. Now let's see how she responds.

"Honey what on earth are you talking about?" My mother asks in a half-honest manner. I can tell her brain is working in overdrive trying to figure out what's coming next. She has probably feared this day for years. Thoughts of this moment have probably been a frequent visitor in her mind. I know the guilt of living with such a secret still lingers.

"I'm talking about my father."

"What about him?"

"My real father," My words are more shocking than aiming a loaded pistol at her. They leave her speechless. Her eyes instantly widen and her jaw slightly gapes.

"How… I hoped and prayed that this day would never come. I guess there's no point in denying it. How did you find out?" She looks intensely at the table as she wrings her hands.

"So it's true?"

"Yes, it is true. I'm sorry for lying to you all these years. I thought it was best if I didn't tell you the truth about him. How did you find out?" She searches my face for the answer, no sense in keeping her in suspense.

"My grandmother told me, she told me everything."

"That's not possible, your grandmother is dead!"

"No she is very much alive. How could you lie to me and marry my father's brother? That's wrong on so many levels!" I let some of my anger out.

"Who are you to judge me? You don't know what went on back then! You don't know the choices that I've had to make then and ever since!" My mother expels with equally matched discontent.

"Oh, so you felt it was a good choice to hook up with your daughter's uncle? Did you feel good about your choice of not telling me about my real father?"

"You didn't know him! I did it for you, to keep you safe! He was involved in things that I never wanted you to know about!"

"What are you talking about?" I ask. Now we're getting somewhere. The truth is finally getting out!

"He was dark… ungodly… he was losing himself in the world the he was creating. He wasn't always like that though. He got involved with the wrong group of people, devil worshippers I think. It was some kind of cult, hands of something or other. After he joined them, he became very secretive. He said that he needed it to go further in his craft. I assume that you already know about his craft."

"Yes I know what he did. And I know that he used the name Armichael when he performed."

"Correct and even though I'm not a super religious person, I didn't feel comfortable with the path he was taking. He was going in the wrong direction. He became completely obsessed with his new way of life. He kept talking about the truth and someone named Amy." I see tears starting to form in her eyes.

"How did my father die?" I ask, all the while hoping that it doesn't correspond with my grandmother's version of the events.

"He... died in a fire. I talked to him earlier that week, and your father, I mean your uncle went out to see him. Your father was so happy. Things were starting to happen for his career, he and your uncle were patching up their relationship, and we were back on speaking terms as well. He said that he would be back for us the following week. He said that he wanted to work on our family. He was really looking forward to being a dad, he—" The sound of a car pulling into the driveway interrupts our conversation. My father's killer has just arrived. The door opens. I hear him take his shoes off and make his way to the closet.

"Hey peaches, I'm home." He announces as he settles in.

"Hi dear,"

"Is Talia here?" He inquires, as his footfalls get closer.

"Yes," she answers as she wipes her face and straightens herself out. I'm so angry. I don't even know if I want to talk to him. I contemplate grabbing a knife and jamming it right into his deceitful evil heart! As he enters the kitchen, a headache starts to make itself known. I'm filled with rage at the sight of him.

"Hey Tal," he says as he greets me with a smile.

"Hello uncle Corvis!" I respond. The look on his face quickly changes from "oh what a pleasant surprise", to "you fucking little bastard bitch", which would be an accurate label considering the circumstances. He looks over at my mother, and then looks back at me. He is caught completely off guard by my response.

"So you told her?" He asks as he looks back towards my mother.

"No, your mother did." she answers with a straight face.

"How... she's dead!" He declares as he begins to pace back and forth.

"No, she's not dead. You tried to murder her just like you murdered my father!" I state in a dead serious tone. He sees the way my mother looks at him and he quickly goes on the defense against my accusation.

"I did what? Are you having mental issues again? What, are you going to pull a gun on me too? I don't know what you're talking about but you really need to check yourself because you're way out of line!" He exclaims as he loosens a tie from around his neck. His look intensifies as he turns his full focus towards me before continuing to speak. "I did not murder or try to murder anyone! I honestly thought that she was dead! I haven't heard from her in almost twenty years! She is crazy!" He exclaims in an infuriated tone "and if you're going to come to my house with such bullshit accusations, you're no longer welcome here! Get the hell out now!" He raises his arm with his finger pointed toward the doorway. I'm so angry that I involuntarily start to laugh. My rage takes over.

"That's good, because I don't want to be around a fucking lying murderer!" I yell as I get up and fume towards the doorway. He grabs my shoulder as I attempt to make my way out. "What the fuck are you doing?" I ask, fully ready to defend myself if need be. He looks at me for a second before speaking.

"You're acting just like him!" He says in a brutally harsh manner.

"Whatever!" I respond as I snatch away from him. I quickly exit the house and hop back into Lindy. I rev her up. She sounds as angry as I feel. I rip out of the driveway and race back home. As I'm driving along, my thoughts are all over the place. I know that he killed my father. How could my mom be such a whore and marry him? I hate them both, almost enough to… KILL THEM!

CHAPTER 19

I'm nearly home when my phone begins to vibrate. Thinking that it may be one of my parents, I apprehensively grab it out of my pocket. I look at the phone screen and see the number is restricted.

"Hello?" My voice spills into the phone, breaking the silence. I hear shallow breathing on the other end of the line. "Hello?" I repeat in a slightly elevated attitude.

"You're dead!" A deep ominous voice on the other end verbalizes.

"You know what, I'm sick of your bullshit threats. If you dare come anywhere near me, I'll have a bullet with your name on it!" I shout before abruptly ending the call. I pull into the driveway and expediently exit Lindy. My headache is getting worse by the minute. As I approach the front door, I notice a small package on the steps. I cautiously continue to move towards it. I've watched enough action/crime shows, to know that there is a highly probable chance that the unknown package may contain a bomb! I build up my courage and slowly pick up the box. As I hold the strange package in my hand, I contemplate whether I should shake it, just say the hell with it and rip it open, or take it inside with me. I choose choice c.

Once inside, I place the mysterious item on an end table in the living room. As soon as I place it down, my phone starts to vibrate yet again. I don't want to answer it. I don't feel like dealing with some asshole that wants to play games. I try to ignore it, but something inside, is really urging me to answer it. I quickly swipe the screen.

"Look, you need to stop calling me with this bullshit!" I scream into the phone. I've had enough with the games.

"Is everything alright Talia?" I recognize the voice immediately, its Aiden.

"Hey baby, I'm sorry about that. Someone keeps playing on my phone and it's pissing me off. Well I'm already pissed off because of other things but the prank calls are making it worse, plus I have a headache."

"So what's going on?" Aiden asks in a concerned sincere manner.

"A lot more than I care to go into detail about," I say in a brash tone. Damn I feel like such a cunt. I didn't mean to project my anger at him. He isn't the cause of my problems; I'm probably the cause of some of his. "I'm sorry for being snappy, there's just a lot going on right now. I have issues with my parents, I just recently had to fire some people at work, some weird stalker keeps calling me, and I keep getting these headaches. Everything is crazy in my world right now."

"It's okay, I understand. I talked to my mother about our situation." Aiden says. Oh great more drama, just what I need to hear.

"So what did she say?" I inquire though at this point I don't even think I care to know. My headache is killing me, and now just isn't a good time.

"Well at first, she was highly disappointed and upset with you. She doesn't agree with us still being together but I told her that I needed to be with you. I threatened to stop talking to her if she kept on about it. Even though she doesn't understand, she would still rather keep me in her life than lose me."

"So she is okay with it because of your father's death, I mean that's what it sounds like to me. It's sounds like she doesn't want to lose another person that she loves, so she will tolerate things that she doesn't agree with."

"It's that and the fact that she just found out Ashley is a lesbian."

"Whoa... Ashley? Your sister is gay?" I was not expecting to hear such jaw dropping information. Ashley is definitely too hot to deny her snatch of the pleasures of a nice hard cock. "So how did she find out?"

"Well we've always speculated it but we never said anything about it. Even my father thought she was. I mean she tried to cover it up by having boyfriends but it just looked so forced and put-on. Remember when we went on a double date with her and her boyfriend at the time, which I think his name was Steve but anyway remember?"

"Yeah I remember that, I thought something was weird but I just assumed it was because she wasn't that into him." I respond as I head upstairs to find something comfortable to change into.

"That's what I thought too but when I asked her about it, she said it was something else but she wouldn't go into detail. Well, it turns out that she has known that she was gay since she was in middle school. She said that that was when she had her first experience, it happened at a sleepover."

"Wow, I'm surprised she didn't say that she was born that way. That's what a lot of people claim."

As I enter my bedroom, I find a bottle of aspirin sitting plain as day on my dresser *"How the hell did that get there?"* I think before grabbing it. When I was having suicidal thoughts, I couldn't find a single pill. Now there is an entire bottle resting in plain view. Filled with disbelief, I rush into the bathroom and open the medicine cabinet. To my surprise, all of the medicines I remembered putting inside of it after the move are there. "Whoa this is too much." I mumble as I hastily exit the room.

"What?" Aiden asks.

"Nothing just thinking aloud, hold on." I respond. With Aiden on hold, I return back downstairs and grab a bottle of smart water out of the refrigerator. I get a glass from the cabinet, open up the bottle, and begin to pour.

"Aiden are you still there?"

"Yes."

"Okay well as I was saying, most of the gay people that I've encountered have stated that they were born that way." I assert before popping two aspirin. I quickly gulp down them down with the water to eliminate the chance of tasting that disgusting medicine taste. You know the taste that you get when uncoated pills are in your mouth too long ugh! I get a bad taste just thinking about it!

"So are —" I cut Aiden off before he has the chance to finish his question.

"I know what you're about to say and the answer is no. Besides I'm not gay, I'm bisexual. There's a difference." I state defensively.

"So does that mean that you won't ever completely shift over to that preference? I'm sorry for seeming ignorant but it's all completely new to me. I mean I've dealt with people who had other sexual preferences, but it was different because they weren't in my family or someone that I'm seeing intimately."

"I understand." I respond, not completely sure of the answer myself. "Well anyway, I've got a headache that I'm nursing so I'm about to lay down for a few. I'll call you when I get up okay?"

"Alright well make sure you do because I miss talking to you. I love you baby," Aiden utters.

"I love you too babes." I reply with my heart longing to have him near me.

I hang up the phone and remember the weird package. Curiosity looms as I stare at the enigma resting on the end table in the living room. I'm tired of waiting and wondering what's inside. I pick up the box. I grab one of the corners of the packaging and begin to tear it open. A faint undesirable smell escapes through the opening. It makes me delay the process. I contemplate tossing it in the trash out back but then my curiosity wouldn't be appeased. Against my better judgment, I continue opening it. The smell grows stronger with each part that I pull off. Once I remove all of the packaging, I see a shoebox. I open the shoebox. I drop it as an involuntary reflex upon seeing what's inside. The box hits the floor. The impact of the fall releases the carcass of a dead rat. The rat has a note attached to it. The smell hit's me full force along with a queasy feeling as I gaze at the mangled corpse. I feel the need to upchuck as the nausea kicks in. I cover my mouth and make a dash for the kitchen. I make it to the garbage can just in the nick of time. The contents of my stomach rush out of my mouth like a volcanic eruption. I feel the stomach acid coarsely flow over my esophagus. I hate throwing up. I always find myself with a sore throat and hoarse voice days after the fact. I finish releasing, clean my mouth, and grab some disposable gloves and a garbage bag from out of the cleaning supply closet. Once my stomach settles, I make my way back into the living room. Someone is really a sick fuck to have the audacity to send such a thing! I take pictures of everything for evidence sake. That way if the person that is out to kill me succeeds, I will have enough evidence for the authorities to catch the sicko. I squeamishly pick up the dead rat and remove the note before tossing it into the garbage bag. I also toss the box and wrapping in the bag before opening the note.

"Your time is up. Now it's time for you to die! All rats must atone for their sins!"

The note is scrawled in blood, which I assume is from the rat.

I toss the note in the bag as well. I want to throw it all away, but I figure it might be in my best interest to call the cops and turn it over to them. I think that that would be a better course of action to take. I seal up the bag, put it outside of the front door, and take off the plastic gloves. I then swipe my phone lock and log onto the security feed. I scroll through the footage. I stop at the sight of a man in all black with his face covered walking up to my front door. I play it back several times trying to get a clear view of the man. He's so well covered, that it's hard to make out a definite identity. After several more attempts of trying to figure out the culprit's identity, I give up and dial the authorities.

"Hello, West Shore Police Department. Please hold," A voice on the other end says quickly, not giving me a chance to speak. I'm placed on hold for a few moments.

"Caller, are you still there?" A woman on the other line says.

"Yes I'm still here. I would like to report threats of violence."

"Okay and, what exactly is the nature of your problem?"

"I've been receiving threatening calls and text messages and today when I got home I found a package on my front porch. When I opened it, there was a dead rat and a note written in blood attached to it. I also have surveillance video of the person dropping it off."

"Oh wow, okay hold on. I'm transferring you to Detective Warner." The woman on the line says before I'm placed on another few moments of silence.

"Detective Warner speaking," rumbles a gravelly voice.

"Hello Detective Warner, my name is Talia Rhodes." It feels so weird saying my last name now that I know the truth. "I'm calling today because I've been receiving death threats."

"Okay Ms. Rhodes and what is the extent of the threats?" Detective Warner asks.

"Talia, just Talia," I correct him before continuing. "First it was just calls and text messages. Today I came home and found a package waiting for me. When I opened the package, I found a dead rat inside with a note attached to it."

"So what did the note say?"

"It said your time is up. Now it's time for you to die! All rats must atone for their sins! I also have surveillance footage of the culprit dropping it off."

"Okay, and were you able to clearly identify the person on the footage?"

"No. The person is covered from head to toe. The only thing that I can decipher from the footage is that it appears to be a man."

"Okay, well do any possible suspects come to mind?" The detective asks. I think about everything that has transpired, leading up to the start of the calls and messages.

"Um well the only person that I can think of is a former employee that assaulted me after I terminated him." Shane is the only person that comes to mind. I know he did it. He has to be the one. That asshole has had it out for me since forever.

"Alright Talia, what is the name of the possible suspect?"

"His name is Shane McGruden. His date of birth is 07-14-1979." Don't ask me how I remember his birth date. I guess when you dislike someone as much as I dislike him it's easier to remember things like that.

"When did you terminate him?"

"Less than a week ago,"

"Okay and when you fired him it led to an altercation correct?"

"Yes. Shortly after I fired him, he left the office that we were in and headed towards my boss's office. My boss is the Department/Operations Manager. I tried to stop him from going to see my boss because as the Office Manager it's my responsibility to handle the office employees. I didn't want to risk looking like I couldn't handle the functions of the job, so I gave my best effort to stop him. Shane was determined to see him. On my final attempt to stop him, he turned around and swung a punch at me. When it missed, he smacked me and then proceeded on his way. That among other things is why I whole-heartedly believe that he is behind the harassment. I know the guy wants to kill me!"

"Okay… so did you report the incident?"

"No."

"Why not,"

"I didn't think it was that big of a deal. I was just happy to see him leave."

"Well you probably should've. I'm going to send officers out to collect the items for evidence and view the footage. They will also need the information of the security company that provides your surveillance service. They should be there within the hour."

"Thank you."

"You're welcome. Have a good evening."

I hang up the line and go into the kitchen. I want to eat but I can still see and smell the dead rat. I know it's purely psychological but I just can't shake it. I decide to put eating dinner on hold. I go to my computer and fire it up. Once I log on, I check my Facebook page. I haven't checked it in ages. I'm surprised that I still have friends on it. I can't even remember the last time I updated my status. I practically have notifications bursting from the little world icon. After getting bored with reading a whole bunch of pointless statuses, I log out of Facebook and go to check my email. Nothing but spam, spam, and more spam! I do a little surfing before getting bored and shutting the computer down. The sound of a car pulling into the driveway catches my attention. I grab my phone and log onto my surveillance system. I see a dodge charger with police decals sitting in the driveway. I go to open the door. I see the same officers from the previous visit.

"Hello Ms. Rhodes, we're here to pick up the evidence and file a report," the male officer says. I guess the whole death threat thing makes my gun-cleaning lie more plausible. I step outside and show them the bag containing the evidence. They open it up and take a peak. The female officer quickly closes the bag, but not before the tart decomposed odor escapes from its plastic drawstring prison. They have me answer a few questions, I show them the video footage, and then they leave. I close the door and plop down on the couch. It's been a long day. I'm tired and frustrated. I grab the remote and click on the TV. I flip through the channels desperately looking for something to take my mind off everything. I really need a temporary escape from my life. An episode of "South Beach Tow" catches my attention. A fight on the show makes me laugh so hard, that for a brief second I forget that I have a headache. The situations that take place on the show are so over the top that they seem scripted. There is no way possible that the stuff that happens on it is real. I end up watching two and a half episodes before dozing off.

The ringing of the doorbell, snaps me out of my brief catnap. I click the cable button to check the time. It's a quarter after eight. *"Who would be coming over unannounced?* I wonder as I wipe the sleep from my eyes. *"Maybe it's Aiden."* I think as I get up from the couch and walk towards the door. I look through the peephole.

Just as I suspected, Aiden is on the other side of the door. I quickly open it. Before I can even give him a proper greeting, he rushes in, wraps his arms around me, and plants his soft cold lips on mine.

"Hey sexy are you happy to see me?" He asks as he takes a break from showing me affection. He has on a dark brown leather coat with a burgundy scarf.

"Yes and I missed you too superman," I joke as I flash a playful smile.

"Ha, ha real funny I'm still upset with you for not calling me when that asshole attacked you." He retorts. Knowing he genuinely cares means everything to me. I feel myself smiling. He is as handsome as ever. I have missed him profusely. My heart has yearned for him.

"I've been thinking, why don't you call Kenna over and we can all hang out," he says, catching me completely off guard.

"So I guess that means that you're okay with everything?" I question as I study his face.

"I didn't say that I was okay with everything but I'm trying to adjust because I really want you. Talia… my life is empty without you. When I wasn't talking to you, it was hell. I'm willing to give us another shot but in order to do that I have to give Kenna a chance. Because, whether I like it or not she's a part of your life. So if I'm with you, then she is a part of mine as well." Wow, it's just like Kenna said. Aiden is definitely beginning to warm up to the situation. While in mid thought, my phone begins to vibrate. I grab it out of my pocket. Speak of the devil, its Kenna.

"Hey babe," I answer as Aiden hangs up his coat and scarf.

"Hey Talia, do you feel like having company?" She asks in a cutesy, timidly sensual manner.

"Actually I do, or rather we do. Aiden and I were just talking about you."

"Oh really," she sounds surprised by my response.

"Yeah, Aiden wants to give it a shot. I figure we can all hang out, watch a movie, and go from there. We'll talk about it more when you get here."

"Okay well I'm on my way as soon as I get done eating. See you soon. Bye."

"Alright bye,"

CHAPTER 20

We are deeply engaged in foreplay when the doorbell rings. *"It must be Kenna."* I think as I stop giving Aiden fellatio. I straighten myself out and get up to answer the door. I check through the peephole just to be certain before opening it. Having death threats loom over one's head can have that effect. I see the sexy red head goddess on the other side of the door. I quickly open it.

"Hey Talia," she expresses in a seductively pleasant manner. She is bundled up in a warm fur lined brown coat. She gives me a hug and attempts to kiss me. I jerk my head back and try to prevent her. "What's wrong?" She asks with a quizzed look on her face.

"Well I don't mean to be vulgar but I don't know of any other way to put this. I was in the middle of something." I try to give her a subtle hint without being too vague. She looks and see's Aiden reaching for a comforter to cover his exposed muscular lower half.

"Oh… so I see you guys got started without me huh?" She says while giving me a playful smile.

"Actually, you're right on time. The party just started." I respond as I take her coat and invite her in. She smiles at Aiden. Aiden smiles back with one of those awkward smiles that a person gives when they're uncomfortable.

"No need to cover up handsome," Kenna says to Aiden as we make our way over to him.

"She quickly bunches up her hair and kneels down in front of him. She then takes over where I left off. Aiden gives me a weird look.

"It's okay." I mouth as I watch Kenna perform. I watch with mixed feelings. I'm turned on and a little jealous at the same time. I wonder if Aiden felt like this when I told him about the situation with her. While deeply engaged in her performance, Kenna starts to remove her clothing. She unhooks her bra, releasing her soft supple breasts. She removes her button up blouse and bra without missing a beat. Aiden is fully under the spell of her lip service. His eyes are closed and his head is thrown back. Sick of feeling left out, I begin kissing on Kenna's exposed soft flesh. My lips passionately caress her skin as I slowly work my way up to Aiden. Before long, we are both engaged in pleasing him. He moans loudly as we continue stimulating him. Kenna stops and speaks.

"Mmm, let's take this upstairs." She says in sultry tone.

"Okay," Aiden says in a low breathy manner. The moment is very thrilling. We are on the cusp of something that I have been secretly hoping for since I accepted Kenna back into my circle. I haven't been this enthusiastic about sex since my first threesome in college. It feels like I'm reliving it. We excitedly make our way upstairs and into the bedroom.

Once inside of the bedroom, Kenna and I strip and sprawl ourselves out over the bed. We begin caressing one another as we stare at Aiden with anticipation. I've dreamt of this moment so many times, now it's becoming a reality.

"Come on Aiden," we both say in unison like a singing group in perfect seductive harmony. I wait on edge as Aiden decides which one of us to engage first. Aiden stares long and hard at the both of us before making his way to the bed. He descends onto the bed and seconds later, I feel him plunge into my soft, moist, warm walls.

"Yes," I moan in approval as he begins stroking and stoking the flames of lust. Kenna begins sucking my fully aroused nipples while Aiden labors away with slow intentional thrusts. Her soft, wet, warm mouth on my flesh in conjunction with Aiden's rhythmic massaging of my walls send an acute tingling sensation throughout my body. It gets so intense that I have no choice but to succumb to the erotic assault. "Ugh, I'm about to cum baby!" I announce before erupting in a series of shakes and twitches. "Oh fuck!" I shout as my nails dig into the mattress.

"My turn daddy," Kenna says as I roll over and she takes my place. She doesn't wait for him to make the first move. She grabs his hard cum soaked cock, and shoves it inside of her moist, "can't wait to cum" pussy. I watch in a satisfied state as my two lovers begin their erotic dance. A smile forms on my face as they share each other's lust. They grind and moan in unison. Each seems to be enjoying the other equally. Kenna turns her head towards me and gives me a naughty sex face.

"Cum for me baby," I utter as I reach over and touch her breast.

"Here it comes!" She groans as her legs begin to shake. "Ahh," shoots out of her mouth as she releases her saucy essence.

"Oh shit," Aiden groans loudly as he follows suit.

"I hope that was as good as it looked." I comment as Aiden collapses to the bed. We lay in the after math of passion. Kenna and I are nestled against Aiden. I imagine Corvis' face of disapproval as I smile with glee. After a while, I feel so relaxed that I end up resuming the nap that was previously interrupted.

"Talia..." the sound of someone whispering my name wakes me from my siesta. I check Aiden and Kenna. They're both sound asleep. *"Talia..."* I hear the voice again, except this time it sounds like several voices in accord. They sound hallow, like echoes. I get up and follow them. They sound like they're coming from downstairs. I slowly inch my way down the stairs. They make that weird sound that wooden stairs that are carpeted make. It's like a muffled, creaking floor shifting sound. The voices get louder as I follow them. I follow them into the living room where I see my

phone lit up. I pick it up from the coffee table. A picture of Jeff is on the screen. Somehow, my phone mysteriously opened up Jeff's contact info. I check my recent call log to see if he called. I find nothing. I think about calling him but I'm sure that he's still pissed over his termination. I mentally play out multiple scenarios before deciding that it's best to leave it alone. I grab my phone and head back upstairs.

The chatter of conversation wakes me up to the new day. I hear Kenna and Aiden chatting away like two old friends. I assume that I'm the topic of discussion. I look at my phone. I still have twenty minutes to rest before I have to get ready for work. I'm still puzzled about Jeff, my phone, and the voices. The incident last night was truly weird. Unable to clear my thoughts, I decide to get up and forego the additional rest time. I make a quick trip to the bathroom before heading downstairs. The chattering ceases as I enter the kitchen.

"Don't stop talking on my account," I blurt out as their mischievous smiles greet me. I know that they were talking about me and I'm guessing that it was in a good way.

"Talia you're silly. We weren't talking about you… in a bad way." Kenna playfully adjusts her words to fit her naughty persona.

"Oh okay, so what were you two great lovers discussing?" I inquire as I grab the orange juice from the refrigerator.

"We were discussing last night." Aiden says as he looks at me with his hypnotic blues.

"Yeah, I think we all needed that! It was so good that I don't even want to leave. I wish I could call off and play for the rest of the day!" Kenna exclaims with great delight. Her words trigger flashbacks in my mind.

"I'm about to go get ready. Join me if you like." I offer the invitation for a little pre-work fun.

"I think we'll take you up on your offer." Kenna responds and gives Aiden a quick look. Life can't get much better than this. I smile at her before leaving the room.

Once in the bathroom, I turn on the shower and wait a few seconds for the water to heat up. While I'm waiting, thoughts about the death threats that I've been receiving come to mind.

Thoughts of the weird incident involving Jeff's contact info and my phone pop up as well.

"What the hell is going on?" I wonder as I step into the warm inviting shower. I hear the door open as I let the hot shower spray over my face. I grab my washcloth and wipe my face. I look through the semitransparent curtains. I see Kenna and Aiden undressing. Kenna steps into the shower followed by Aiden. I'm glad that my house came with a slightly larger shower/tub. It definitely has its advantages. I lust as the water rolls down our bodies. I lose track of time as we engage in an intense exchange of kissing and fondling. Caught up in the heat of the moment, Aiden make a move to insert his love inside of me. I reluctantly halt his efforts.

"If we start something, we might not make it to work." I say in a seriously truthful tone.

"She's right, because you're going to have to give it to me right after you give it to her." Kenna adds as she takes a time out from placing light kisses on my back.

"I guess you have a point. How about we finish this later?" He asks as I grab my body wash and bath sponge.

"Um, that sounds like a tempting offer but only if you promise to give a performance as equally pleasing as last night." I murmur as Kenna's breasts lightly brush against my back.

"Yeah because it was definitely enjoyable," Kenna says concurring with my sentiment.

"Oh I most certainly can deliver." He responds with an air of confidence. We finish our shower and get ready to face the day.

"So do you want to ride to work together?" I ask Kenna before Aiden heads out to warm up all of our vehicles.

"I would but I have to make a stop before I head into work." Kenna responds.

"Okay," I reply.

CHAPTER 21

"Talia I really must have a word with you." Mr. Beck says after entering my office. From the look on his face, I can't tell if it's something good that he wants to discuss, or something bad. The last time he needed to have a word with me, it ended with me having to fire someone. I brace myself before responding.

"Okay sir what's up?" I inquire as I slightly rearrange the papers on my desk. He takes a seat and gets himself situated before he resumes speaking.

"I know that you're probably expecting me to say something bad like requesting you to fire someone but I just stopped by to commend you on the great job that you're doing." I'm completely thrown off by his praise. Wow, I was definitely not expecting it.

"Well thank you for noticing sir," I respond in a surprised manner.

"I just wanted to say keep up the good work and everyone in the office is doing fine. Oh and by the way, we have some interviews scheduled for next week. I also put a few projects on hold. I figured it would keep you and everyone else from being burdened by the extra workload. Sorry it took so long, but I told human resources to be stringent on the applicants. I'm not trying to hire another Shane or Jeff and I don't need some temps coming in and expecting to get hired in either!"

"Understood sir, I wouldn't want to have to fire another Shane or Jeff, especially Shane. I don't think my face could take another one of those!" I infuse a joke to lighten the mood. Mr. Beck lets out a slight uncomfortable laugh before responding.

"That was a good one Talia. Once human resources have selected the applicants, I need you to do the first round of interviews.

"Whoa, you want me to do interviews? I'm—"

"I know that you don't have much experience with doing interviews but don't worry. I will have the interview questions prepared for you. All you have to do is ask them and feel the applicants out."

"Okay sir, you can trust me. I'll take care of it." I respond in a confident manner. I've only conducted one interview in my entire life and that was a mock one in college but how hard could it really be? Mr. Beck leaves in good spirits. I'm glad we have a good rapport, truth be told he is a great person to work for. I guess that makes doing my job a little easier.

I manage to get everything on my agenda done, including a practice interview with Jessica. It took a couple of tries but I managed to get serious honest answers out of her. I finish my day and get ready for the long drive home through traffic. As I'm making my way out of my office, Mr. Beck stops me.

"Hey Talia just one more thing before you leave." He says as he approaches.

"Um okay," I respond while zipping up my coat.

"I don't mean to be in your personal life but there has been word traveling around the company that you and another female employee are carrying on a relationship outside of work." Mr.

Beck's inquiry is confirmation. It's official. Pretty much everyone in the company knows. Mr. Beck is always the last person to know about workplace gossip. So if the news has gotten to him. Then it's spread to everybody. I hate that have to lie to Mr. Beck because he has always been upfront with me but it would be absolute suicide to confirm to rumor.

"If you're referring to our friendship, then yes we have a relationship outside of work."

"Okay well I was asking because I was told that it was something more than a friendship. If that is indeed the case, one of you may have to find employment elsewhere. Company policy states that relationships of that nature may pose a conflict of interest."

"I understand."

"Good. Have a great weekend." I feel my phone vibrate as Mr. Beck finishes his statement.

"You do the same and thank you for having this talk with me. See you Monday." As I head out of the department, my phone begins vibrating again. I grab it out of my pocket as I reach the elevator. It's Kenna. I missed her call by a mere second. I quickly unlock my phone and call her back. She answers just as the elevator doors are opening.

"Hey babe, what's up?" I ask while pressing the garage floor button.

"I'm pretty sure you've heard by now that everyone knows." Kenna responds in a solemn tone.

"Actually, my boss approached me as I was heading out. You didn't tell anyone did you?" I know what the obvious answer is but I ask anyway.

"Of course not, I denied everything but I don't think my supervisor is convinced. I'm not feeling so good right now. Can I come over later?"

"Um, I don't think that that would be a good idea." I respond as my mind switches gears from workplace gossip to the persistent death threats that I've been receiving.

"Why not, what's wrong?" Kenna asks. I'm tempted to tell her a lie. I don't want her to be worried about me. I contemplate my choices as I reach Lindy. I stick in the key and turn her on. Even though it goes against my better judgment, I decide to go with the truth, there are already enough lies in my life.

"I don't know how to tell you this, but I think Shane is going to try to kill me."

"Are you still getting the calls and text messages?" She asks with concern evident in her voice.

"Yes but it's a lot more serious now. Yesterday, before you and Aiden came over, I received a package.

"Okay… what kind of package?"

"Uh, well… I received a package with a dead rat that had a note written in blood attached to it."

"Oh shit! Are you serious?" By her response, I can tell that she's going to be a worrywart. I have to think of something to say that will put her at ease.

"I already got the cops involved plus I have the security system so even if he tries anything, he won't get far. Trust me, the cops in my neighborhood would be on the scene in a matter of minutes. The only reason that I didn't want you coming back over yet is because I'm still kind of freaked out by it. Besides, I need some time to myself to recuperate from last night

"Talia I honor and love you." Kenna says in a glum low voice.

"I love and honor you too Kenna." I respond. "I'm about to

start driving, so I will call you as soon as I get home honey."

"Okay Talia, take care and make sure that you do."

"I will." Thinking about Shane makes my blood boil. I'm so angry that I don't even bother turning on the radio. I think about what would happen if he actually did succeed in killing me. I refuse to let that happen. I nearly avoid hitting a dumbass that swerves into my lane without using their blinker. "Fucking idiot," I yell as I forcefully mash on my horn and drive past her. The heated altercation with Shane replays in my head as I battle my way through traffic. After a fifteen minute dead stop on the freeway, I finally manage to get into the clear. I get off at my exit and continue my trip home.

As I reach my street, hunger makes itself known. I feel my stomach rumble as I pull up to my house. I park Lindy and I take a careful scan around the area before proceeding towards the front door. The coast is clear, no weird packages, letters, or other unpleasant surprises. I grab the mail and immediately notice coupons from one of my favorite pizza places, PJ's. *"Hands down, PJ's has the best pizza around!"* is the familiar jingle that plays in my head as I examine the sales flyer. I feel my stomach continue to rumble as I visualize the order I will soon place. Thanks to the coupons and pleasant memories, I'm dying to get some PJ's pizza. I haven't had a pie from them in ages. A handwritten attachment offering free delivery for any order only sweetens the deal. *"I'll definitely order something in a few."* I think as I put my key into the lock. Once inside the house, a weird feeling comes over me. A light bulb turns on in my head. *"The alarm isn't beeping."* It's not making the sounds that it would normally make before I punch the code in to disarm it. I look at the system. From what I can deduce, the power source has been interrupted.

"Shit." I mumble as I make several more attempts to get it back online. All of my efforts are useless. I call the security company to see if they can resolve the issue.

"C.T.S. security, please hold." A man's voice on the other end says followed by a horrid jazz rendition of an Alicia Keys' song. I hate when they do that! Is there anybody alive that still listens to jazz? "Hello this is Keith speaking, how my I assist you today?" The person on the other end of the line says. I'm thankful that my ears are rescued from the torture of jazz.

"Hello Keith, this is Talia Rhodes. I'm calling because my service is having an interruption. I just got home and when I opened the front door, I noticed my alarm system didn't start beeping. Now it keeps saying power source low."

"Okay let me transfer you to our tech help desk."

"Alright thank you." I respond as I try to keep my lack of patience to a minimum. Once again, I'm placed on hold. Back to crappy music hell!

"Hello Thomas speaking, how may I assist you?"

"Hi Thomas, this is Talia Rhodes. I'm calling because as I explained to the previous person, my service is having some type of interruption. When I arrived home and opened the front door, the alarm system didn't start beeping. The words "power source low" keeps flashing across the screen."

"Alright Ms. Rhodes, that sounds like and electrical issue, I'm going to get my electrical specialist on the line."

"But I thought that you were going to help me. I mean what's the point of me explaining my problem to you if you're not the one that's able to help me?" I say in an agitated tone. I hate when I call a customer service line and get placed on hold and then transferred.

I really hate when one or the other happens more than once during the same call. It really pisses me off when I'm placed on hold and forced to listen to crappy music, or prompts. Then after suffering in hold limbo, I'm taken off hold while they attempt to transfer me, but what really adds insult to injury is when they end up disconnecting me instead.

"I'm sorry if this is causing you any inconvenience. I'm just doing my job. May you please hold again while I transfer you?" I spend a few moments in defiant mode, not uttering a single word.

"Ma'am is it okay if I put you on hold while I transfer?"

"Don't call me ma'am. It's Talia and yeah okay, whatever." I grumble as I mentally kick myself for not going with a major provider. I'm placed on hold yet again!

"Ms. Rhodes?" A new voice on the line rescues me from a jazzed out cover of Nirvana's "Smells like teen spirit." I don't know who decided that it would be a cool idea to do a jazz version of it.

"Talia and yes I'm still here." I respond as I get more agitated by the second.

"Hi Talia, my name is Scott and I'm going to try my best to

355

help resolve your issue. Now it appears that the area you live in has experienced a power shortage. According to the electric company, a squirrel got into a substation. It happened earlier while you were at work I assume. Several customers near your location have called in with same type of problem. We're working with the electric company to get things back up and running. Now I need you to check all of the rooms in your house for electricity."

"Okay I'm going to check them now can you hold for a second please?" I ask while checking the lights in the vestibule. Next, I test the TV and lights in the living room before moving on into the dining room and the kitchen. So far, everything else is working. The dining room and kitchen lights are working, and the refrigerator is running. I quickly check the rest of the house before getting back on the line. "Scott, are you still there?" I ask while heading back down stairs.

"Yes, is everything working?"

"Everything but the alarm system," I shoot back in a negative disappointed manner. "I have been receiving death threats, which is why I really need my security!" I didn't want to reveal my reason for urgency but what else could I do, it's just like what I learned in my marketing class back in college. A sense of urgency goes a long way.

"Oh wow... well, we're temporarily short staffed and booked up with tech issues because of the power outage. However, due to the severity of your issue I'm placing you on the priority waiting list as we speak."

"Okay so by what time should I expect a technician?"

"Well since I placed you on the priority list, you should expect them within the next four hour block of time. That's typically how we schedule it. The technician will call when they're en route."

"That's not acceptable; maybe I should cancel my services and go with one of your competitors." I infuse the threat into the conversation with an obvious tone of dissatisfaction in my voice.

"We really want to keep your business, so I will personally make sure that you are the next person in your area." Scott says, as a means of saving my account. Little does he know it's of no use, I've already made up my mind to cancel.

"Alright Scott, thanks much." I say in a slightly sarcastic manner.

"You're welcome Ms. Rhodes. Have a good evening." He

responds in a polite manner, obviously not picking up on my

cynicism.

"It's Talia, and you know what… just cancel it and transfer

me back to customer service!" I've had enough. I'm sick of the

system anyway. It's not really keeping me safe. If a person really

wants to kill me, they will find a way to do it, security system or

not, that's why I have a gun.

"Hello Talia, are you still there?" Scott says as he gets back on

the line.

"Yes I'm still here." I respond in a less than pleasant tone. I'm

irritated with the whole experience. I'm done. C.T.S. security is

horrible.

"Okay Talia, I have Donald on the line with me and he's going

to handle your cancellation."

"Hello Talia I'm Donald. For security purposes, this

conversation may be recorded. I'm going to be asking you a series

of questions. Do you understand everything so far?" I hate when

people ask me stupid questions like this, why can't he just get on

with it?

"Of course I understand I'm not retarded!" I respond in a nasty manner. If Grandma Mariana were around to hear how flippant my last statement was, she would've slapped me upside my head or cleaned my mouth out with soap. A smart mouth is one thing she didn't tolerate.

"I was not insinuating that you are in any way mentally challenged ma'am. It's just a question that I have to ask everyone."

"Not ma'am, Talia! Now can we just get this over with?" I'm trying hard to keep my temper under wraps.

"Okay Talia just so you're aware, there is an early termination fee of one hundred dollars for cancelation of the service before your contact expires." I hate how companies screw people over with cancelation fees. I guess I shouldn't have been in such a rush to get the service. I also probably should've read the contract more thoroughly.

"I don't care. Just do it." I reply.

"Alright Talia I have your service cancelled. You should be receiving an email as well as a physical copy of the conformation by mail. Thank you for choosing C.T.S. and have a good evening."

"Yeah, mmm hmm," I hang up the line and try to calm down as I settle in. I remember that I took Max outside before I went to work. I quickly go to the backdoor and retrieve him. After giving Max warm bowls of chow and water, I go upstairs to change. As soon as I reach the upstairs, the sound of someone running startles me. *"What in the hell,"* I think as I feel the hairs on the back of my neck stand on end. I fear the worse as I try to decide what my next course of action should be. Considering the possibility that the noise could've been caused by an intruder, I decide to get my gun. I quietly make my way to my bedroom and quickly duck inside. Once inside of the room, I hear more strange sounds coming from one of the other rooms. It sounds as if someone is looking for something. I nervously retrieve my weapon. I make sure it's loaded and the safety is off before venturing back out into the hallway. I cautiously trek further down the hall towards the sound. I do a quick inspection of the bathroom. I know the chances of an intruder being in it are slim but I have to eliminate every possibility. I feel a lump form in my throat as I reach the first guest room. I take deep breath and slowly step inside. I'm relieved with my findings, nothing. All is clear. Everything looks normal. I let out a sigh of relief before continuing my search. With two of three bedrooms and the bathroom clear, I now know for a fact where the intruder is. There is only one option, the last guest room. I muster up all of my courage, and bravely tip toe towards it. I'm inches away from the doorway when the noises stop. The sudden ceasing of the noises is disturbing, more so than the noises themselves. Possessed by an unyielding need to solve the mystery, I carefully step into the room. Just like the others, it is devoid of life as well. *"Was I hearing things?"* I wonder as I take a quick peek inside of the closet. I search every square of the room before returning back downstairs empty-handed. *"Maybe the noises were coming from outside."* I think as a means of coming up with a logical solution to the mystery.

After finishing his grub, Max comes in the living room and plops himself down beside me. I start to smell a weird funky odor.

"Max, phew you need a bath!" I state as I begin watching one of my favorite movies, "The Notebook".

I make it to one of my favorite scenes, the one where they're in the rain and Noah tells Allie that he wrote her a letter every day for a year, when my appetite interrupts my viewing. My stomach growls like a ravenous beast as I struggle to keep focus. I really need to get something to eat. I grab my phone and look up the nearest PJ's. I find one located just minutes away. I click on the phone number and the phone places the call.

"PJ's, home of the Midwest's best pizza Jeffery speaking and ready to take your order." That's weird. His name is Jeffery and he sounds a little like the Jeff that I fired.

"Hi Jeffery, I'm calling to place an order for delivery." I respond, as the rumbling in my belly gets louder and more frequent.

"Alright, may I have your phone number?"

"My number is 216-555-4347," I state while fantasizing about tasting one of the best pizzas on earth!

"Okay…" he pauses for a moment before speaking. "I have you listed as Talia… Rhodes?"

"Is everything okay?" I ask as I wonder what in the hell is going on.

"Yes, everything is fine. It's just these darn computers freeze up from time to time is all. What would you like?" I shake off the suspicion and focus my mind back to ordering. I know exactly what I want. As a creature of habit, I've grown accustomed to certain things. Maybe in the future I'll feel adventurous and try something different.

"Give me a personal size PJ special with a side order of honey barbeque wings."

"Do you want regular or boneless wings?"

"Regular please."

"And do you want your pie with thin or hand tossed crust?"

"Give me hand tossed."

"Alright, I have you down for one personal size hand tossed PJ special and a side of regular honey barbeque wings. That comes out to $11.45. How are you paying?"

"That's correct and I'm paying with cash."

"Okay you're all set it'll be—"

"Wait don't you need my new address?" I ask as I remember that it's been a while since I've ordered delivery from them.

"No, we have your address. You're at 5525 hope drive in West Shore Village. We will be out to you within the next thirty minutes."

"Wait but—" Jeffery hangs up before I can finish my

sentence. "Wow that was fucking rude and weird!" I say aloud as I contemplate calling back and asking to speak to a supervisor. I figure I will let it slide since I already have enough on my plate without having to worry about a disgruntled bumpy faced pizza kid, (which I assume Jeffery is) trying to get payback for my complaint costing him his job. I put the phone down and resume my movie.

As I'm watching the movie, the possibility of Jeff being the PJ employee works its way back into my thoughts. *"Wait… was that… it couldn't be… it would really suck if the Jeff I fired ended up working at a pizza shop."* My attention shifts from my thoughts of Jeff to Max as he stands up and begins growling in the direction of the dining room. Suddenly, everything in the house goes dark. I start to feel a chill sweep across the room. I hear the door to the basement open. Paralyzed with fear, I try to remain calm and not panic. Whatever is going on is far from normal. Every fiber of my being wants to get up and head for safety but I decide otherwise. This is my house and I'm not leaving! I grab my gun and aim it at the dining room entrance. I look on in terror as the dark semitransparent shadow figures from my nightmares emerge from the dining room. "Oh shit…" I utter as I rise from the couch. In a complete state of panic, I squeeze the trigger on my gun. CLICK, nothing. Supernaturally fast, the creatures surround me. It seems as if time freezes. Everything is silent and still. Undeterred by the first failed attempt and the fact that I'm now surrounded, I aim my gun and prepare to fire. Before my finger can squeeze the trigger a second time, the shadow creature in front of me waves its hand and the gun flies out of my trembling palms.

"Go away!" I scream at the top of my lungs, all the while hoping that Heaven, Hell, and everything in between will hear. I know what these things in my house want. They want me! It's not all in my head. It can't be all in my head, they're here right now. My dreams are coming true, unfortunately not in a pleasant way. I can see my breath in front of me as it escapes my warm ninety-eight degree body. I feel the sting of the cold numbing air. The temperature in the room has dropped significantly. Death or something like it is present. Max stands near me paralyzed with alertness; his fur is standing on end, his growl guttural. I feel an icky crawling sensation invade the surface of my skin as goose bumps form on it. I'm flooded with intense fear as I stare deep into something that is there but not there. A shadowy semitransparent creature with red piercing eyes stands in front of me. Its eyes are like small intense fires burning their way into my core. I feel helpless and alone. I know that there is no way to escape; this is it. I wish Aiden were here. I wish I had his protective courage to rescue me in my darkest hour.

"It is your time, you must transcend. You must become what we need you to be. Spill the blood of the unworthy one and fulfill the divination. He is near. Sacrifice him to your cause." The menacing figure says in unison with the others surrounding me. Who or what they are referring to is unclear. I feel their strong cold hands grab my wrists. I attempt to break free, but my efforts are futile. The more I struggle, the stronger they become.

"No, get off of me!" I yell while struggling for freedom. Suddenly, the creature that I'm directly facing removes its hood and reveals its identity. It is... me! We appear to be the same person, which is utterly impossible. *"How can there be two?"* I ponder as my heartbeat intensifies. My other self, has a sinister look of glee. It is as if she is feeding off my fear.

I never really did take much stock in ghosts, demons, angels, or the paranormal world at large. I figured that only people craving attention or afflicted with mental illness believed in those types of things. Now I don't know what to believe. I really thought that ghost-hunting shows were just a bunch of Hollywood hyped entertainment. Orbs, EVPs, doors opening, mysterious footsteps, haunting reoccurring dreams; these things didn't happen to someone like me, Talia Rhodes. I was the type of person that stuck strictly to facts. If I couldn't see, taste, smell, or touch it, it didn't exist. Now I'm trying hard to cling to my belief system. *"What's really waiting for us on the other side? Where do we go when our time is up? What happens when the clock stops ticking, when we leave this world? When bills become irrelevant and saving for the future ends."* All of these thoughts are rumbling around in my head as I stare face to face with a woman that is not supposed to be there. She reeks of brimstone. Her eyes are filled with an all-consuming malevolence. She extends her hand towards my head. As she extends it, her form begins to change. I jerk back, a futile effort to prevent her from touching me. I watch in horror as she turns into a grotesque oddity, the likes of which I have never seen.

The sheer horror of her appearance is indescribable! She turns into an exact personification of evil. I fight and frantically move my head. I mustn't let her touch me. She looks as if she is enjoying every moment of it. The shadow creatures grab my head and hold it still as my dead ringer's hand gets closer and closer. I feel an intense burning sensation as her fingertips touch the skin on my forehead. Her fingers begin to merge into my flesh, which is something I know there is no known explanation for; the laws of science are being broken as I cry and wince from the intensifying pain forming in my head. My head starts to throb and a loud ringing sound begins to bounce around in my ears. The pain is so intense. It's like having an earache to the tenth power combined with cramps. I feel myself getting weak. My legs are getting heavy. The muscles in my abdomen tighten and throb as well. My posture begins to slump. The pain is unbearable. She merges further and further into me. A dizzying sensation sweeps over me as everything begins to fade.

CHAPTER 22

The sound of birds chirping and rays of sun sneaking in through the slats of the window blinds work collaboratively to awaken me. I try desperately to rustle out of my semi-comatose state. I'm in my living room sprawled out over my couch in a weird unnatural manner. I notice dark red spots smeared in its fabric, as well as on my hands, arms, and torso.

At first, it doesn't really hit me. However, as I continue looking myself over, I begin feeling uneasy. My feet have caked on dirt and remnants of dead leaves stuck to them. "What the…" I sit up. My body feels rigid and my head is throbbing uncontrollably. I manage to stand sloppily to my feet. I look around the room and begin to assess the situation. The room is in complete disarray. The coffee table is broken and lying scattered in pieces across the once pristine carpet and someone or something has made a huge hole in the chocolate colored accent wall. Something definitely isn't right. I try to remember the night before but most of it seems like a dream. It's all pretty much a blur. I can't distinguish the difference between reality and fiction.

Panic begins to set in and my body starts to tremble involuntarily. *"Keep it together."* I think while on the verge of hyperventilating. I tightly wrap my arms around myself as I try to calm down. I desperately want to close my eyes and not accept what I am seeing but a weird compulsion forces me to do exactly the opposite. I continue glossing over the room. My eyes stop at a trail of bloody footsteps leading into the dining room. I lift up one of my feet and check the bottom of it. It's covered in dried dirt and blood. The footsteps appear to be my own. I lower my foot and continue my trek. While walking through the dining room, I look over myself again; this time checking for any cuts or other fresh wounds. I don't find a single scratch. "What have I done?" I mumble as I reluctantly follow the mysterious trail out of the room.

I step into the kitchen, and immediately notice a shovel with pieces of fresh dirt caked on it. I can tell that it's fresh because it still has a clumpy, moist appearance. *"Did I kill someone? And how did I dig through the cold hard pre-winter soil?"* I question mentally as I try to CSI the facts. I walk through the kitchen and head out the back door. I examine the backyard for any freshly dug or covered holes. I'm glad that my backyard has a tall wooden fence that encloses it. The last thing I need is a neighbor to see me covered in blood looking like a deranged killer. I see a small hole near a tree. I proceed over to have a look in it. It's empty. Now I'm confused. *"What did I remove from the hole?"* I rack my brain trying desperately to retrieve any memories of what transpired the night before.

I try to recall the last person with whom I came in contact. *"Kenna,"* quickly illuminates in my mind. In a panicked haste, I run back into the house and scramble around for my phone. I begin removing every couch cushion and metaphorically leaving no stone unturned. I find it of all places, in my back pocket. I swiftly swipe in the pass code and scroll through the recent call list. I tap on the last call log with Kenna's number. Her contact info pops on the screen, accompanied by the sound of ringing. The phone picks up.

"Hello," interrupts the silence.

"Kenna," I respond feeling partially relieved to hear her voice.

"Hey Talia what's up?" She says, while obviously in the middle of something, I can tell by the amount of noise in the background on her end. "So did you have a good night?" She inquires.

"Uh yeah sure," I blurt out, not really giving my full attention to the question.

"You know I miss you," she says warmly.

"Hey let me call you right back okay?" Like a flash of lightening, another person pops in my head, *"Aiden,"* I quickly hang up and scroll until I locate his number. I click on it and it begins to dial. I say hello as soon as the rings stop.

"Hey, I was waiting on you to call me," Aiden says in longing sincere, somewhat angry manner.

"Hi honey," I reply.

"Why didn't you tell about everything that's been going on?"

"I see somebody is happy to hear my voice," I respond sarcastically.

"You don't have to be a smart ass! All I'm saying is that you could've filled me in, I'm sick of finding out things after the fact! Kenna told me everything. I called you like I don't know how many times and it kept going to voicemail!"

"I'm sorry," I reply, which is a rather weak response given the circumstances but I can't think of anything to else to say. Most of my attention is preoccupied with the mystery from the night before. "Hey honey..." I pause, midsentence. In the midst of panic, I clearly forgot to check for one thing, *"Where is Max?"* is the latest addition to the mystery. "Hey Aiden baby, let me call you right back okay?"

"Okay," he responds angrily before abruptly hanging up.

"Max," I yell as I search throughout the house. I check the rest of the rooms on the first floor, no Max. I check the upstairs rooms, still no Max. I make my way to the basement… surprise, no Max. The sound of scratching stops me dead in my tracks. I follow the sound; it leads me to the front door. I open the door and see Max! Whew am I relieved to see him. His tail wags as he looks at me with his bright grayish blue eyes. He begins to bark and runs past me. I turn around and my eyes follow him. He stops at the kitchen table. My eyes detect something that I didn't notice before.

"How did I overlook this?" I think as I walk over to my kitchen table, all the while staring at the black dirty locker that rests on top of it. In all of my haste, I didn't even pay attention to it. I examine the box and notice a small rusty lock attached to it. As if on cue, I reach into my pocket and recover a small key. *"How did that get there?"* I wonder as I examine it. I insert the key into the rusty lock and twist. The rusty little lock reluctantly releases its hold on the black box. I open up the box. Its contents seem vaguely familiar to me. It's a bunch of papers with what appears to be spells or rituals on them. Pentagrams and other symbols appear throughout most of the text. One symbol in particular, catches my eye. "It's the hands of Aka Manah symbol!" I say aloud as I remember the business card I received from Doug. My phone begins to vibrate. I pull it from out of my pocket. A number that has no contact picture, or name associated with it, is on the screen. Thinking about the bloody motif in my living room makes me hesitant to answer. After the same number calls a second time, I answer it.

"Hey Talia," a voice says on the other side of the line I'm sure

I know who it is. The name is on the tip of my tongue.

"Doug?" I respond as I match a name to the voice.

"Yeah, you called me last night but I missed your call." I don't remember calling Doug.

"I did? Are you sure that it was me?" I question as I try to recollect calling him.

"You called me and left a message. You were talking about joining us. You were saying a whole bunch of other things too but I think it would be best if we discussed them in person." I'm not sure what he's talking about but based on how my house looks, it can't be anything good.

"Well I have something very major going on and I can't talk right now." I have to get this place cleaned up! There's blood everywhere and I have a feeling something worse is about to occur.

"Alright well just call me later okay?" Doug says in a concerned manner.

"I will," I reply before hanging up the phone and thinking of what I can use to remove all of the blood stains splattered across my couch and carpet. If what I think happened actually did happen then it won't take long for the cops to show up. I should probably stash the black box somewhere for safekeeping. One person quickly comes to mind. "*Kenna*," I waste no time calling her. She answers right away.

"Hey, I need you to do me a big favor!" I skip the pleasantries and get right to the point.

"Anything for you Talia, what's going on is everything okay?"

"It's too much to explain on the phone, I need you here ASAP! I gotta go, see you soon!" I hang up and resume organizing my task. I rush into the cleaning closet and pull out the needed supplies. I do a mental checklist several times to make sure that I have all of the needed items before getting started. I remember everything Grandma Mariana taught me about getting bloodstains out of fabric and carpet. Sometimes when Grandpa John would return from hunting, he would somehow manage to get bloodstains on various things throughout the house. Grandma Mariana would be pissed but after she mastered the art of removing them, it didn't bother her as much. Especially, after she started making him help! I have a bucket, five white towels, and a cleaner with enzymes. I also have a toothbrush and some dishwashing liquid. I waste little time getting the arduous task underway. I mix the dishwashing liquid with the cold water. I apply it to one of the stains and brush it in with the toothbrush. Then, I spray on a thin layer of the enzyme cleaner. Finally, I use the white towels to sponge the stain until I no longer see any traces of blood. I repeat the same exhausting method several times until I completely remove all of the stains. After brushing and wiping so many times, it feels like both of my hands are going to fall off. I hear a car pull up in the driveway. *"It must be Kenna."* I think as I gather up the supplies and give everything a quick glance over. I set the supplies in the kitchen and sprint to the door. I open it just as Kenna is about to ring the doorbell.

"Hey, come in," I utter in a hastened manner and follow up with a quick peck on her cheek. "Have a seat but don't sit on the couch!" I instruct as I get back to disposing of the blood soaked towels and dirty bucket of water. Once I dispose of everything, I grab the black box and all of the stuff I found in the basement. I neatly pack everything up and return to Kenna.

"I might be in some major trouble. I need you to take all of this stuff for safe keeping." I try to convey the urgency as best I can while trying to get her on her way.

"Talia you're scaring me, what's going on?" Kenna inquires. I wish I had an answer for her but I don't even have one for myself! I still can't remember most of what happened last night.

"I'm not sure but I know it's not good, I… I think I killed someone!" The look on her face matches my feelings to a tee. Confusion, concern, and panic, are the emotions that are bouncing around in my head.

"You did what? How…?" She asks in slightly elevated voice. I want to hold and console her. I want so desperately to give her comfort but I'm pressed for time and helpless to do so.

"I… I don't know…" I look down as I search for a way to explain it. It's no use. I place my hands on the sides of Kenna's face and look deep into her eyes. I need you to take these things for safekeeping. Give the box to Doug. He'll know what to do with it." I place a passionate kiss on her lips before escorting her out with the items. Once I see her off, I rush upstairs and quickly jump in the shower. The water has a tough time getting the dried blood off. I scrub like a maniac until all that remains is reddened skin. I hop out of the shower and quickly get dressed. As I'm in the middle of buttoning my shirt, I hear a knock on the door accompanied by the ringing of the doorbell. I disregard fastening the last buttons and run downstairs. As I reach the first floor landing, a second louder series of knocks echo through the house. I reach the door and peer into the peephole. I instantly feel a sense of dread upon seeing what lies on the other side of it. I see several cops. Some of them are suited up in swat gear. "Oh shit," I utter as I realize the severity of what is about to occur. Not wanting to risk getting my door kicked in, I reluctantly unlock the door and twist the knob. A cop with full riot gear bursts in before I get a chance to open it completely. The impact forces me to the ground.

"Freeze you fucking murderer!" He yells as he aims an assault rifle directly at my face. Now I know how my mother felt. I realize the severity of what happened last night. I realize now that, I did in fact kill someone!

"You have the right to remain silent. Anything that you say can and will be used against you in a court of law!" The aggressive police officer yells while steadily keeping the rifle aimed at me. Another officer swarms in and damn near dislocates my shoulder while forcing my arms behind my back.

"Aah," I yell in pain as they yank me from off of the floor. My emotions and thoughts are all over the place. I'm in such a state of panic that it feels like my heart is going to burst through my chest! The officer roughly handles and searches me for weapons and illegal substances. The whole process is so degrading. To make matters worse, they forcefully sit me down right on one of the freshly scrubbed areas of carpet. I feel the wetness soak through my clothing. I just sit and take it. I dare not move and give them a reason to beat the shit out of me or get trigger-happy. I know the neighbors are having a field day. This is probably the most exciting thing that has happened in this neighborhood in ages. I feel sick to my stomach at the sight of all of the law enforcement invading my domicile. Max begins to bark at the strangers as more make their way in. I know he's probably nervous and frightened at the same time. Poor pooch. He probably would've been better off staying at the kennel. I watch as the officers tear through my house looking for weapons and evidence. My 9mm is one of the first things they spot. In the haste of cleaning, I somehow failed to put it back in its designated place in my bedroom

"I found a .22 and some ammo!" An unseen officer yells from upstairs. Based on how they're handling the living room, I can just imagine how they're treating the rest of my house. After sitting on the wet freshly scrubbed carpet for what seems like forever, a heavily biased police officer forcefully removes me from my home. In his eyes, I'm already guilty. He probably perceives me as some murderous bitch on the rag. I feel a massive headache starting up. I try to ignore the gawking stares of onlookers as I walk to the patrol car. They probably notice the wet stain on the backside of my pants and assume that I pissed myself. I feel so degraded. The news crews filming and snapping pictures, only make it worse. I dread the finished product of what the shots will produce. My hair is a mess and I have on zero makeup.

After the walk of shame, I'm thrown into the back of the cruiser with little regard for my welfare or comfort. I feel like a second-class citizen as I wait and look away from all of the nosy bystanders. Now I understand how the animals in a zoo feel. I feel like a zoo attraction, all of these gawkers and hecklers surrounding me. I glance up just as another news van pulls up. I've really fucked up! Now I'm desperate. All of the chips are down. The deck is stacked against me and the odds are a gazillion to one. The shit has officially hit the fan and splattered all over the walls, flies enjoy! My headache is hanging on for the journey. I'm beginning to feel that same throbbing sensation that I've felt many times before. The ringing is starting up as well. I wish my hands were free so I could cup my head in between them. The noise from the circus gathered around the car only makes the headache worse. I close my eyes and try to tune out the throbbing and ringing. The front car doors open. I open my eyes and see that the officers assigned to the vehicle have finally returned. The sound of the engine starting is like music to my ears.

After a long anguishing ride, we arrive at the West Shore Police Precinct. I'm thankful that I didn't end up going to "The Justice Center" county jail in downtown Cleveland. I hear that it's one-step above hell. This one girl that I used to work with got into an altercation after having too many drinks on a Friday night and ended up staying in the place for a week. She told me all kinds of horror stories. The thing that stuck out the most was a meal that the inmates refer to as "Fear Factor". Not having to go there is the only bright side to this whole situation.

The vehicle slowly pulls into the parking lot. Once the car is parked, they waste no time escorting me out of the vehicle and into central processing. My heart beats in triple time as I take in the environment around me. Jail is one place I never in a million years thought that I would end up. Getting checked in is as bad as I expected it to be. Once released from the cuffs, they make me spread my legs and put my hands up against the wall as they search me one last time for quote UN quote "weapons or contraband". I believe it's just an excuse for the hard up officer to get free feels. After it's determined that I'm clean, they lead me into another room for the infamous mug shot. Next, I'm finger printed and led into yet another room where they force me to relinquish all of my personal belongings (belt, cell phone, and all of the change in my pocket.)

"Alright, you got one phone call and don't forget to dial nine first!" The officer says in a stern tone as he points at the phone stationed on the desk. I dial nine as instructed and call the first person that comes to mind, I call my mom. The line connects and the phone begins to ring. I get more anxious with each ring. I silently pray that it doesn't go to voicemail. She finally answers.

"Hello," I blurt into the phone the second that the ringing stops. I'm anxious for her to hear my plight.

"Tal is that you?" My mom says in an inquisitive manner.

"Yes, it's me. I really need your help!" I frantically spill my words into the receiver.

"What's wrong Tal, and where are you calling from?"

"I... I'm in jail!"

"You're where? Are you serious?"

"Yes. They're trying to charge me with murder!"

"Oh God," my mom responds before I hear the phone drop. I wait worriedly in silence for her return back on the line. Someone returns on the line but not the person I expected, Corvis is on the line.

"I guess you've really done it now! Your mom is a hysterical mess because of you! What is your problem, how did you end up in jail?" Corvis questions in a manner similar to that of a drill sergeant. I feel myself tense up as the headache resumes.

"Look I know what you did. I know you're behind this, so don't think you're going to get away with it. I'm innocent! I feel myself elevating. I quickly regain my composure.

"What are you talking about and why should I care? I'm not your father. If you weren't in a bind, we wouldn't even be talking! You probably got all paranoid like when you pulled your pistol out on your mom. I told you to get help. Now look at you. You should have never started digging. From this point on you're on your own. You made your bed and now you have to lie in it!" Corvis says before ending the call. His words cut deep into my soul. It feels like a part of me is dying. I'm left hurt and speechless. I hang up the phone and the guard leads me to a holding cell. I step into the cell feeling numb and dead to the world.

The cell is just as one would expect it to be. It is a small room with no windows. An all-metal lidless toilet is positioned in the corner farthest from the door, with a generic sink positioned adjacent to it. A lone plastic chair sits in the corner closest to the door. A raggedy cot rests on the floor a few feet from the entrance, a thin itchy wool blanket, a pillow, and a couple of standard issue sheets are neatly stacked on top of it. The reality of it all must really be contributing to my headache. It feels as if it's getting worse by the second. As the cell door closes, I submit to the pain. I fall to my knees on the cheap jail issued cot. The throbbing and ringing gets overwhelming. I start to see spots before my eyes. Everything around me begins to fade away as my alertness slips into the recesses of mind. Right as I'm on the verge of losing consciousness, something grabs me. Images begin flooding into my head. A bright flash temporarily blinds me.

Once the light dissipates, I realize that I'm no longer in the holding cell. I'm back in my house! The time of day has changed along with the location, it is now night. My body begins to move, but I'm not the one moving it. I have no control over my body, I feel like a person on the passenger side of a vehicle. I'm just along for the ride. I'm watching everything from a first person point of view. Even though I'm not in control of my body, I still sense everything. I feel the plush carpet underneath my bare feet. I smell that familiar smell of the lilac scented air freshener. I walk to the front door. I feel my arm extending to reach the door lock. The metal of the lock is cold to the touch. I twist it to the unlocked position. I feel my hand wrap around the doorknob. I try to gain control over it but it's useless. It's like playing a first person shooter in which the game goes into a cut scene. The only thing I can do is watch as some unknown force acts as a puppeteer, making me open my front door. The door opens. It reveals a man with a blotched out face. He is holding a large object in his hand but it's blurry. It's weird because everything else is clear. I invite the unknown person in.

Everything fast-forwards and stops right at the point where I turn to go into the dining room. After a few seconds of walking, I feel myself spin around, I face the stranger just as he is about to plunge a knife into me. I successfully manage to thwart his attack and remove the knife from his hand. Once he is unarmed, I grab the assailant by the throat. He squirms and attempts to free himself from my grip. I feel my fingers tighten around his neck. He gasps for air, as my grip gets tighter and tighter. I begin to laugh maniacally as the man fights for his life. I release my grip. He falls to the floor, catches his breath, and lets out a weakened scream. I laugh even harder.

"I'm sorry, please don't kill me!" He pleads as I toy with him like a cat toys with a mouse before the kill. I wave my hand and he lifts into the air. I wave my hand again and watch as he slams into the coffee table. I hear a loud crack as the weight of his body breaks the table. He resumes begging for his life. I wave my hand once more and he flies across the room like a rag doll. He collides into the chocolate accent wall like a crash test dummy, leaving a hole in the wake of the impact. I watch myself physically grab the unknown man and begin punching him repeatedly. The man's blood, splatters over me as I continue pummeling him in a brutal merciless fashion. After beating the man into a gory mess, I throw him and fall to my knees. A strange weird draining sensation sweeps over me; I sit motionless like a robot that has run out of power. I remain idle as the man gets his bearings. It feels like whatever was controlling me has relinquished its hold. I watch as the bloody mess of a man barely escapes out of the door with his life. I hear the roar of an engine revving up outside, followed by the screaming sound of tires peeling. I snap out of my trance. In the blink of an eye, I'm back in the holding cell.

"If that's what happened last night, then why am I being charged with murder?" I question as the door to the holding cell opens.

"Step out of the cell." A guard instructs in an emotionless manner. I stand to my feet and do as instructed. "I need to take you over for questioning," he says as he removes the handcuffs that are clipped on the side of his waist. I turn around and position my hands behind my back. He clamps the cuffs around my wrists and then leads me out of the cell. We walk past the other cells. I definitely feel like a stray animal in the custody of a kennel. We continue to walk until we reach another section outside of the jail area.

We stop at a room on the other side of the building. He removes his set of keys from a clip fashioned near his belt. He fumbles through the keys before finding the right one. Once he finds the right key, he jams it into the keyhole. He turns the key inside the lock as the other free keys rattle. We enter the room. It has the smell of stale coffee mixed with dirt. A metal table and two plastic chairs are in the center of it. It looks like something out of a crime drama show. The whole room fits the comparison to a tee, including the two-sided mirror taking up the top half of one of the walls. This is what my life has become. I went from the road headed towards success, to the one leading straight to hell.

"Have a seat," the guard says before turning to leave the room. He exits the room and locks the door behind him. I sit down in one of the plastic chairs. I try to calm myself down. My anxiety level escalates with each second that passes. I'm past distraught. I feel my hands begin to shake as I picture myself being in prison. If it's anything like how they show on those prison reality shows, I know for certain, that I won't survive it. I don't want to end up as a burly dyke's bitch! I would rather die before submitting to such a drastic lifestyle change! I keep thinking about last night, Aiden, Kenna, and my job. My career as an Office Manager is over. Sorry Mr. Beck, I'm going to miss having the office with the sweet view of the city. As far as the job goes it's over, but my life is far from over, I didn't do it! I didn't kill the man! The vision showed it! I hold my head down in shame. I wish I could wake up from this bad nightmare. I pray to God that this is just a dream, just another nightmare to add to the collection.

"Give in to your true self," the disembodied voice that I have heard many times before says. It breaks up my pity party. I quickly raise my head and glance around the room. It's empty. I start to feel a cold chill. Something is in the room with me. I know it is. I can feel a presence. The lights in the room start to flicker. Just when I thought it couldn't get any worse, I begin to feel a deep sadness. It feels like a part of me is dying. *"Your true self will be*

your way out," the voice states. It sounds stronger and close, like it's standing right next to me. Now I know for certain, that I'm not hearing things. The rattling of keys catches my attention. The door opens. In walks an intimidating figure of a man. He looks like a husky ex-boxer. He reeks heavily of sweat and some type of musky cologne. A long scar along his jawline only helps to add to the intimidation factor. He takes off his suit coat and places it on the chair across from me before speaking.

"Ms. Rhodes, I'm Detective Burnside. I'm going to ask you some questions and I want straight honest answers. If you cooperate, things will go as good as they can, well given the circumstances of course."

"I didn't do anything!" blurts out of my mouth like an involuntary nervous reflex. "I don't know why I'm here… can you please tell me what's going on?" I plead with the detective. I need clear concise answers. I need to know if the vision is true. I truly feel like I'm losing my sanity.

"Are you serious, you really don't know why you're here? Oh, I get it you're going to try to go for the insanity plea or better yet, you're probably going to try to use the fact that you're a female to gain leniency in the eyes of the court. Well I'll tell you right now, you can throw those ideas out right out the window. I don't give a fuck what you are, man, woman, child, dog, if you did the crime your damn sure doing the time!" Detective Burnside says as he paces back and forth. He looks like a tiger on the verge of attacking. "I'm going to tell you exactly what happened. You attacked a pizza deliveryman. I don't know what occurred prior to the altercation but I assume it was something that brought out the worst in you. I played the angles from all sides, I added up all of the clues. Here's what I came up with, the guy that you killed was actually someone that you used to work with."

"I killed Shane?"

"No. Shane is not the victim. Actually, you killed Jeff, Jeff Blake. I noticed that in your file there is an incident report stating that you were receiving death threats. I looked into the surveillance footage as well. I understand what all of that can do to a person mentally especially considering the fact that you were nearly raped a little over a year ago.

"What... how..."

"Surprised are we? I know all about you, the nightmares, the altercation at work, pointing a loaded weapon at your own mother." There is no possible way that Detective Burnside should know those things unless... he spoke with Corvis! "You're a real piece of work. You should've gotten help like your father recommended. Now it's too late. He said that he and your mother did all they could, but you were just too much of a loose cannon." Just as I suspected, Corvis' twisted half-truths have already swayed the detective's judgment. "I understand your mindset for possibly committing the crime but I also realize that Jeff had plausible motive to attack you. I mean, you fired the guy and he ended up having to work at a pizza place just stay afloat.

The fact he was a delivery driver, gave him the freedom he needed to leave the gift that you found on your doorstep. It's quite odd how he ended up being your delivery driver last night. I was thinking, maybe it was self-defense but then we apprehend you and there's not a single scratch on you! Jeff on the other hand, looked like a team of MMA fighters ganged up on him! He tried hanging on but his body had taken too much damage. Even if he came to your house with the intention of doing something, it's going to be hard proving self-defense, especially when you add your guns into the mix. So anyway you cut it, you're going to have to do some time. The proof is in the evidence."

"I didn't kill him! He came to my house and tried to stab me with a knife!" I respond in an angrily excited manner. I would rather die before doing any time in prison!

"I thought that said you didn't know what happened? Now you're saying that he had a knife, you've got to be fucking kidding me!" Detective Burnside slams his open hand down on the table. "You need to get your story straight, because right now your story is Swiss cheese! Meaning that, it has far too many holes in it! We found a knife but your prints are on it, not his!"

"That's because I managed to deflect his attack!" I have to restrain myself from becoming too animated.

"Well, all I have to say is this; you need get your story straight or kiss at least ten years of freedom goodbye!" A guard comes into the room as Detective Burnside grabs his coat off the chair. "Take her back to her cell. She's not ready to cooperate!" Burnside says to the guard before he leaves the room. I'm so angry and in dismay that I remain silent and hold my head down as I force the tears to stay in. I pull myself together before I stand up and allow the guard to place the handcuffs back onto my wrists.

Around dinnertime, I receive some type of bland basic meal to eat. I'm so distraught, that I can't even force the slightest appetite to manifest. Kenna, Aiden, and the murder stay on my mind. Everything is fucked-up! All hope is lost! I finally give in to the anger and hurt. Tears escape from my eyes like rats from a sinking ship. I feel their wet warmth, as they roll down my face. I think about what Grandma Mariana and Grandpa John would say if they were around now but I guess it doesn't matter what they would say, because they're dead. The phrase *"give in to your true self"* keeps making its way into my conscious thoughts. *"What is my true self?"* I think back to what Isaac and Doug talked about. I'm not doing something right. If I were, I wouldn't be where I am right now.

Thinking and worrying have left me drained. I just want to escape from it all. I begin crying out to God. I haven't prayed in years. I fall to my knees and begin praying feverishly. After praying for what seems like forever, I start to feel stupid. The voice from one of my nightmares begins speaking to me, *"That God can't save you!"* It makes me stop my prayers and focus back on the insurmountable odds that I face. Exhaustion is starting to set in. I'm fatigued. I can't fight any more.

After making one last honest effort to eat, I shove away the tray and collapse onto the cold uncomfortable cot. I close my eyelids and welcome the darkness. I focus on the quiet solace of the holding cell. I snuggle up underneath the thin itchy jail issued blanket and try to block out the cold. I guess whomever is in-charge of the jail really wants to make the prisoners suffer.

CHAPTER 23

Sleep doesn't come easy. I toss and turn throughout the night. I keep having reoccurring nightmares of being an old woman in prison. After finally managing to get a few hours of shuteye, I wake up determined regain my freedom. I will do whatever it takes, even if I have to sell my soul! I get up off the second rate makeshift bed and relieve myself. The sound of keys rattling on the other side of the door gets my attention. I finish my deposit and quickly wash my hands in the metal sink. A different guard comes in with a tray of food. It's a female guard. Her physical appearance is rather dumpy and weary. She looks at me with pity. I feel dreadfully self-conscious as her somber eyes examine me. Aside from feeling determined, a small urge to eat is growing inside of my stomach. I suppose I should appease it seeing as how I didn't eat a single thing yesterday. I guess I owe myself that much. I begrudgingly take the food provided. I force a slight smile as I try my best to be polite in spite of the circumstances. The guard smiles back, which is a good thing because I'm not trying to shit on her day. She's not responsible for any of this; she's just a person working to pay her bills like everyone else.

I prepare myself to eat as she leaves the room. I look at the tray, there is a bowl of what I assume is cornflakes and a slice of some type of cornbread cake. There is also an individual serving size carton of milk and a small microwaveable pizza. I scarf down the pizza even though it's not all the way heated. Once I devour the pizza, I try my luck with the cornflakes. I pour the milk into the bowl and give it a go. The taste is far from what I expected. The cereal tastes like raisin bran minus the raisins, which is utterly disgusting. Less than pleased with the cereal, I try a piece of the cake muffin thing. I bite into it expecting some kind of nasty weird taste to hit my taste buds. Surprisingly, it's quite the opposite. I finish the cake and drink the milk out of the bowl of cereal before placing the tray by the door. I don't even think twice about consuming another spoon of the awful tasting cereal.

Hours pass as I await an update on my fate. I bet the local news sources are going crazy with my story. It hasn't even been a full twenty-four hours and it's already getting the best of me. Bored and stressed out of my mind, I begin speaking aloud, pleading to any being or entity that will hear.

"Please somebody get me out of here! I will do anything! I just need to get out of here! God, the Devil, anybody please help!" A quick thought of Amy flashes into my mind. I remember my grandmother telling me that Amy was my guardian spirit. I begin praying to Amy. "Amy please come to my rescue, I can't—" in the middle of my plea, the lights in the room go out. I frantically look around. The temperature begins declining as well. Something weird is going on. Out of nowhere, a bright blue flame appears in the middle of the room. It briefly blinds me. The smell of fire and brimstone fills the air. The flame dissipates. Amy is standing before me. She is dressed in a jet-black business suit with a blood colored blouse and shoes to match. Her eyes are glowing brightly with a fiery red hue. Her presence makes me tremble. I'm afraid and relieved at the same time.

"You require your freedom Talia?" She asks in a deep but still feminine voice. It echoes off the walls in the room. I sense the power in her voice. It sounds like one of those voices from a dream sequence.

"Yes I need to get out!" I state adamantly. "I will do whatever it takes to get out of here!" I have nothing but my life to lose, I'm desperate. Amy smiles at my desperation.

"You can be free after you give yourself to the truth. You must devote your life to your true master. You must dedicate yourself to my lord Lucifer." A chill runs through my body at the sound of the name.

"You want me to sell my soul to the Devil?" I ask as I study her movements. She moves in an unnatural manner. It's hard to explain it but it's different from the previous times I've encountered her.

"No. Not sell, dedicate it to him. Your soul is already his. We want you to dedicate your life to him. We need you to kill your old life and embrace a new one. You are already his. It is your destiny. It is time for you to fulfill your obligation." I take a moment to weigh my options, which doesn't take long at all. I have no other choice.

"I'm ready to do it." I respond. I'm ready to do whatever it takes to get back to life on the outside.

"Good," she says as she smiles at me with a "more than meets the eye" grin. In the blink of an eye, she grabs my left hand and exposes my index finger. I try to jerk my hand back but it doesn't budge. Her grip is extremely strong. I have to remember that I'm not dealing with a mere human. She could probably snap me in two if she desired to. She extends one of her fingers. The nail on it grows and forms into a small sharp blade. She swipes the nail across my finger. It breaks the skin apart. Within seconds, blood begins to make its way out of the wound. She takes my finger and sticks it into her mouth. I feel a stinging cold pain. After a brief moment, she releases it. I withdraw my hand and examine the finger. I can't find a single scratch. My wound is healed!

"It is done. You will be free before today's sunset," she says while giving me a serious no nonsense look. I step back, still in awe of what has just transpired. The blue flame reappears and she disappears within it just as quickly as she arrived. The holding cell light turns back on, and everything resumes back to how it was before. I feel a great weight lifted from off of me. I have confidence in what Amy has stated. I will be free again! Minutes after Amy vanishes, the guard returns with toiletries.

"It's time for you to get washed up Ms. Rhodes," she states as she hands them over to me. I look over the items. All of it is basic, an economy toothbrush, an off brand tube of toothpaste, a very basic bar of soap, a bottle of generic shampoo, a white washcloth, and a matching towel. Another guard comes in to assist her with walking me to the showering facilities. As we walk down the hall, I think about the black box and its contents. I wonder what Doug made of it. I also think about Max. Poor pooch, they probably took him to animal protective services. Oh well I can't worry about it now. My only concern is getting out.

The shower room reminds me of the one at my old high school, minus the lockers. I wash yesterday's funk off and get right to cleaning my oily matted down hair. I end up using the whole bottle. Upon getting out of the shower, they give me an orange jail uniform that's at least two sizes too big, and some weird prison issued flip-flops. They take my street clothes and put them with the rest of my personal items. Instead of going back to the holding cell, they escort me to another cell with other inmates.

"Please let Amy make good on her end," I think as they usher me in.

CHAPTER 24

I stand before the altar draped in a dark crimson robe with red, blue, and black lit candles surrounding me and positioned before me. The smell of burning incense fills the room. An athame, a dry pen, an aged bell, a lone blank sheet of paper, a silver chalice, and a silver bowl rest before me. Doug and Isaac are beside me. I look out at the sea of black and crimson robed figures gathered before me. The moment is surreal. As I'm taking in the significance of it, Isaac steps forth and begins to recite a prayer.

"In Nomine, Dei Nostri Satanas, Luciferi Excelsi. In the name of Satan, ruler of the earth, true God, almighty, and ineffable, who has created man to reflect in thine own image and likeness, we invite the "Forces of Darkness" to bestow their infernal power upon us. Open the gates of hell to come forth and greet us as your children of truth.

Deliver us o' mighty Satan from all past error and delusion. Fill us with truth, wisdom, and understanding. Keep us strong in our faith and service so that we may abide always in thee. Allow us to lift thy name with praise, honor, and glory forever and ever." Isaac finishes the prayer and lifts a chalice from the altar. "Let us all drink," he says as he comes forth with his chalice raised. Doug and I step forth and grab chalices from the altar as well. We raise them in unison with the rest of the people in the room. We begin to drink the sweet tangy intoxicating tonic. That same possessed feeling as before sweeps over me.

"Whenever you are ready to begin sister," Doug says as he waits and watches with the rest of those gathered for the ceremony.

I place the chalice down before removing the bell and athame from the altar. Doug and Isaac both step back as I remain in the foreground. I ring the bell and begin turning counterclockwise. I hold the athame out in a pointing manner. First, I point east and call out Aka Manah. Next, I turn north and call out Beelzebub. Then, I turn west and call out Lucifer. Finally, I turn south and call out Amy. I return my focus back to the altar. A blue aura like glow of energy surrounds it. I look at the athame clutched in my hand. The cold metal blade dares me to use it. It practically begs to dig into my flesh. I take a deep breath. Then I lightly scrape it across my left index finger. Within seconds, blood rises to the surface of the wound. I walk up to the altar, and drip some of the blood from my wound onto it. I then grab the dry pen, dip it into the small puddle of blood, and begin to write on the blank sheet of paper.

"Before the supreme and indefinable God head Lucifer, the gatekeeper Aka Manah, and in the presence of all true original gods in his service I, Talia Elizabeth Rosette, renounce any and all past allegiances. I renounce the false Christian God Jehovah, I renounce his vile and worthless son Jesus Christ, and I renounce his tainted, detestable, and putrid Holy Spirit.

I proclaim Lucifer as my one and only God. I promise to recognize and honor him in all things, without reservation, desiring in return, his diverse aid in the conquering achievement of my undertakings.

In honor,

Talia Elizabeth Rosette, "

Once finished writing, I read the letter aloud for all those present to hear. After reading it, I fold up the paper and hold it over one of the candles. It catches fire from the flame like a bad cold. I drop the paper into the silver bowl. The flames turn an electric blue, completely engulfing the paper. I raise my chalice to say a final toast before the indulgence session begins. Doug steps up and begins a special announcement.

"Brothers and sisters this indulgence session will start unlike any other," he says before turning toward a group of people positioned on the side of the stage in front of a set of double doors. "Bring them out!" He commands before looking at me. The group leaves through the double doors "I hope you're ready for this." He whispers while flashing a sinister smile. A few moments later, they return with two people bound by rope with hoods over their heads. They bring the people over in front of me and make them kneel down before me. "Go ahead, remove their hoods." He instructs with glee. I grab both hoods and remove them simultaneously. I look over at Doug and smile. Corvis and my mother are kneeling before me. They look so pitiful bound up and gagged. Fucking liars, my whole life has been one big sick fucking lie! How could people that say they love you day in and day out keep such a fucking dirty disgusting secret? I now stand before my true family, the crowd looking on. I can tell by the expressions on their faces that they are in agreement with me. My old family must die! Doug and Isaac move the altar and afterwards, Doug places his hand on my shoulder before speaking. "Brothers and sisters, we are here today to witness a new chapter in the life and history of our sister, Talia. Our godly spirits have stated that in order for one to walk in his or her destiny, that individual must purge their past, to purify their future. Tonight sister Talia will make this transition. Tonight she will cleanse her life in blood. The hand of Aka Manah will guide her to complete this task. Talia we are ready."

Filled with anger and hurt, I step forward and grab my athame. I remove their gags. Fear is evidently present on their faces. Now comes the hardest part, choosing which one to sacrifice first! After a moment of debate, I turn towards Corvis. If he had it his way, I would still be in jail on my way to prison or even worse, dead! He never really gave a fuck about me and my mother is weak. She goes along with anything that her worthless husband does. I feel my true father's presence strong within me. I look the deceiver straight in the eyes. He knows his life is over. He knows tonight is the night he pays for a life of deceit.

"How could you murder your own brother? Furthermore, how could you take his life and blessing as your own? How could you lie to me and try to keep me from my true destiny?" I search his eyes, trying to find some ounce of truth in them. He begins to speak

"You really wanna know why I did everything I did? Since I'm going to die anyway fuck it, I might as well get it off my chest. I hated your father! He always got everything! He was a product of love; I was a product of hate! Our mother loved him because he reminded her of her beloved dead husband! She hated me because I reminded her of her rapist and his murderer! My father killed his father and raped our mother! That's how I was conceived, a product of fucking rape! As I got older and started to look like him, she spared no expense at showing me how much she hated me. It wasn't my fault! I did nothing wrong but she still punished me for the sins of my father. Your father got everything in life, talent, love, looks, admiration, and a destined future to wealth courtesy of the bloodline blessing. I wanted everything he had and was on the verge of getting, so I killed him. Your mother didn't know..." he looks over at my mother. She has a shocked look on her face. "Honey I'm sorry..." he stops when he realizes apologizing is futile. She turns away in disgust.

"She doesn't want to hear it Mr. Rosette. It's your fault that she's here. You wanted to let her only child rot in prison. You wanted to let me stay in a fucking cage! My real family cared enough to prevent my demise and made sure I regained my freedom! It's too late for apologies Corvis!" My cold demeanor is rightly appropriate. I remove my hood as I mentally prepare myself for what I must do. I step forward in his direction. I take a deep breath. I'm ready. "Time is up for everything." I proclaim as I raise the dagger over his head. With brute strength and rage, I plunge the cold sharp dagger into his skull. He lets out a loud groan. His eyes roll in the back of his head. His last moments of life are agonizingly painful and shocking. His body shakes and convulses uncontrollably. Within seconds, blood begins oozing from his mouth and wound. I retrieve the dagger from the top of his skull as his lifeless body falls to the ground.

I feel a burden lifted. I have avenged my father's death and restored the blessing. Well almost, I look over at my mother. I feel a sense of sadness. She didn't kill my father. She didn't even know that he was murdered, let alone who did it. I move over in front of her. Her green tear-filled eyes, focused intensely on me. I feel a conflict of interest rising from within.

"Talia is this really what you want?" She asks as tears start to flow down her reddened cheeks. "I only wanted you to have the best life that I could possibly give you. I didn't kill Michael... I loved him! We just became distant after he got deeper into the occult and went to New York."

There is a moment of awkward silence in the room as I struggle to regain my focus. I feel the heat from the tears swelling up in my eyes. Memories of my childhood flash through my mind as I stare at my mother. Even though she didn't kill my father, she brought dishonor to his name by passing me off as his murder's child. She added more insult to injury by marrying him, my father's own brother! What a fucking whore! Who would marry the sibling of their deceased lover? I feel the anger rising back up. I wipe away the tears as I ready the dagger.

"It's true you didn't kill him, but you dishonored his name! You tried to keep me ignorant to the truth. You raised me to believe that the man that spilled my father's blood was my father! You are now dead to me. I disown you. The daughter you knew is dead as well..." Memories of my childhood continue to flash through my mind. I try to go through with the task but the emotions triggered by the memories take hold of me. More warm tears begin to run down my face. I turn away as I discretely try to wipe them. I have come too far to turn back now. If I allow her to live, she might betray me again. I can't take that risk. "You were going to let me stay imprisoned. You don't love me. You will now die like the dishonest whore that you are!" With one swift swing of my arm, the dagger slices across my mother's neck. Her eyes widen with shock as she gasps for her last breaths. She frantically grasps her throat as blood flows from the perfectly slit wound. She struggles to hold on, but to no avail. Death claims her all the same. I stand silent. I can feel the eyes of my brothers and sisters intently focused on me standing over my deceased parents. I look down at my handy work. I start to laugh. It starts out as a small giggle, and then it inflates to a hysterical, maniacal laugh, almost on the verge of sinister. An energy sweeps over me. I am intoxicated with a rush of power that surges into me. The spirit of my father, Armichael appears in front of me. He looks exactly as he does in my dreams. After a few seconds, he fades away. Doug raises his chalice and makes an announcement. "Brothers and sisters let us drink to a new beginning!"

I look down into the chalice that is in my hand. The dark crimson liquid intimidates my stomach. I feel it turning at the thought of drinking more of the mysterious substance. *"Well here goes nothing."* I think to myself as I quickly gulp down the rich warm liquid. I look around. I see Kenna staring at me with admiration. My life feels like it has just begun. This is a completely new book, not just a chapter. The blood on my hands is the price that I had to pay for future wealth, success, and the continuation of the Rosette lineage. Nothing in this life is free, not even the truth. I've been denied it my entire life! My whole life was just one big illusion. I now walk in my true destiny, my preordained purpose. I will never deny myself again. I am a God among mortals. I am no longer Talia Marie Rhodes. From this day forward, I am Talia Elizabeth Rosette. **END**

DEMONS

BEELZEBUB – ONE OF THE KINGS OF HELL

According to early scriptures and religious text, Beelzebub is the original fallen angel. Many believe that he is the embodied identity of Satan himself, or an alternate incarnation of Baal or Bael. Beelzebub is one of the most dangerous demons there is. Out of all of the demons, Baal Zebub (as he was referred to in ancient times), is the dominating factor to two of the seven deadly sins. He is the master of pride and gluttony. Many lost souls are under his hellish influence. Many secret societies exist solely to worship and praise his unholy name, as well spread his influence to future generations. Beelzebub is supposedly a part of hell's unholy trinity.

AMY – GREAT PRESIDENT OF HELL

Amy is a great president of hell. Amy is a female entity that often appears in a blue flame of fire. She sometimes lends her guardianship to lineages of musicians or others highly proficient in the liberal sciences. Amy uses her demonic wiles to entrap familiars, master human sciences, and manipulate religious politics. Throughout mankind's history, Amy has primarily appeared as female to those that she seduces, although in some rare instances she has assumed the form of a man. She often leads those with great influence, down a road of self-destruction. It is rumored that Amy is responsible for the premature deaths of many famous pop icons. Although Amy has her hands involved in the affairs of men, she is particularly focused on moving up through the demonic ranks. Amy aspires to be one of the greatest forces of evil. She has often used the talents of men to help her rise through the ranks and gain momentum for her campaign.

LUCIFER – "LIGHT-BEARER"

Lucifer, meaning 'morning star', is the fallen archangel. He is the ruthless power hungry proposed ruler of the underworld with hell's legions under his charge. Like Beelzebub or Beezebub, Lucifer is speculated be Satan. Historical records refer to Lucifer as being the main force behind the great heavenly revolt. Seeing himself as God's equal, Lucifer, the angel of light gathered a group of like-minded angels and sought to overthrow the creator's heavenly rule. He and his fellow conspirators received the ultimate wrath of God. They were stripped of their titles and cast out of heaven, never to return, thus the term fallen angel. Some believe that Satan is in fact a representation of Lucifer, Leviathan, and Beezebub and that hell has only one king, and his name is Satan. It is believed that the unholy trinity is a warped wicked replica of God's Holy Trinity (the Father, the Son, and the Holy Spirit). He commands all in the realm of hell and is the one demon all humanity agrees is most powerful and most dangerous.

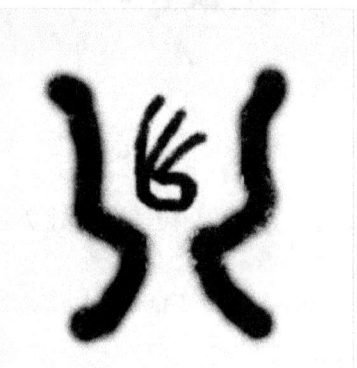

AKA MANAH – MASTER OF EVIL THOUGHTS

Aka Manah also known as Akem Manah, Akoman, and Akvan, is the highest-ranking arch demon in the realm "carnal desire", also known as "evil mind", "evil purpose", "evil thinking", or "evil intention". He is the primary demon of sensual desire and is rumored to be the gatekeeper to Hell's throne room. According to some sources, satanic followers wishing to gain greater access to Satan, Baal, or Lucifer, must first be in service of Aka Manah. None shall pass through the gates of supreme demonic influence and power, unless they deal with him. Ancient Iranian/Persian religious writings mention this demon. His eternal opponent is the angel known as Vohu Manah.

ABOUT THE AUTHOR

Anthony D. Phillips was born in Cleveland, Ohio 1980. He lives in Cleveland, Ohio with his wife Tonia and their cats. He is also a father of three and stepfather to two. Creating stories for others to enjoy has become an all-consuming passion. He is deeply engrossed in his work as an author. Simply put, he loves what he does.